Buzz

THE RILEY BROTHERS BOOK 1

E. DAVIES

Buzz / E. Davies. – 2nd ed.
ISBN: 978-1-912245-00-0

CHAPTER

One

CAMERON

Ice squeaked as his blades cut clean lines down the center of the ice. Foot over foot, a swerve, a sudden swoop around the net, and back down to the other end. It didn't matter if he was sick, injured, or heartbroken: the cool breeze across his face grounded him. He spun to skate backward down the ice a few dozen feet, then turned again to swoop around the corner again behind the net.

It was second nature at this point for Cameron Riley. He'd been skating since he was three. Four years later, he was playing hockey. Then, he became the star forward of the junior team. Back then, the other kids hadn't been competition for him.

Now...

"Heads!"

The weight of one of his teammates slammed into him from the side. They crashed into the boards, pulling their feet up and out of the way of each other.

"This isn't the fuckin' bunny league, Cam! Keep your head up!"

Coach Walker was right.

This was the minor leagues, but there was nothing minor about the upcoming big games. The series was tied. It was going to game seven. Just as important: the scouts in the crowd would take note of who was responsible for their win or loss.

The *big* job offers were coming in the next couple of months. Everyone on the team who was serious about their pro career had their head up and eye on the puck. They couldn't pass up the salary, the fame, and the chance to do what every one of them had been training for over the last five, ten, even twenty years.

"Sorry, coach," Cameron recited, focusing on the puck as he swept around to join the drill. It flashed back and forth between Matty and Lou's sticks.

"Get to it, then. All of you. I want a good, clean game. Not too boring, not too flashy. Play to win, both sides."

They split into practice teams. Another wave of dizziness swamped Cameron as he thought about what they were practicing for.

It was a big deal. Tied series weren't won on game three, but the tone was set for the fourth, fifth, even sixth games.

Their opponents – fucking Montreal, to add insult to injury – were good at nailing them on their weaknesses. Their goalie played aggressively on the crease, and their defense players moved lightning-fast. Cameron liked to figure out the *best* pass, not just the most available one, but their defense were aggressive. They wouldn't let him get away with anything.

He was getting dizzy a lot lately when he thought about it, but that was a common reaction to stress. He pushed through on the ice every time. He'd mentioned it to the team doc after the last game and they'd figured he'd been sneaking in too many extra-salted chips. He liked to rationalize it away by saying the fat gave him extra bulk.

Nathan hated it, but Nathan hated a lot of stuff he did. He was in the bleachers, scrolling through his phone and glancing up now and then. Like some of the hockey wives, he dropped in to watch now and then. He expected extra praise and sex for doing it.

When the puck dropped, Cam easily won the scramble and took off down the ice with it. *Pace yourself, Cam.* Fast games weren't everything. He was going to get the most ice time of any of his teammates – Coach Walker had pulled him aside yesterday to tell him that.

Coach Walker wanted him to be drafted this year.

Lou deked left, then right, then whipped the tip of his stick around Cam's. He lightly nudged the puck around the edge of his blade and took off the other way.

Much as it made his blood boil, Cam admired the move. Lou was the master of subtle grace on ice, underplaying what he was about to do until he took off at a sprint. He was light, fast, and would be infuriating for Montreal to deal with tomorrow.

Cam pursued, but it was too late: the puck flashed across the ice toward Mac as Chris tried to intercept it. The bleachers were gone, his focus narrowing to the ice. His heart pounded. His breath was ragged. *Control yourself. Don't burn out in the first five minutes, rookie.*

He didn't succeed, but after a quick skirmish, Mac had it – for a few seconds.

Mac passed to Chris, who broke out of the pack with the puck and sprinted down the ice. Cam spun on his heel for a two-pronged maneuver. Sure enough, Chris passed the puck to him and they rushed past Lou and McKay.

This was their game-winning move.

Cameron's heart pounded. He slipped Chris the puck, then crossed in a quick dance of blades. He feinted like he had the puck, drawing McKay's eye for long enough to get Chris into position, and *oh shit*, he was *very* dizzy, and his heart was racing and he couldn't breathe, the pounding in his ears drowning out the screeches of metal on ice, and then--

--the ice rose, jumping up at him, flying into his face.

Blackness.

Loud voices. Screeching, a spray of ice across his cheek. His heart fluttering helplessly, beating one-two-three-four-five before he finished each thought...

Somehow, in that split-second that had passed since he'd fallen, there was a stretcher under him. He was being carried, and--

"Wha--?"

"Lie down," Coach Walker told him. He was strapped down anyway, and – fuck, that hadn't been five seconds, had it?

He was dizzy and sick and there were voices again. Mac was asking someone if he'd be okay, if this was just a spell or "something more serious" in a carefully calm tone.

An authoritative voice from near his ear told Mac they were doing everything they could.

"What about the game tomorrow?" That was Nathan.

"We don't know yet. The doctors will make that call."

Cam struggled to open his eyes and see his boyfriend, but it was bright. And warm. They were outside the arena now. His practice shirt clung to him with sweat at the warm spring air compared to the refreshing cold of the arena. He nearly protested about having to go into the warmth, but he kept his mouth shut.

Fuck, his lip throbbed and his head... He wasn't wearing a helmet, but he had been, hadn't he?

"You're with us again, aren't you, Cam? You mind being called that?"

Cameron blinked, focusing on a friendly face as his stretcher was lifted into the ambulance. A man a couple years older than him, with light brown hair. He was smiling, and Cam's lips instinctively twitched. The man had a calming air about him.

"Yeah, s'fine," Cameron mumbled, clearing his throat. "What-- what happened?"

"You fainted on the ice," the EMT answered, swinging himself up beside Cameron into the seat. That was right, he was an EMT. He had a uniform. Cam appreciated uniformed men, especially those who helped people. Including himself right now.

That reminded him – Nathan. He spotted his dark-haired boyfriend standing outside the ambulance.

"Are you coming with us?" Another EMT was talking to Nathan this time.

Nathan hesitated.

In those few seconds, the sinking truth hit Cameron: he wasn't planning on staying with him. The last time they'd gone on again, they'd agreed to keep it quiet. To the outside world, even to his own team, as always, they'd be good buddies. The team knew the truth, but nobody said it.

Fuck.

What had he done wrong this time?

"Otherwise, I'm coming," Coach Walker spoke up, and there was something in his voice – a threat? A reprimand?

Nathan's deep, thrumming voice sounded. "I guess I am."

"Sit up front with me, then," an EMT directed.

Nathan caught Cameron's eyes for a long moment, those dark eyes penetrating yet veiled. The ambulance doors slammed shut.

I guess so?

Cameron gulped for air.

This time, when dizzying blackness struck, Cameron welcomed it, if just for a moment.

CHAPTER
Two

CAMERON

BEEP, BEEP, BEEP.

So it was true that when you woke up in the hospital, you were attached to a heart monitor.

It was far from the first time Cam had used one. As he fidgeted with the cushioned plastic clip around his finger, the gaps between spikes on the screen narrowed.

What the *hell* was wrong with him?

"You're awake," a nurse smiled, stepping around the curtain. He guessed he was in an emergency room.

"Yes. I... how long was I out?"

"You've only been here for a few minutes," she assured him. "How do you feel?"

"Frozen crap," he answered, then winced. "Pardon me." *Can't say what I'd say on ice.*

"Your heart rate is back to normal," she told him, not fazed. "The doctors will want to do tests on you, of course."

"Right."

"Let me know if you need anything – the doctor will be by shortly."

Cameron murmured, "I'm fine," then glanced around. Nobody was there with him. "Uh, did anyone come with me?"

The nurse shook her head. "There was someone here for a few minutes, but he seems to have left."

Of course he did. Cameron lay back, gazing at the green curtains. "All right." His voice was soft. He didn't want to sound defeated, but it was hard to feel any other way.

Nathan can do whatever he wants. Maybe he has something urgent to get to...

He wasn't sure how much time passed, but he wasn't passing out again. Instead, he focused on staying calm, picturing the plays they'd gone over that morning.

Damn. He'd never gotten a chance to test their new deep right wing penetration and hook. That would have been a fun move. Hopefully he'd be able to pull it off tomorrow. He'd skate tonight if he had to.

"Cam?"

It was Coach Walker's voice.

"Here, coach." Cameron nodded as the familiar gray-haired man pushed his way around the curtain, carrying his gym bag. Thank god he'd washed it after spilling Gatorade all over it.

"How you doing, buddy?" his coach asked, his tone gruff but a little warmer than usual. "I brought your stuff and called your brother."

Fuck. He's feeling sorry for me.

Oddly enough, even being in the hospital wasn't serious to Cameron. He'd been there enough for stitches, concussion checks, a broken arm...

But having this man sound even slightly concerned?

That was fucking terrifying.

"Fine, fine," Cameron assured him. "Thanks. I passed out in the ambulance, but I've been awake since then."

"You never told me or the doc anything was wrong," the coach said, and that was definitely a reprimand.

Cameron blushed and shrugged. "Sorry, coach. That was a big fuck-up, I know. I just... didn't think it was this bad. Doc thought it was too much salt. I've never just... passed out."

"You wiped out pretty bad. That'll be a colorful lip," Coach Walker added. "And you're definitely not fit to play the next game."

Cam's heart sank.

Of all the punishments Coach Walker gave out, benching was among the worst. Benching him for one of the biggest playoff games against their bitter rival?

His heart monitor sped up in the background. He gritted his teeth for a moment before letting his breath out.

"Fine," he answered with a slight nod.

Coach Walker eyed him for a moment, then sank into his chair. "You misunderstand. This isn't to punish you, kid. You're twenty-three – you're on the cusp of success. You can't fuck it up now. Push too hard, at the wrong time, and you can bench yourself for *life*. Or, worse, lose your life. Heart problems, if that's what this is, are nothing to screw around with."

Cameron wanted to argue, wanted to jump out of the hospital bed. He wanted to do ten one-armed pushups just to prove how in-shape he was. He had to prove that he wouldn't faint again, but... he didn't know if he would.

Maybe his coach was right.

"This one game, then. Hopefully the doctor will be here soon..."

The curtain swung. A man in the stereotype of a doctor's image – older, white coat, aloof – stepped through.

"Ah, my star hockey player," he greeted. "And you must be his coach."

"Walker."

They firmly shook hands.

"Dr. Lenny. And you're Cameron?"

"Yeah," Cameron confirmed, fidgeting with the finger clip again.

Dr. Lenny pulled Cameron's paperwork out of the file for a quick glance. "There's nothing out of the ordinary on your records. Anything you want to tell me?"

"No, sir," Cameron answered. "Except I've been getting dizzy whenever I get stressed for the past... well, for a while. I went to the team doctor and she told me it's probably salt. I *was* eating too much."

"No other dietary changes?"

"No."

"What about drugs? Legal or illegal."

Coach Walker looked sharply at him.

Cameron's cheeks flushed at the implications. "No," he snapped. "I don't do anything except multivitamins. I can't afford to fail those tests."

"All right," the doctor nodded, making notes. "We'll need to keep you for today for testing if you want us to get to the bottom of this. I'll order the battery of tests." He stepped out around the curtain again.

"You can't be passing out on ice again," Coach Walker said, rising to his feet. "Take the time to get better. Even if you miss the rest of the playoffs, we don't want you sending the net flying again."

"Shit, did I?"

"You hit the boards and then crashed into the net."

Cameron raised his free hand to press his fingers to his lip. Not the worst he'd ever had, but he felt like he'd been thrown through the boards. Then, he touched his chest – there were cardiac monitor pads already stuck to his skin, and he winced. Those were going to be a bitch to get off.

"Yeah, you're still pretty, don't worry," the coach snorted.

That made Cameron laugh, at least.

"Where's your – uh, where's that kid, Nathan?"

"I'm... not sure," he admitted.

Coach Walker knew the truth. Cam had walked into the coach's office on his first day on the team, scared and shaking and sure he was about to lose his chance at pro sports. The coach had coolly told him he wasn't the first and he wouldn't be the last. Then, he'd said to keep his head down unless he was ready to be the poster boy.

When Nathan had shown up to practices along with the other guys' girlfriends or wives, Coach Walker had put two and two together. He'd just told Cam not to let him distract him.

Nathan did nothing *but* distract him.

He was always trying to prove himself to Nathan – that he wouldn't sleep with the rest of the team, let fame get to his head, forget about him... Nathan complained he had his head in the clouds; he tried to stay grounded by cooking every meal when he was home. Nathan said he didn't pay him enough attention; he'd learned sensual techniques to mix up his sports-focused massages.

And now, for the third time, Nathan had walked out on him.

Coach Walker smiled dryly. "Not the best time to decide he has other priorities, kid. Watch out for yourself."

"I will."

The coach stood up and clapped his arm. "I'll check in on you later. I gotta get back to practice."

The arena felt a million miles away from him.

"Could you, uh, grab my phone first? I wanna make sure my brother knows I'm alive." Jackson would be out of his mind by now, and Cameron didn't want the whole family panicking. "It's in the end pouch."

The coach fished it out and handed it over without looking at it, then clapped his arm again. "See you, kid. Get better."

"Will do, sir."

Holding the phone was awkward without one finger, but he managed it one-handed.

Both his brothers and Nathan had messaged him.

Jackson's message was first: *Hey, I heard what happened. Call when you can. Haven't told Mom & Dad yet. On my way, should be there tonight.*

Cameron hadn't seen Jackson since Christmas. Even if the reason wasn't the best for the visit, his big brother would look out for him in the hospital system.

Thomas's message was next: *Thinking of you, lots of love.* Simple and sweet, just like Thomas. He worked as a bank teller, which suited his reserved personality. Cam secretly wondered if he would turn out to be the third gay brother in the family. Cam was only halfway out, but everyone had guessed; Jackson had been out since high school. Thomas just... didn't talk about dating. Not before or since moving out to Halifax, the big city.

Finally, though his stomach twisted with dread, he opened Nathan's message. His heart sank, but he forced himself to keep reading through the end.

I'm done. Don't want to indulge you in drama. I've blocked and deleted your phone number and email and I'm moving out soon. I can't put up with your attention seeking anymore. Have a good life.

Cameron choked back a sob that threatened to escape his

lips and closed his eyes, pulling the thin hospital blanket up over him a little more.

He'd always expected it, but somehow, hadn't prepared for it. Now that the moment was here, he couldn't process the mix of anger, grief, and fear.

Why fear?

His coach shouted that at Cam when he held back from a good move. The answer was all too clear.

I'm not good enough even for a guy like him.

Cameron was exhausted and cranky by the time the doctor walked into his tiny section of the emergency room. He was about sick of nurses giving him tests, asking about his condition, checking his heart monitor... They were nice, but they couldn't give him a prognosis.

This new specialist, a short man with close-cropped hair and a brisk attitude, first checked his file. "Cameron Riley?" His tone was authoritative.

Cameron fought the instinct to sit up straight. "Yes, sir."

"I've been going over your test results and all your physical records from your team doctor. Neither of us can find anything wrong with you."

Cameron's cheeks burned as his jaw dropped. *Is he implying I made this up...?*

"You obviously experienced some anomaly, but we can't identify it."

"No..." Cameron murmured. "No, you don't understand. I can't play until this is diagnosed."

"Ah. That's the thing."

No.

Cameron raised his hand and eased himself into a sitting position to hear this. He couldn't think how to explain the desperate desire that pulsed, throbbed, hummed through him. He *needed* to skate more than breathing. Fuck, that was a cliché. He just needed to tell them to fix him.

There were a few moments of silence before the doctor spoke up, his voice quiet. "We'll keep you here for a few days and try to get a diagnosis for you, but you won't be out in time for your next game. I already told your coach."

Cameron shook his head. There wasn't a lot else he could say. He didn't want to hear the doctor telling him he was useless.

"So, you don't know what this thing could do to me, when it'll happen again...?"

"Physical exertion is the only clue we have tying together the dizzy spells you reported before and this incident," the doctor answered. "That's why we're keeping you here in a controlled environment. We'll contact your insurance regarding a private room... I'll send the nurse in to explain everything."

Cameron had to bite back all the venom in his veins to manage a quick, "Thanks."

What had he done to deserve this shit?

Abso-fucking-lutely nothing.

CHAPTER
Three

JACKSON

TONGS WEIGHED DOWN ONE OF JACKSON'S HANDS, THE blowtorch heavy in the other. He stretched the steel rod, shaping the rough draft with precise hands.

Of all things to be working on, an art piece about a hockey player was an oddity, but Jackson was enjoying it. It made a great change from all the construction jobs.

His cellphone rang and he frowned. He had "do not disturb" on for all but emergency calls.

Oh, shit.

He backed away from the glowing steel, then fumbled under his leather apron and yanked off his gloves to grab his cellphone.

Coach Walker.

Who was that?

It took him a second to remember: his little brother's coach who'd led his team to a near-perfect season record last year. So far this year, it was a less perfect but grittier record – whatever that meant. Cam had given Jackson the coach's number to reach him on short notice during a game, but Jackson hadn't expected the other way around.

"Oh, *shit*," he whispered, out loud this time. He fumbled to slide a finger across the screen. "Jackson speaking."

"Jackson Riley, right?"

"Yep, that's me. You're Coach Walker? My little brother's coach?"

"Yes. Don't worry, your brother's fine."

Nothing in the world would make him fucking panic more. "What happened?" he demanded.

"He fainted during practice. There's some kind of... medical issue going on with him. It's not dangerous so far as we can tell. But it's serious enough to bench him until we get a diagnosis."

"Is he in the hospital now?"

Jackson yanked his leather apron off, shutting off the forge damper to stifle the fire. He groped for his keys with his other hand.

Toronto was a damn sight away from his small New Brunswick hometown, but he was gonna drive there if he had to.

"Yes," the coach told him. "The doctor's told him that he's benched."

"Jesus, I bet he didn't take that well." Jackson double- and triple-checked the forge, then transferred his phone to the other ear to open the door to his workshop and step outside.

It was still early enough in the year to need a jacket, but only a light one. The temperature was always in the plus during the day.

"I haven't talked to him yet. He'll launch himself out of bed to explain why he can play after all." Jackson laughed. *That* sounded like his kid brother.

Cam had always hid any perceived weakness. Once, he'd

knocked out a tooth on the fence while climbing trees. He'd come into the house cool as a cucumber, hand hiding his bloody mouth, and told their mother he needed to see the dentist.

"How long has this been going on?"

"We don't know. He talked to the team doctor a couple times about dizzy spells and we thought it was a nutrition problem. Then, suddenly... Well, this is the first time fainting we know about, and I trust him to have told someone if it had happened before."

Jackson wasn't so sure, but either way, he was going to find out what Cameron had been hiding. He just worried it had something to do with that dick boyfriend... Nathan whatshis-face. He'd never liked the guy, but for some reason, Cam was stuck on him. Not that Jackson's taste in men was much better, but he pushed that thought aside.

He unlocked the car door. "Right. Thanks. I'm gonna fly in, I think. I'll break the news to our brother and parents."

"Thanks," Coach Walker answered. "Appreciate it, man. I'm sure we'll see each other when you visit him."

"Yep. Just text me the details of his hospital and stuff so I can get in when I get there," Jackson requested.

"Of course. I'll make sure they expect you. Want me to let him know?"

"Nah, I'll surprise him," Jackson told him. "Thanks, Coach."

When they hung up, Jackson leaned against his car door while he searched for flights to Toronto.

The hospital was sterile and cold, and Jackson hated it. Getting his wisdom teeth out had been enough experience with hospitals for him. They were ugly and white and architecturally displeasing. Not that he was an architect, but he worked with enough design stuff that he thought he had a better eye than most.

Give him some steel columns and twisted chandeliers and blown glass windows any day.

He was built like his brother, broad shoulders and firm jaw and around six feet tall, but Cameron was more nimble and lithe, an athletic build. Jackson was muscle and had always been goalie in their boyhood ball hockey games. He'd been all right. Cameron had kicked everyone's ass until he talked their parents into letting him do hockey when he was seven. The rest... well, was about to be history.

God, he hoped his brother didn't have to quit. From what he understood, his agent was certain he'd get signed this season. Cam wasn't going to take it well if he had to quit now.

He knocked on the door to Cameron's room, then cracked it open and stepped inside.

His little brother was at least dressed in jeans and a t-shirt, but he was lying down on a hospital bed surrounded by machinery. He was pale and stressed as hell. In this environment, Cam looked younger than his twenty-two years – no, twenty-three now. Like the last four years, Cam's birthday had been spent in constant training.

"Hey, bro." Cameron glanced up quickly. The mix of expressions on Cameron's face made Jackson smile: confusion, then surprise and joy. It had been a couple months since they'd last seen each other just before Christmas.

Jackson strode across the room as Cameron sat up in bed, leaning in to hug him. Jackson refrained from his usual strong back-clap, but Cameron hugged him as tight as ever.

"Hey, Jackson," Cameron answered, his voice quieter. He was alone in the room, a fact that made Jackson frown.

"Where's everyone? The coach? That boyfriend of yours, Nathan?"

Cameron's expression shifted strangely and he looked away.

Oh. Shit. Jackson hadn't meant to pry at a recent wound. "...No."

"Yeah, he, uh. He's gone." The words were sour and succinct on Cameron's tongue. From his tone, Jackson knew the bastard had dumped him.

"Fuck." Jackson sank down into the chair next to the bed. He scooted it closer and leaned in to half-hug his brother again, clapping his back this time. "Sorry, man. Just now?"

"Yeah, earlier today."

Jackson's head spun. The last few hours in airport hell and on planes had thrown him for a loop. It hardly seemed like the same day Cam had been admitted. It was late now, past visiting hours, but he'd talked his way in. "I wish I could've been here in person sooner. The bastard was no good for you."

A little smile cracked through Cam's stress and grief. "Tell me what you really think."

"I always do," Jackson reminded him, grinning back at him. "I'll stay here with you 'til you're out, all right?"

Cameron's eyes widened. "You can do that? Work-wise? Oh, shit, do Mom and Dad know?"

"Yeah, and Thomas. I told them all before I left. They send their love and so on," Jackson waved a hand. "Work's no problem. Don't worry about it, man."

"Cool." He was clearly trying not to let on his relief, and Jackson couldn't blame him. It had to suck to be all alone, dealing with some life-threatening mystery condition. And in

Toronto, a soul-sucking hellhole at the best of times. Well, Jackson thought so; Cam disagreed, but never bothered to defend it too hard.

"So, it's just a waiting game? Your coach mentioned specialist test results. They got you doing all those fitness tests and heart monitors and shit?"

Cameron nodded.

Jackson stretched out his legs and breathed out, settling into the chair at Cam's bedside. "Well, we've got all day and night."

All day and night to plan to grab Nathan by his greasy hair and chuck him out if he tried strolling back into his little brother's life yet again.

CHAPTER
Four

CAMERON

After the first night, the hospital insisted that Jackson couldn't stay in Cam's room. Cameron tried to pay for a downtown hotel, but Jackson said he had reward points to use up. When he came back, he smuggled in a pizza to share between nurse visits.

Cameron fucking loved his big brother.

Jackson had always been there for him, and now was no exception. Not that he blamed their little brother, Thomas, who was stuck in Halifax with work. He'd texted back and forth for a while with Cameron to pass on his best wishes and concerns. He was clearly worried, but Jackson and Cameron had both insisted that he should stay at work for now.

Having Jackson there for him was so much better for Cam. Those first few crushing hours facing the prospect of no passion, no job, and no boyfriend had passed. With company, he was more grounded and optimistic.

The first day or two of bed rest was a nice break from the constant intense training schedule.

By day three, Cameron was ready to break out of the hospital. Coach Walker had visited, as had many of his teammates. Most of them met Jackson for the first time, many for only the second or third, and all instantly liked him.

Everyone did. Jackson was just easy to get along with, for the most part. It made Cam smile.

Then, the doctor asked to see them all together – the coach, his brother, and him. That was reason enough to stop smiling.

Cardiac specialist Dr. Whitfield had been working on his case for the last couple days, but no tests had been conclusive so far. As he gazed at them all from across his imposing desk, Cameron already knew where this was going.

"So, you said you have answers for us?" Coach Walker wasn't buying into the ominous silence for a second.

Jackson nodded with the coach's words. Coach Walker sat on one side of Cameron, while Jackson flanked the other side.

"Yes." Dr. Whitfield fidgeted with the file folder on the desk in front of him. "Here's the thing, gentlemen. I've been going over it, over and over, and... nothing adds up. Cameron is going to need to get some serious testing done with a cardiology team... assuming it *is* a heart problem. There could be some other invisible illness causing it."

"Lupus?" Cameron quipped. Both Jackson and Coach Walker shot him looks. "Sorry."

Dr. Whitfield nodded. "Something like that. It's... you know, we can't guarantee your safety or even your life if you keep playing. All we know is that reaching peak physical exertion seems to trigger the response. Dizziness at first, escalating to fainting, obviously. Our fitness tests haven't replicated that yet, so we can't see *what* it is. It's stress-linked, too."

"So you're saying he should stop playing." Coach Walker's eyes were difficult to read. He wouldn't let the doctors slide away under some BS excuse.

Dr. Whitfield nodded. "Avoiding prolonged periods of elevated heart rates or short periods of highly elevated heart rates is best."

There was a long moment of silence while Cameron's stomach churned with distaste. *Come on, talk to him. Make them do more tests before they let me go.*

"You're not the first guy who had to leave right before he got an offer."

No.

"Or even after."

"No way," Cameron gritted, trying to keep his voice from cracking.

"You're young, you can find another career and kill it, whatever you choose. You've got the guts and strength. You're driven and loyal. You're *able* to do it."

Coach Walker had never talked to him this frankly, and Cameron wasn't ready to handle what that meant. "But--"

"Take two weeks off first, Cam," Coach Walker told him, and from his voice, there was no negotiation. Jackson watched him closely, just as the doctor and his coach were watching. "Spend time with your family and friends before you decide. Doc, how long before the referrals come through?"

"We can try to fast-track you if you go private, but... months."

"And private isn't--"

"Cam," the doctor said, and the nickname from the professional made Cameron recoil and pay attention to him. "That first referral won't fix everything. How long have you been living with these symptoms?"

Cameron bit back his retort. Months, if he was honest, but it had started so small he hadn't noticed. There had been a little dizziness he'd attributed to performance anxiety every time he was on the ice. Then, numbness in his fingers or toes, a moment of heartsick tension in his stomach…

"That's what I thought," the doctor said. "This has been escalating, and it's not worth your life. If you're meant to play, you'll play in a year or two, when this is settled."

"Can I at least stay in shape?"

"Yes, but you *have* to stop at the first sign of relapse," the doctor said sternly. "No stressing out over it, no pushing yourself to your limits. You can rebuild muscle later, but your heart…"

Jackson reached out to grip Cameron's shoulder. "I'll make sure he doesn't push it," he promised.

Fuck, he didn't want to go home and face that shame – well, no, face Nathan. Would they become ugly roommates now? The kind who brought home men to spite each other?

"The whole family's gonna be home this weekend," Jackson told him. "Everyone has things to talk about. This has been… a scare for everyone."

Fuck. Stubbornly sticking around and killing himself over this sport would be selfish as hell.

With the weight of his involuntary decision lifted a little, Cameron nodded. "I'll come home with you."

The shuddering underneath became a smooth glide. The plane whined in the background, its props fighting through turbulence. Cameron leaned against the wall, gazing out the window as the plane climbed into the sky.

There went the tower, the harbor, the island, the arena…

Fuck, the arena.

He'd wandered past the shining glass and chrome, the giant

red letters spelling out the center name, so many times. He'd sat in the bleachers, studying games, and he'd been invited into the locker rooms a few times.

It wasn't the coliseum where *his* team played, but... it was the home of the team he *dreamed* of playing for.

As they banked in one more smooth swoop before turning east, Cameron pushed the window shade down and leaned back in his seat.

He was leaving his skates, stick, and goddamn heart in Toronto.

CHAPTER
Five

NOAH

Noah groaned as he rolled over in bed. His cellphone never stopped ringing these days. Even on a nice Saturday morning when he wasn't scheduled to work the exhibits, he couldn't have a moment's peace.

Then, he got over it and stirred awake, grabbing his phone and clearing his throat before he answered.

"Hello?"

"Hey, Noah, it's your uncle Bill."

"I know who it is," Noah laughed as he sat up. He'd had his number in the phone for years, but Bill still didn't get that cellphones had caller ID. "What's up?"

"I have a favor to ask."

Noah had a pretty good idea he knew what it was. It was farmer's market day. Every Saturday, Bill sold his honey, beeswax candles, honeycomb, beekeeping supplies, books, and more. His stand was well-known among the locals now and many people stopped by just to chat about the bees and how they could help save them.

His uncle probably needed help running it. Of all the things to do on a Saturday morning, the market wasn't bad. He knew all the other vendors by now.

"There's a swarm."

"Ah." That made it more urgent, then. Noah climbed out of bed and opened his drawers to find a clean, presentable outfit to wear. He was almost out of clean laundry. No time to do it while negotiating loans and commissioning pieces for the new hockey exhibition he was running at the local arena.

He resisted the urge to groan. It had been a fucking long week, one of those weeks from hell. But he wasn't going to say no to his uncle. "Um, give me... half an hour? I'll try and be faster."

"Thanks a bunch, kid."

"See you, Uncle Bill." He hung up and tossed his phone onto the bed, then ran his hands over his face.

A lot could happen to an unguarded swarm in half an hour. He headed straight for the shower, grabbing a towel along the way. There was no time to waste.

***

"Early swarm this year," Noah greeted his uncle when he managed to slide through gaps in the crowd and duck behind the table.

Bill shrugged helplessly. "I don't know why. The homeowner's panicking."

"Right. Go on, you better catch 'em," Noah encouraged him. "I'll take care of things here."

"Thanks a lot," Bill answered, clapping his shoulder as he rushed for the parking lot.

Finally, Noah breathed out. He hadn't even grabbed a proper breakfast – just a banana. He'd have to ask Susan or

Lucy from the fudge stand if they'd watch the stall for a minute while he grabbed a pastry later.

He liked to be presentable all the time, even though he wondered why he bothered sometimes. On his sloppiest days, he styled his hair and wore a short-sleeved t-shirt over his long-sleeved t-shirt. He joked that he wanted to be ready to propose a date to some hottie.

Even when he had a boyfriend, he believed in looking his best at all times. It only ever earned him attention from the ladies at the fudge stall, but at least he scored free fudge.

Hmm. He could do fudge for breakfast. There was a brief gap in the crowd and Noah raised a hand to wave. "Morning, Susan!"

By eleven in the morning or so, the market was always at its busiest as people who woke up late came to shop or socialize. It was exhausting keeping up with everyone who wanted his attention.

Large groups of people wandered past the stalls together, pausing to glance at jars of honey or pollen. It was a whole different atmosphere – one that required a more extroverted touch than the morning sales did.

Noah sold all the honeycomb by noon, plus half the honey jars and three books. He even passed out business cards for people who were interested in buying beekeeping supplies.

Now and then, he had a chance to chat.

"Hey, Ray!" he called out, waiting to attract the attention of the man at the houseplant stand on the other side of the aisle. "The game tomorrow's at three." Ray nodded, then kept wolfing down his sandwich.

Noah helped run a little field hockey league – nothing serious, and he was pretty bad, but everyone involved had fun. Whoever won, they drank and laughed at bars downtown after each game.

That sandwich looked good and Noah's stomach was growling, too. He was considering stepping away from the stall to grab a samosa and run back. Before he moved away, though, someone approaching the table caught his eye.

Noah was starstruck.

This man was tall, broad, yet subtly muscled – not hulking with gross veins popping out everywhere. He wore a light t-shirt despite the spring morning, and Noah tried to drag his eyes away from the nipples poking against his white shirt.

Holy shit, his face was gorgeous. The stranger had dark brown eyes, a slightly crooked nose, and a smile that would charm the pants off a monk. And Noah's gaydar was going off like *crazy*, which made him ten times more nervous than if this had been some hot straight guy.

The stranger fidgeted as if nervous, too. He let another section of the crowd pass by, then slipped between them nimbly. Once he reached the table, he glanced down at the honey instead of at Noah.

Say something.

This was the moment to clinch the sale. Noah drew a breath, trying not to act completely nervous. He rested his hands on the table to keep them from shaking. "Hello. Can I help you?"

CHAPTER
Six
CAMERON

Holy shit, Jackson's house was cramped.

His brother had been trying to find a bigger place for a couple months now, but he'd never gone through with it. Something was always wrong – a flood risk or it needed too much work or it was *too* finished.

Cameron was grateful to stay with his brother, though he was getting too familiar with Jackson's basement laundry corner. He was wearing the same few outfits over and over from the duffel bag Jackson had grabbed from his house while he'd been in the hospital, and laundry was getting old.

As Jackson paged through real estate listings, Cameron tried to ignore the morning news. He hated watching the news. It was depressing and it never actually told him anything useful. Just more stabbings in Halifax and shit, and he didn't need to be worrying about Thomas all the time.

"I'm going down to the market," he told his brother. The farmer's market was something of a Fredericton tradition. A lot of people went to socialize in their small town and catch up with old buddies, not just get their produce. It would be nice to run into a few people he knew, even if most people he knew here had been in his high school graduating class.

A lot of that crowd was still hanging around, most of them done with university by now. Some had moved back home and some had never left. Then there were the older folks, friends of his parents' or teachers, who were glad to see him back home. He told them all it was a vacation back here after too long away and they always agreed.

"You should think about moving back," his old English teacher, Ms. Crawford, encouraged. "There's a lot going for young people. All the tech companies moving here. It's all from that town Internet access program."

"Right, right," Cameron nodded. He knew shit about Internet access programs, but it sounded like it made sense. "I've thought about it."

"I mean, unless your big sports career keeps you away. But a lot of folks here would be glad to see you back," she assured him.

Cameron smiled. "Well, you never know," was all he'd commit to. "It depends which teams want me."

"There's one starting up here."

"Really?" There had been rumors for years. Cameron would believe it when he saw it. The town just wasn't big enough to sustain a pro team of its own. Minor leagues here never lasted long before getting bought out by another team and moved.

"Oh, yes. You should talk to people about it," Ms. Crawford told him. She juggled her vegetable basket from one arm to the other.

"That looks heavy. I won't keep you," Cameron nodded. "See you, Ms. Crawford. Great to meet you again."

God, he'd sucked in her class.

His cheeks burned as he remembered the red ink on one

paper with a typo in the title and three Wikipedia sources. He waved goodbye, then escaped through the crowds.

Honey? Sure. He could use honey... save the bees and all.

Oh, shit.

The man *behind* the honey table almost stopped him from going over to it, but not because he was unapproachable. Quite the opposite: he was *beautiful,* and there was no way in fuck he was straight. He stood tall, but he hadn't quite spotted Cameron yet.

It wasn't a rebound fling if Cameron just wanted to have a word with him. There was no way he'd wind up being single.

Cameron approached, picking his way through the crowd until he reached the table and the man greeted him.

"Hello. Can I help you?"

He sounded cheerful and bright, his voice warm and somehow familiar. It was the kind of comforting voice you'd expect from a nurse or physiotherapist.

No, I need to get out of that mindset. Not everything was about sports anymore.

"Hi," Cameron answered, dragging his gaze from the honey jars up to the man. Angled cheekbones, the full, feminine lips, the bright brown eyes... the scruffy blond hair gelled up, then messed with.

He was offering Cam a smile and not the distant, suspicious expression he'd expected. His stereotypical once-broken nose and general broad build made people think he was a bouncer or a scrapper sometimes.

"Um, just taking a look at your honey," he answered, gesturing at the jars.

"Well, we're sold out of our fresh honeycomb, but we have lots of liquid honey left. There's small sample jars of a hundred mill's," the man gestured toward them. "And larger ones, of course."

"Is it all local?"

"From my uncle's hives."

Cameron licked his lips. "Oh, cool. He sells it to you?"

"Oh, no, this isn't my stand," the man smiled. "It's his. He's off catching a swarm, actually."

"A swarm?"

"Bee swarm. When they leave the hive en masse."

"Wow. I see." Cameron tried to think of something else to say just to hear that warm voice again. Sometimes it caught when he drawled his way through a syllable and that gorgeous Atlantic accent came out.

Cameron had missed the accents from home.

"Yeah. He has several hundred hives of his own, and manages a network of about a thousand more through a co-operative profit-sharing agreement." That sounded like a spiel.

"On his own?"

"Yeah. He wants an apprentice, but it's hard to find anyone our age who's interested in it. He tried twice and the guys left a month or two later. We're all leaving for Toronto or Fort Mac... you know how it goes."

Cameron frowned. *I was one of the kids who left for Toronto too. Not doing the oil fields, though...* "Uh, is he still looking?"

The man stuck out his tasty lower lip in thought. "He might be. If you wanna stop by next week, he'll be here and he can talk to you about it. Or I can take your number..."

"Oh, I don't – I don't have a local number yet." Cameron didn't want to give away his Toronto number and get charged long distance – or worse, sound like he was trying to pick up this guy for a fling. Most Ontarian visitors did that: fucked their way through town on vacation and left. He needed to sound interested in the job, though. "But I'll stop by next week."

"Okay. I'm Noah, by the way."

"Cameron. Or Cam's fine. Everyone calls me that." What was wrong with him? He usually got quiet, not chattery, when he was nervous.

"Nice to meet you, Cam." Noah reached over the table for a firm handshake. This was something else he'd missed: everyone did business with a handshake here, not sleazy contract lawyers and agents and the media. "See you later."

This wouldn't be a bad place to move back to, relatively speaking.

"See you." Cameron's skin tingled as he drew back, his heart still flip-flopping. For the first time in days, it wasn't in a bad way.

On his way out, Cam passed a plastic house-shaped box with a stack of real estate listing booklets. He opened the creaky metal handle to pull down the door and reach in for a brochure, then let it snap shut.

He flipped through the brochure as the scents of food and the sounds of excited residents faded. One listing in particular caught his eye.

Score this hat trick of houses.

He rolled his eyes but scanned underneath.

A triple listing: great for an investor or a big family.

Cameron's mind raced as he scanned through the three houses. They were each priced the same and had roughly the same features, but differed slightly in their upgrades. One had a better garden, another a better kitchen, the third had a good media room in the basement, and so on.

They all needed a little fixing up, but that was nothing he couldn't handle. He knew his way around light home renovations. He'd learn more from the hardware store or YouTube tutorials. Plus, the summer was coming up and it sounded like there was a job opportunity for someone to make a living as a beekeeper...

As Cam waited at a red light to cross the street despite no cars coming the other way, he thought the small town life was kind of tempting. Maybe moving back here would be the kind of change Coach Walker was talking about. Hell, maybe he could stop blaming himself for everything.

"Thomas! God, it's great to see you," Cameron grinned as he held the door to his parents' house open for his little brother.

Thomas was a couple years younger than him, clever as a whip after graduating at twenty. Cam and Jackson had looked out for him, because the two of them had actually *been* gay, yet scrawny Thomas had wound up labeled the gay one at school.

Then again, Thomas hadn't actually told any of them about dating a girl, even since moving to Halifax. Cam quelled speculation by saying the chances of all three brothers being gay were pretty fucking small, but he wondered.

Their little brother kept himself to himself, but he was sweet and as loyal to their little family as could be. He was beaming, a grin breaking across that narrow face as he strode up and crushed Cameron in a hug.

Cameron pretended to stagger to his knees. "Mom! Thomas is picking on me!"

"Settle down, boys," she laughed. Their father was laughing from the living room as he waited to greet their son.

"Welcome home, Thomas," Mom added, hugging and

kissing his cheek. She sent him into the living room to greet Jackson and Dad.

As they caught up on their trips home, everyone headed to the table for supper. Cameron ate even more than the other two, but he always had, to fuel his muscle growth.

"So, you're better?" Thomas finally broached when they were done their main course.

"Yeah, I'm good," Cameron assured Thomas, feeling the nervous silence descending. "I'm just taking a couple weeks off to visit you guys and... you know, recover."

"It was a shock for all of us," Mom spoke up, her voice a waver. Cameron had hugged it out when he'd first gotten back, but she still seemed upset. Not that he blamed her – he still couldn't even provide a diagnosis or explanation.

"Well, now that you're back here... I mean, are you gonna... go back?"

Dad cleared his throat, but Cameron shook his head. "No, I don't mind," he assured them with a quiet laugh. He was a grownup. He'd tell Thomas to fuck off if he had to, but he honestly didn't. They shared many of their decisions and fears in this family. "I'm thinking about it."

"His coach thought it was a good idea," Jackson added. "He was pretty firm on that."

Cameron rolled his eyes. "I'm not just gonna stop playing, but... if that means getting out of competition..."

"Oh, Cam," Mom breathed out.

"Yeah, you worked so hard..." Jackson frowned, sympathetic despite his clear views that Cameron should quit.

No way would Cameron admit how much it stung. He just shook his head. "No, really. If I'd gotten signed, I'd have been moving all over the country, never seeing you guys... I mean, I missed it here a lot."

"You've barely been home," Dad agreed.

"Yeah, and that sucks. I mean, the money doesn't, but then all the guys blow it on..." *Hookers and cars and anything that won't show up on a test...* "You know, just empty stuff. Nobody banks it away." *I would have.*

"That's not a good lifestyle to be around if you don't want it," Thomas spoke up. Youngest or not, he was a voice of wisdom sometimes.

"No, exactly. What, are your bank coworkers partying too hard?" Cameron teased to take some of the attention off himself and find out a bit more about his younger brother. They hadn't properly talked in so long.

"No," Thomas laughed, then grew a little quieter. "No, but things are kind of sucking there, too. The new branch that opened up, where I'm working now-- uh, by the way, I transferred..."

"Yeah, I know." Jackson had filled Cam in on Thomas's transfer. He'd switched branches last month to move to a brand new branch downtown, and Cam felt bad that he'd had to be filled in on something that big.

"Okay. Um, things are pretty harsh there. The new boss is bad, and we don't have any loyal regulars yet. There isn't the atmosphere I liked," Thomas admitted, pushing his wine glass around. "I've thought about transferring here."

Their mother was concerned but growing tired. She tried to hide her drooping eyelids, but Cam spotted it. She'd been working all afternoon on supper. "How about we go out to the bar and talk about it?" Cameron suggested. *I gotta talk to them about the houses, too.*

"Yeah, good idea," Jackson smiled. "Mom, Dad, you can get some rest. Now that Thomas is in town, he'll be getting us all up early for family bonding time..."

"Shut up," Thomas laughed. "That was *one* Christmas."

Mom interrupted with a wave of her hands and a laugh. "Go on, all of you. We'll get the dishes."

"We can--" Jackson started, but Dad shook his head.

"Just buy us dinner next time," their father teased. "I'm sure you boys can manage that."

"Oh, yeah, of course," they all clamored to agree. They all got to go out together so rarely that there'd be a fight to pay.

"Go on, scram. Let us get some peace, then," Dad added.

After the obligatory hugs and kisses, all three brothers set off for the bar.

***

"So, I had an ulterior motive," Cameron confessed over his beer, pulling out the folded real estate booklet.

They were all settled around a table in their favorite bar. It was the one Jackson had taken Cam to when he turned nineteen, then Cam had taken Thomas to last year on his nineteenth.

I wonder how they'll take this.

"You're looking at real estate now?" Thomas exclaimed while Jackson choked on his beer.

"Just look at the ad."

Both men leaned in across the table and Cameron pushed the ad toward them. It took a minute before it sank in.

"You're thinking... the three of us?"

"I'm not pushing you," Cameron hastened to tell them. "Thomas, you can always transfer back to your old branch, but if you were serious about wanting to come here..."

Thomas's eyes had lit up, and Jackson was beaming.

"No way, man," Jackson exclaimed. "You're serious?"

Cameron drew a deep breath and let it out. "Well, it's worth investigating."

"We never thought you would wanna move back here after a taste of the big life," Thomas murmured. "Jackson and I even talked about splitting a duplex before..."

"Really?"

"Yeah," Jackson laughed. "But, man, this could be perfect. Thomas, do you think you can get a transfer again so soon?"

"I can swing it somehow," Thomas nodded. "Pull strings if I have to."

"I'd have to go home and get the other place cleared out and all that," Cameron shrugged. "But if we're serious... We can help take care of Mom and Dad when they need it, and... you know, be together."

"I like it," Jackson nodded. "But then, I'm already here. It's up to you two."

Thomas and Cameron exchanged looks.

When Thomas nodded, Cameron let his breath out.

I can't believe I'm walking away from that dream.

But, as he'd been trying to do all day, he did his best to reframe it in his mind.

*I'm **getting** something out of this, not losing everything.*

"And, for the love of God, we can all get boyfriends or girl-friends or whatever." Jackson held up his beer in a toast. "And get our shit together."

Cameron laughed and clinked glasses. "I think you two have your shit together. It's just me."

"Doesn't feel like it sometimes," Thomas laughed. "I always thought *you* two did."

Jackson shook his head. "I thought *you* two did." They shared in the next laugh. When they settled down again, all three of them were glowing with pleasure. Cameron's chest was tight with pride he tried to hide: he'd brought them together again, at last.

"What about Coach Walker?" Jackson asked Cameron.

Even that didn't dampen Cameron's spirits. He had to face his coach sometime; the sooner, the better. Cam didn't yet know if he'd be proud or disappointed.

Cameron rose to his feet. No time like the present. "Be right back."

He picked his way around rowdy students celebrating the end of exams and stepped outside, enjoying the cool breeze as he searched for his phone. Before he took it out, though, he spotted a familiar face and the other guy saw him at the same moment.

It was Noah, from the farmer's market. His lips were turned down, but the moment he saw Cameron, a smile broke across his face.

Cameron's cheeks flushed, and he told himself it was just the chilly April air. He didn't believe in signs, but he'd bumped into Noah just as he was about to change everything.

"Hi."

Noah's eyes glimmered, his rich voice a little strained with emotion. "Hello. Fancy meeting you here. Weird timing..."

"It is for me, too." Cameron hesitated. "You all right?"

Noah nodded, that cute blond hair bobbing in the light breeze. "Yeah. I'll be fine," he promised, his eyes flickering back and forth between Cameron's.

"Yeah?" Cameron wished he knew how to offer comfort, but whatever he was doing was working.

Noah's smile only grew. "I'll be great."

CHAPTER
Seven

NOAH

IT WAS THE FIRST TIME NOAH HAD BEEN STOOD UP FOR A DATE since university. He was an ancient twenty-four years old now, and he hadn't had a lot of dates lately. It was a slap in the face after taking the time to get dressed up.

Flaky-ass guys around here, Jesus. It had seemed like a promising first date at a nice bar with an art appreciator. It wasn't that Russell was late; Noah had waited half an hour. He'd never had a date show up more than half an hour late and it wasn't like there was heavy traffic here.

Noah patted his hands together to ward off the spring chill. The nights were still damp, with most of the snow having only melted two weeks earlier. There were still tiny patches here and there in the shade.

That was it for dating, then – blind dating, at least. Noah would wait until someone showed interest in him. Someone like--

The bar door banged open, and the physicality of the man who walked out made Noah glance over. With Noah's pretty lips, swishing hips, and clingy jeans, he was always on guard.

But he didn't have to worry about Cameron.

Despite the chill, Noah's cheeks were warm. His heart pumped, blood rushed through his body, and his jeans were a little too tight. His fingertips tingled, so he pushed his hands into his pockets as he faced Cameron.

The way Cameron's eyes widened made Noah smile. He wasn't the only one who had taken note of the man at the market, then.

He struggled to get over Cameron's physical good looks and respond to small talk. Cameron picked up on his roller coaster of emotions. Far from feeling like a last resort, the way Cameron watched him made Noah feel like the center of the world for a few seconds.

"You all right?"

Noah managed to assure him that he'd be fine. In fact, a smile burst across his face.

"Well, that's better. You're cute when you smile."

Noah's cheeks flushed red and he knew it. He could handle compliments like a grown man, but fuck, Cameron's roguish bad boy air set him off-kilter.

"Th-Thanks," Noah answered, laughing under his breath. "Glad you think so. I just got stood up."

Cameron's expression went from teasing flirtation to furrowed brows. Noah raised his eyebrows. Despite barely knowing him, the man was angry on his behalf.

"That's not right. I'm sorry, man."

Noah shrugged, not wanting to be a downer. He wanted more attention – compliments, physical closeness... "It's my fault. He was a flake, in retrospect. I meet loser 'alpha' dudes who decide they don't wanna be seen in public with... you know." The lisp slipped out despite his best attempt to prevent it, his *losers* and *seen* slipping through the night air.

Cameron didn't cringe. "Just out for a little Grindr action." He nodded sympathetically. "Sorry. I mean, I'm sure everyone says it, but... what about someone more like you?"

"More feminine?" Noah teased, and he was thrilled at the pink staining Cameron's cheeks. Maybe it was just the cold, but maybe it had been *him* having that effect on Cam. "Don't worry. I don't mind people calling me that," he added. "I've tried, but... we end up being friends. I just don't feel the chemistry. They don't turn me on like a guy who can haul me around."

Like him. Oh, fuck. He hadn't even finished the sentence before he realized that Cameron's short t-shirt sleeves showed rippling muscles and strong forearms. They were lightly hairy and Noah wanted to run his palm across the hairs and make Cam's skin tingle. Cam's thumbs were tucked into the pockets of his jeans. *How isn't he cold in just a t-shirt?* As he dragged his gaze back up Cameron's body, a knowing smirk lingered on Cam's lips.

"N-Not that, you know, that's everything... but it just tends to be... a factor..." Noah bit off his sentence before it continued, watching Cameron smirk.

Then, Cameron leaned in and Noah's whole *body* tingled, even though they didn't touch. Cameron's feet shifted until their bodies faced each other. Cameron's foot was between Noah's. Warm breath tickled his jaw as Cameron murmured, "You'd be cute to haul around, believe me."

Noah licked his lips. He *wanted* the burn of this man pressing up close to him, his strong hands closing around his arms or ass...

"But first," Cameron added, pulling back enough for them to make eye contact, "I'd like to hang out and... get to know you."

Noah hadn't expected the just-friends line right after *that* line. *Friends with benefits? Is that what he wants? Or is he looking for a... mature relationship, too?* Either way, he was interested.

"Yes."

Cameron laughed quietly. "I haven't even asked."

Noah cleared his throat. Cameron's eyes sparkled and nose scrunched when he laughed. "To a date. A get-to-know-you date." *He'd better not fall through and get shy at the last moment.*

"Are you asking me?" Cameron teased, but before Noah answered, he nodded. "That's what I'd like. I'd like your number first, though."

"Oh, yeah," Noah murmured, fumbling for his phone to pull it out of his pocket.

They swapped numbers and Noah raised his eyebrows at Cameron's first few digits: 905. "From Toronto?" he asked. Cameron nodded. "How long are you visiting? When works?"

"I'm mid-move, actually. I'm here for another week and a half, and then I fly back to Toronto to finish packing up and properly move."

Oh, so he's very new to town. Why move here without a job lined up? Noah nodded. "Um, you free this weekend?" That was the obvious choice. "Oh, no, I have a hockey game."

"Ah." A startled expression crossed Cameron's face, and Noah fought his immediate reaction: annoyance. Most guys built like Cam had been the star hockey kids. They could never believe that "someone like him" would be into playing hockey at all.

Noah decided to continue. "And next weekend, I'm building wooden boxes for my uncle's beekeeping business."

"I've done carpentry." Cameron winked.

Oh my god, is he offering...? "Oh, I – I can't put you to work on the first date!" Noah laughed, and Cameron joined in with a chuckle. "And honestly, I don't want to wait that long."

Cameron wasn't turned off by his frank admission. "This week, then? Monday evening?"

"Yeah. Perfect," Noah nodded. Monday evening wouldn't force him to wait *too* long, but it was going to feel like an eternity anyway.

"Can't wait." Cameron gave him another of those perfect, gleaming, genuine smiles. How did his teeth glow in the darkness? Had he had them whitened? Noah tried not to let it distract him.

"Me, too."

I should get home before I embarrass myself. Jesus. Noah's hands almost shook with nerves. "O-Okay. I'll see you. Text me and we'll set up the details."

"Will do," Cameron promised, lingering near the door of the bar and waving. It was a sweet moment, and Noah relished it.

Noah raised a hand. He strode down the sidewalk, thankful that the concrete was bare now. It was a quicker getaway when he didn't have to tiptoe across slick patches. He resisted the urge to glance over his shoulder.

Despite the chill, a pleasurable glow deep in his belly warmed him.

Eight

CAMERON

"HELLO, MS. HENLEY? THIS IS CAMERON RILEY. I'M IN TOWN at the moment and my brothers and I saw the ad for the three-house package. I know you might be off Sundays, that's no problem, but we'd like to get a tour on Monday, if possible. Here's a number where you can call me back..." Cameron hated leaving messages. He gave Jackson's number to call back so Rogers wouldn't nail him on long-distance.

Jackson loved working in the early hours, so he was already at his workshop while they waited for Thomas to wake up. Cam was used to waking up early for practice in pitch dark, bone-chilling winter.

"Well, no sense waiting around." Cameron grabbed his jacket and headed for the door. If they couldn't get a formal tour that day, he'd go check out the neighborhood, at least.

The day was brisk but sunny, for which Cameron was grateful. His winter in Toronto had been snowier than usual, so it was nice to bask in sunshine without choking on the cold. Sure, Cam had grown up on skates and handled the cold better than most. Didn't mean he didn't love the warmer weather of cross-training season.

Cameron found the package – three empty houses in a row, but spaced apart well with privacy fencing. That wouldn't work for their family, so he'd install gates. The siding needed painting on all the houses for curb appeal. Those front porches looked old, too... and there wasn't much landscaping. That wasn't even counting updating the dated rooms inside.

But Cameron wanted a project to stay busy while he sat on his ass instead of training like he'd done every summer since he was eight.

"They look good," he murmured under his breath, just for some company. As he walked back past the three houses, he headed downtown to window-shop in the boutiques.

He soon met more people he knew: his parents' friends, a family doctor, and a professor. Everyone was happy to see him – and everyone asked about his hockey career. He brushed them all off by telling them it was a vacation.

He didn't want to tell them all he'd fucking *failed* the one thing he'd been born to do.

Cameron grabbed a newspaper and fresh pastries, then walked to one of his favorite parks to eat and catch up on local news.

The paper was filled with small-town matters from fundraisers to opinion letters on the town council. By chance, Cameron spotted an Events article about an art show coming up at the hockey arena, curated by a Noah.

The same Noah whose pretty dark eyes and smile enchanted Cameron already? He *did* look like an art curator. He'd have to ask.

There was also an ad for a casual men's hockey club. Cameron flipped the paper shut. No sense tempting himself.

Time to get home and make the most of the day with Thomas and Jackson. Having his brothers around all the time would be a change, and they still had a lot to catch up on. Thomas and Jackson had been closer than him since he'd always been away for practice or camp.

And then, of course, he had to get in touch with Noah's uncle about that beekeeping job...

Cameron had to pull his weight wherever he could until he found a new purpose.

CHAPTER
Nine

JACKSON

Jackson had barely stopped work to grab lunch when his phone rang.

"Hi, it's Jessica Henley. I got a message with this number from a Cameron Riley, inquiring about a real estate tour."

"Yeah, that's my brother." Jackson untied his apron and shrugged it off, hanging the heavy garment on a rack. "He's got a Toronto number still."

"Oh, I see. I understand you and he wanted to tour the package of three houses?"

"Yes, with our brother Thomas. The three of us want to move home – well, I'm already here, but they'd be coming back."

"That's wonderful that you're serious buyers. I'm available this afternoon at three, if that's a convenient time for you."

"That's perfect," Jackson agreed. Thomas had the next couple days off before he drove back to Halifax. "Shall we meet you in front of the houses?"

"Yes, is that fine? I'm assuming you know where they are if you live here?"

"Yep, of course," Jackson invited her chuckle with his own. "In front of them at three?"

"Perfect. I'll see the three of you then."

"Thank you, Ms. Henley," Jackson answered, and when they hung up, he pumped his fist.

With his brothers in town, he could have the family reunions he'd always sort of daydreamed about. He'd never thought Cam would come back to Fredericton after getting recruited to Toronto. Superstars never came home until they retired. Million-dollar mansions and celebrity parties outshone the four or five fancy restaurants here.

Jackson tidied up his tools before he left his rented workshop space. He'd be glad to get a backyard workshop set up after they moved.

Cameron worried him, though. That fucking ex of his. He always wormed his way back into Cam's life with a few apologies and a sweet gesture, and Cam always fell for it. He was too kind. Could Cam tear himself away from his sport and his old love all at once?

He called Thomas first to tell him the news. The phone rang twice before his brother picked up, his voice rough around the edges. "Hey, Jackson."

"Afternoon, lazy boy," Jackson teased. "You up and around?" He liked to poke fun at the guy for sleeping in whenever he visited town for a weekend.

"I've been up for an hour, thanks," Thomas grumbled. "Some of us have real jobs, you know."

Jackson just laughed off the snide comment. Thomas *definitely* hadn't been up for an hour if he had that attitude, but he didn't call him out on it. "So I heard back from the realtor. We can do the tour today."

"You told Cam yet?"

"No. Um, listen, on that note…" Jackson trailed off.

"Yeah?"

"I'm worried about him." Jackson didn't want to talk about Cam behind his back, but this was a pretty big change. "You know about his ex, right?"

"Yeah, Nathan? You told me." The scorn dripped from the name when Thomas said it. It was pretty much how Jackson felt, too; but when Thomas let such strong emotions slip, he was pissed.

"Well, that asshole's always had that way of, you know…"

"Winning him over again."

"Exactly. And what with that and having to quit hockey, you know…"

"He might not be thinking straight? I don't know. He seems more clear and grounded than he has in years," Thomas told him.

Cam *was* more focused, especially over the last day or so. He was getting his feet back on the ground. "Yeah. But if Nate comes back…"

"We'll sit down with him," Thomas promised.

"I've told him before, but he never listens. Exes should stay exes. You broke up for a reason, fuckin' stay broken up." Jackson pushed back the living room curtains to check for Cam.

Thomas didn't say anything.

Jackson hesitated, then shook his head. *It's probably nothing.* "Anyway, you comin' over or what? I can put on lunch for us all and we'll head out to the house tour."

"Sounds good. I'll be there in half an hour," Thomas promised.

"Soon as you get out of bed?"

"Bye," Thomas groaned and Jackson laughed when the line

cut off with that. He sent a quick text to Cam to let him know the news, then headed to the kitchen.

"Hey, I'm back! Holy crap, that smells good."

Jackson laughed at the early feedback from his brother. "Thanks," he answered, glancing around the kitchen corner. Cam was kicking off his shoes. "It's just sauteed onions, but it always smells like supper. My home ec teacher taught me how before I switched out for workshop class."

"I'll keep that in mind. So, we got the house tour!"

"Yep," Jackson smiled, and his heart lifted at the smile on Cam's face. His brother looked his age again, his nose and smile a little crooked. He hadn't been moping about his diagnosis, then. Good.

"Thomas's on his way. We'll have lunch and then he just has to drop off something to Mom and Dad and escape again before the tour."

"Cool. Need a hand with anything?"

"Nah, I've got it. Grab a couple beers for us, we can eat outside."

"Before he's back, though, I wanted a word." One-on-one, Cam wouldn't feel cornered.

"'bout what?" Cam cracked open two beers, putting one beside Jackson and leaning on the counter nearby. His sideways gaze was sharp and perceptive as he watched Jackson. No wonder he'd been considered for captain: he was a lot smarter than he gave himself credit for.

"Are you gonna be... okay moving back here?" Jackson asked. It was the most hands-off way to ask the question.

"Oh, yeah," Cam assured him, his chest swelling as he lightly punched Jackson's shoulder. "Getting cold feet already?"

"No," Jackson laughed. "I just worry. I'm a big brother, it's my job."

He'd said it for years, but for the first time, Cam looked at him – really looked – when he said it. Cam's face was set in a light frown, his eyes roving across Jackson's face while he fidgeted with his beer can.

"Are *you* okay?" Cam echoed. "I mean, man, I've hardly heard about your life lately. I was... pretty absent for a while."

"No, man, we all knew that was gonna happen." Was Cam feeling guilty now? Bullshit. He'd been training for one of the highest-paid and most demanding careers in the country.

"I mean, you're not dating or anything."

Jackson grunted. That was down to a couple bad relationships, a lack of eligible guys, and his focus on learning new work skills. He wanted to be the go-to blacksmith for everyone in the area from house builders to art galleries.

Didn't mean he didn't want to date, but Cam was one to talk.

Oh. Wait.

This was his way of trying to broach it, wasn't it?

"Neither are you now," Jackson pointed out, watching him. Cam looked away first, peering out through the small kitchen window to the picnic table. He had something to hide, then. "Or is Nate back?"

"No." That was far more vehement an answer than Jackson had expected, but it set him at ease. Cam didn't lie like this. "No, it's not Nathan. He can fuckin' stay gone. I'm just saying, I'm not *not* dating. I'm open to it."

Has he already met someone? "Oh. Good."

"Yeah." Cam was done with the conversation. A purr of an engine shutting off in the driveway announced Thomas's arrival. Talking about boyfriends was awkward one-on-one, let alone around their presumed-straight brother. Jackson let it go.

The doorknob jiggled. "You locking him out until he gives the password?"

"Oh, shit, I locked it after me."

"Toronto boy." Jackson laughed as Cam jogged to the living room and called out his apology. Maybe too much of a big-city kid right now, but his brother would adjust.

He'd be okay.

CHAPTER
Ten

CAMERON

"WE'RE LIKE THE THREE STOOGES," CAM LAUGHED AS THEY ALL piled out of Thomas's car. Broad-shouldered Jackson and lean, yet muscled Cam contrasted slender, baby-faced Thomas.

A woman in tailored trousers and a blazer smiled as they approached. "You must be the Riley brothers," she greeted them all with handshakes and introductions.

"It's our pleasure," Cam responded, speaking for the other two. He'd always been the spokesman, for no particular reason. Jackson was talkative enough and Thomas wasn't reticent, but they both yielded to him when he was there. "Which house should we go to first?"

"Let's start at this end and work down."

The houses weren't anything Cam hadn't seen before and the first two were especially plain, but he reminded himself they weren't million-dollar postage stamp lofts.

The first house caught Jackson's eye because it had a large, prime workshop space. He said he could easily bring it to code for his forge. The second needed more work, but a gorgeous feature nook in the living room caught Thomas's eye.

As they reached the third house, Cam's stomach clenched. Was he going to like it? Compared to a condo with a view of Toronto stretching out in front of him, minutes away from shopping malls...

Compared to having to share that view with Nathan, he reminded himself. That was enough to jar him to attention as they walked up the path.

"This one's a bit different," Jessica told them. "People touring it are very hit or miss about it. It wasn't built by the same builder like the last two – which was why they were both similar."

It took just one look before Cam saw what Jessica had meant.

The living room was extremely bright with windows on two sides, and tall. Exposed beams crossed an open loft ceiling. A staircase snaked up to the top floor that overlooked the vaulted space. A semicircular nook against the bannister would serve as a small spot to relax. It was braced by a support post downstairs and he made note to find the engineering plans.

The kitchen was the most up-to-date of the three houses, and the open plan meant they already saw clear through to the glass back door and a spacious yard.

Cam loved it. He even had options for carpentry space: a walkout basement and a small outbuilding that needed roof repairs.

"Not my style," Jackson chuckled when they concluded the tour, and Thomas nodded his agreement. It was a city loft in a house, which wasn't their style. Just as well – Cam wouldn't have to fight them for it.

"So, that's it for the three houses. Let's lock this one up and head back out." Jessica led them back to the front sidewalk while Cameron followed, taking one more glance up at the gorgeous vaulted living room.

Thomas asked the question they were all thinking once they reached the sidewalk. "Are there any offers in on this place?"

Cameron held his breath for a second until Jessica shook her head.

"Someone was going to move here from Alberta and put in an offer, but... things didn't work out for him, I understand," she answered. "So the owner's open to offers."

"That's great," Jackson spoke up. "We'll have to have a chat and call you by – say, five?"

Cameron noticed Thomas's startled little glance his way. Their kid brother still rented out in Halifax. He didn't know how fast the market moved.

"That's fine by me. You have my cellphone number," Jessica told them, shaking hands again. "See you soon."

When they were all back in Thomas's car, Cam leaned forward to brace his arms on the back of Thomas's seat. He watched Jackson as they pulled away from the curb for the short drive back to his house. "So?"

"Wow," Thomas breathed out. "That's... that's a lot to take in."

"What is?"

"They all need some work."

"Luckily you know a guy who did a carpentry apprentice-ship and has a lot of free time," Cameron teased.

"You said you're a retired hockey player." Jackson repeated, twisting in his seat to make eye contact.

Cameron swallowed but nodded firmly. "I already made up my mind at the restaurant when we decided to do this." He avoided the emotional moment by switching right back to the subject of the house tour. "Did you guys like the first two? Neither of you were sold on the third one."

"I liked the first one, and I think you liked the second, hey, Thomas?"

Thomas nodded. "And you were sold on the third from the moment we walked in."

Cam couldn't deny it. "Yeah. I didn't know anywhere here had that kind of architecture."

"It did suit you," Jackson admitted. "I suppose you'll want me to custom-make some railings, huh?"

Oh, shit, that would be cool. Cam's jaw dropped as he stared at Jackson, already imagining the possibilities.

"Don't strain his heart," Thomas teased. The joke was cautious and even Jackson glanced at Cameron to make sure he laughed before chuckling.

"Fuck off," Cam told Thomas, slapping his shoulder and leaning back in his seat again. "Anyway, I'm sold."

"Do we wanna risk losing it? Offer lower?"

Thomas cleared his throat. "Well, I was doing some research and it's been on the market for a while. She even said the owner's willing to negotiate. I'm guessing a three-house package is harder to move than they expected."

*Man. We can actually do this. **I** can actually do this.*

Cameron was a little worried about the mortgage, but it would be way cheaper than Toronto rent. He'd find a way to make it work – by manual labor, if he had to. It wouldn't be the same kind of stress that triggered his heart problems. Carpentry, beekeeping, teaching kids to skate – anything low-stress... He'd do whatever he had to.

"So, when are we gonna put in the offer?" Cam asked.

"Today?" Jackson asked, glancing in the rear view mirror.

Cam met his gaze and nodded firmly. "Today."

"Today," Thomas repeated in a murmur. Silence fell until they pulled up to the curb outside Jackson's cramped house – which, if all went well, would soon be up for sale.

Jackson shook his head before Cam climbed out of the car. "Don't drop us off. Let's go tell Mom and Dad."

Their parents were ecstatic, and the brothers' offer was filed with only a few hours' worth of phone calls and paperwork. Jessica had told them it would likely be a few days. They'd had to sign an irrevocable clause to leave their offer on the table for two days so the seller could receive other offers.

Once they left the stuffy real estate office, Thomas headed to their parents' home while Jackson and Cameron headed to Jackson's house for a quiet supper. Celebrations would come after the offer was accepted... if it was accepted.

While Jackson flitted around looking at his furniture and muttering about boxes, Cameron's phone went off. He didn't even have to reach in his pocket to know who it was. Cameron had been expecting this call all weekend.

"Be back in a bit."

When he sat on the picnic bench, Cameron pressed "answer" on the incoming call. "Hey, Coach."

"Hey, kid. Haven't heard from you in a while. I thought I know what that means, but I wanted to make sure."

Cameron swallowed. That was Coach Walker reprimanding him for not having the guts to call first and admit that he was deserting the team. "Yeah. Uh, I've been doing some thinking."

"Don't hold back."

"I'm moving back home. I'm quitting. At least... until I get my heart fixed. Maybe later, if I'm still... anywhere near the skill level I'd need to be to get back on the team..." Cameron trailed off.

There was silence for a long minute – near-silence, anyway. Spring birdsong was loud here. He lay back on the bench, staring up at the bright clouds as the sun tried to burst through.

"You sure about that?"

"Yeah," Cameron said, his voice quiet. "I can't let it kill me."

"I'm proud of you, kid. Everyone says it's quitting, but it takes guts to walk away while you're ahead. And to look after yourself. Can't say I'm not disappointed I'll never see your full potential, though. You had a lot more in you."

Fuck. This sounded so final.

"Thanks, Coach Walker. I was gonna call, but... got caught up in the house hunt," *and meeting gorgeous men,* "and wrapping my mind around it all is still pretty... you know."

"I know." After a moment, his voice quieter, the coach repeated, "I know. Look, I'm glad you're choosing your family and your future. The other guys might laugh, but in ten years they'll have a lot less than you if they don't play their cards right. I hope they all do, but you've got a good head on your shoulders."

The coach had never said these kinds of things to him, let alone all at once. It only reaffirmed Cameron's suspicions: this *was* goodbye.

"Um, you guys still having the season-end party after locker clean-out?"

He didn't dare mention the game. The series was tied three-three and game seven was on Thursday.

He wasn't gonna be there, even in the stands.

Traitor, his brain said.

Coach Walker knew what he was thinking.

"Yeah. You're coming, of course," the coach told him in a voice that left no room for argument. "You gotta tell the guys yourself."

"They already know, don't they?"

"Yeah, but they deserve to hear it."

"I know," Cam admitted. Coach Walker was right, as always.

"Are you coming to locker clean-out day?"

Cameron rubbed his face. He had to. It was in his contract. But all the media questions: what was he doing next? Was he drafted? Why hadn't he been on the ice? If the guys lost on Thursday, did he feel responsible?

"Maybe. As long as the journos don't fuckin' skin me."

"I'll make sure they don't," Coach Walker promised. "Come by later, around four."

Cameron's flight back was early morning, so he could make it if he packed fast. Besides, he wouldn't miss the party for his life. "Pass on my love, a'ight? They're gonna do great."

"Will do. See you there, kid. Take care." There was warmth in the man's voice, and Cameron smiled.

His own brain still screamed at him that he was being a traitor and letting the others down, walking away from the chance of a lifetime. At least he had someone on his side who understood that voice in his head, and that made all the difference.

CHAPTER
Eleven
CAMERON

MONDAY PASSED WITHOUT WORD BACK ON THE OFFER. NONE OF them expected to hear back until Tuesday, when the owner would have to accept or reject it. It was a frustrating distraction, but also good since Cam had his date that day.

He forgot about all his stresses when he spotted Noah waiting outside.

As always, he was *gorgeous*. His light blond hair was wispier, gelled up in a nice textured cut that Cameron kind of envied. He'd always kept his hair close-cropped to keep him safer in fights. He greeted Noah with a cheery, "Hey. Nice haircut – did you just get it done?"

Noah spun on his heel, then beamed. "Thanks! Yeah, I went out on my lunch break today," he admitted, shifting from foot to foot. Adorable.

Cameron tried not to let on that he was just as nervous.

"Let's head in," Cameron told him, opening the door to the trendy new bar and restaurant.

"You chose a good place," Noah told him. They approached

the maitre-d's station and waited for someone to seat them. "I come here sometimes after work."

"Oh, yeah? You work nearby?"

"At the gallery just down the road."

"The national gallery?" Cameron's eyebrows rose. "Nice."

"Thanks," Noah smiled.

"Evening, gentlemen. A table for two?" the waiter greeted as he approached.

Cameron nodded. "Thanks."

They followed along to a cozy, romantic private corner booth with a lit candle on the table. "Will this do?"

"Great, thanks," Cameron approved. Had the waiter guessed that it was a date?

"Let me run over the specials with you."

After hearing about a warm cheesy chicken pasta, Cameron safely tuned out. His mind was made up. He asked for something local on tap, and Noah guided his choice.

Once they had their beers and were settling back in the booth, they finally got a proper chance to see each other.

Noah had a delicate build with a thin face, full lips, thick brows, and a beautiful angular jaw. Jesus, he looked like a model.

Cameron's heart skipped a beat. He was a sucker for a pretty face like anyone else, as much as he was trying not to make this about a rebound. Noah had been studying him at the same time, and Cameron wondered what he saw and if he liked it.

"So," Noah broke the silence with a smile. "How was your day?"

"Uneventful," Cameron admitted. "I was waiting around all day in case a real estate agent called..."

"Oh, are you house hunting?"

"My brothers and I found these properties we think are great," Cameron told him. "We should hear back by tomorrow, and I fly out Thursday to pack up and move out of Toronto."

"So you're coming here," Noah said with a marveling smile. "What a time to run into you."

"Yeah, I know," Cameron chuckled. "It's kinda nice. I'm not moving here knowing nobody."

"Are you from around here? I'm not," Noah admitted. "My uncle wound up moving here to buy a business about a decade ago, but I was born in Alberta and raised in Ottawa."

"Oh? I'm from here, yeah. How'd you end up in Ottawa?"

"My parents' jobs."

Cameron liked the smoothness on his palate followed by a hint of a bitter twist at the end of his beer. It wasn't the bland stuff he drank at team parties just to get drunk. "What do they do? Or did they do?"

"My mom was an art gallery curator."

"Oh, so you're following in her footsteps," Cameron smiled. That rang a bell. "Hey, are you curating a show at the arena?"

"That's the one! You heard?"

"Saw it in the paper."

Noah pumped a fist and Cameron laughed, nearly spilling his beer from surprise. "Sorry," Noah blurted, holding out a hand to steady the glass.

Their fingers brushed.

Cameron's hand burned, a tingle shooting straight up his arm. His heart squeezed with warmth and even his thighs tingled, a shiver running down his spine.

Holy shit, they had chemistry.

Noah's lips were parted as he drew his hand back slowly and sat straight again, their eyes locking.

Fuck, he had pretty eyes.

"Well," Cameron chuckled under his breath. Better to acknowledge the moment than pretend it hadn't happened.

"Yeah."

"I'm trying to be good," Cameron admitted, bracing his elbows on the table. "I mean, I was never the type to just... you know, go home with anyone... but I broke up not long ago."

Understanding flickered across Noah's face, but instead of being wary, he just smiled. "Aw. Yeah, I get it. Sorry."

"No, it's fine. That's part of coming back home. I'm moving out of the place I was living with my ex. But I don't want to dump all that on you."

"Were you living together for a long time?"

Thank God, no. "No. The last year, off and on, but only steady for the last two months," Cameron told him. "But we're through now for sure," he assured Noah. "It wasn't working out. I want something more... mature, but it doesn't have to be right away."

Noah nodded along. Those sweet dark eyes flickered between Cameron's as he fidgeted with the hair at the back of his neck with a couple fingers. His wrist bent loosely across his shoulder. The intense focus of his gaze made Cameron almost trip over his tongue.

"What about you?"

"I've been single for about a year and a half, I guess."

"Is that a long time for you, or are you the infrequent dater?" Cameron asked.

"I... well, I dated through college, and then I sort of stopped when I got here. Like I said, I tried to go on dates but nobody here wanted to come out, and those who're out already have boyfriends."

Cameron nodded. "It was a lot like that growing up, but even more strict. Things are better now. But after Ottawa..."

"Exactly," Noah chuckled. "But I like it here. The slow town pace... there's just something enchanting, you know?"

Cameron nodded. He would have nodded even if he had no idea what Noah meant, his voice was so persuasive in its subtle, gentle tones. "What about family? Mine are all here. Yours still in Ottawa?"

"Yeah," Noah sighed. "That's my one regret. We haven't always got on perfectly, but things have been better lately. But I had to come out here for my career. Curator jobs don't always open up, especially in the capital."

Cameron didn't notice time passing, their conversation was so smooth. Over supper, they talked about Noah's experiences at the art gallery and Cameron's memories of the city.

It was just *easy* to spend time with Noah. He kept thinking about how much he wanted to crowd into Noah's space and pin him against the bedroom wall and kiss him so slowly he begged for it...

Heat staining his cheeks, Cameron pulled himself out of the thought to choose a dessert.

By the time they were done, they were loose and relaxed around each other. They joked easily and brushed their hands together as they left the restaurant.

Noah was nice and normal – especially compared to certain exes. He was sweet, career-driven, loyal to his family, a little self-absorbed about his appearance, but clever when it came to art. Cam had no idea what he meant when he talked about trends and movements, but he tried to learn.

For his part, Noah could hardly keep his eyes off Cameron, either.

As they reached the sidewalk, Cameron cleared his throat. "So, you've got work in the morning, huh? I should walk you home. You live nearby?"

"Yes. Oh, that's *sweet!*" Noah's lisp was so strong even Cameron had to laugh. Noah joined in with a sheepish expression.

"The lisp's cute," Cameron assured him. "Not something you hear around here a lot. I *can* use it, I just... you know. Don't."

"Gay as the day is bright," Noah shrugged with a carefree smile at Cameron. He nodded down the street toward his house and they started to walk. "I like it that way."

Cameron glanced over. He'd been contented to spend years in that space between the closet and public knowledge, but Noah faced things he didn't every day. At least Fredericton was better now. Jackson had gotten suspended four times one school year while he paved the way for Cam's class. "Yeah? You don't ever get annoyed with people... I don't know, assuming things?"

"Of course. They assume things when they look at you, too, don't they? That you're a big, fit, straight guy with a sweet girlfriend... you work on a farm or the oil rigs..."

"I hope not," Cameron laughed with surprise. Before he even drew breath, Noah's hand was slipping into his. His heart squeezed as he laced his fingers with the thinner ones between his own. Noah's hand was cold, and he wanted to radiate warmth even as his skin tingled with pleasure at the contact. "Yeah. That's true." It was a weird conversation for a first date, but he appreciated Noah's direct, sly humor.

"So, you're not closeted, or...?"

"No," Cameron assured him. "My family all know. I've always been kinda quiet at work, but not because I'm hiding. Everyone knows. I think they just don't want to make comments because I'm usually bigger than them. Then they stopped caring." He'd been one of the bigger, tougher guys on the team. It had only taken a couple months for the mildly homophobic bros to learn better.

They turned the corner toward the graveyard and cut through it.

"That's good," Noah approved. "So, why leave Toronto if you don't have a job lined up here?"

"I want to be around my family. I've got some savings so I can float 'til I find something. I'm a decent carpenter so I can find work through my brother's business if I have to. If the beekeeping thing with your uncle works out, so much the better. I have some skills I can teach. I'll figure things out," Cameron told him with a confident smile, and Noah mirrored it.

"It's nice to be around a guy who isn't moping about work, you know."

"Yeah, the same about you," Cameron agreed. "Hearing you talk about the... post-Atlantic-fishery periods, or whatever..."

"Close enough," Noah chuckled as he squeezed Cameron's hand. They waited to cross the street on the other side of the little park. "I'm glad it's not too nerdy."

"Nah," Cameron assured him.

"I live right over there."

"Cute little house," Cameron approved. It was only a fifteen-minute walk from Jackson's place and ten minutes from the potential new house. Noah's white-sided house had a small front yard and three floors. "An apartment?"

"Nope, the whole thing."

"Cool." They crossed the street to stand in front of the stairs, still holding hands. Cameron finally moved to drop Noah's hand and face him. "Man, this was a great first date."

"Wasn't it?" Noah agreed, his teeth flashing in a sincere smile. "I liked it, too." Noah looked him up and down.

Cameron's groin tingled with the desire to slip his hands around Noah's narrow waist and down his straight hips to the curve of his ass.

It wasn't his imagination: Noah's breathing was heavy. His gaze slid down to Cameron's lips and he licked his own in a clear invitation.

Cameron leaned in, cupping Noah's cheek in his palm as their lips met for the first time.

Oh, fuck. He wanted to turn their fascination with each other in conversation to curiosity about each other's bodies and pleasures...

Noah's lips pressed hard against his. When his tongue pressed at Cam's lips, Cameron plunged his tongue into Noah's mouth and Noah moaned under his breath.

Smooth hands cupped Cameron's face in a clear signal not to pull back. Cameron stepped closer instead, slotting his thigh between Noah's and pressing their chests together.

"Mm," Cameron murmured, pulling back from the kiss for long enough to catch his breath and make eye contact. He wanted to make sure Noah was good with this.

Noah was *more* than good with this. His breathing was harsh, his body angled toward Cameron's. His eyes were wide and dark with hunger. Cameron loved the pink flush across Noah's cheeks, and it was easy to feel his grip on the back of Cameron's neck.

Noah yanked Cameron back in to kiss him. Cameron laughed with surprise before warm lips sensually slid against his own again. They breathed together through their noses, their bodies melting together in the cool spring evening.

Cameron's cock hardened in his jeans. Noah's hands were wandering and it made his stomach clench with arousal.

The images flashing through his mind were hard to control.

This man was a goddamn great kisser. Noah's lips pinched around Cameron's lower lip to suck it before letting it gradually pop free from the kiss.

Cameron yearned for an invitation inside, but this *wasn't* a rebound. He had to control himself.

When Cameron finally pulled back, sparks still flew between them. Noah's eyes were on Cam's lips like he wanted to lean in for a third round.

It was a sentiment Cameron shared. This was the hottest chemistry he'd felt for *years*.

"Wow," Noah breathed out, his voice a little shaky as his hands slipped from Cameron's shoulders. "Um, that was a good night kiss for the ages."

Cameron burst out laughing, his cheeks burning with heat. "We might have gotten carried away..."

"Good," Noah murmured. Even though they weren't touching, he still stood just inches away, his breath warm against Cameron's chin.

"So, we'll see each other... soon?" Cameron asked. "When are you free?"

"Wednesday?" Noah suggested.

Cameron grinned. *He's feeling just the same, I bet.* That was the night of *the* game, but... "Wednesday's great," he murmured, his eyes flickering between Noah's. He took both of Noah's hands, swaying closer for a proper good night kiss.

This one was slower and sweeter, but there was a sensual tinge to it, too. Parted lips rubbed across each other's for a few moments before he pulled back. The brush of warm breath, the tingle of firm, kiss-swollen lips together... "Good night," Cameron murmured.

"Good night," Noah answered, letting go of Cameron's hands with a smile and a wink. He trotted up the wooden steps to his door, fumbling for his keys. Cameron waited until Noah had them before walking off.

This time, Cameron glanced back at the same moment as Noah. They shared a smile just for a moment, and then Cameron crossed the street again through the early evening.

Cameron's whole body still tingled. He was certain he was going to be glowing even when he got back to Jackson's place.

Fuck, I can't wait for a house of my own. More than that... Fuck, I'm crushing on Noah.

It wasn't the closely-guarded affair he'd expected. It wasn't secrecy and trying to tiptoe around to keep this potential new guy in his life happy. It was... light, fun, and sexy.

A date the same day we'll hear back about the house.

What a day that was going to be.

CHAPTER
Twelve

NOAH

THAT WAS THE BEST FIRST DATE NOAH HAD EVER BEEN ON.

At first, he hardly remembered why he was rolling out of bed with a smile on a Tuesday morning when it was raining outside. It took just seconds to remember: the guy who had listened so well to him, walked him to his door, kissed him like a fucking *rock star*...

"Oh, man," Noah groaned as he rolled out of bed for the shower. Even thinking of Cameron made his body tingle, and then there was their good night texts. Only a couple, back and forth:

I had a great time. Thank you for coming out with me. Safe walk home, Noah had sent.

Minutes later, Cameron had answered, *So did I. You're cute. Can't wait for Wednesday. Good night xx.*

Were those hugs or kisses? Noah had fallen asleep last night trying to decide.

He scrubbed his body, well aware that he craved the attention he hadn't gotten last night.

Oh, fine. What could it hurt? He had a spare few minutes to

spend thinking about Cameron holding him firmly, kneading into Noah's back to drag him closer...

Even if it was just friends with benefits, Cameron was fucking hot and Noah would agree to it. He just... hoped for more. Cameron's words had been so promising.

Instead, Noah turned his attention to the memory of Cam's "gonna fuck you" eyes.

***

Noah hunched into his raincoat for the walk to work and grimaced when his cellphone rang. The number was the director of the hockey arena hosting his art exhibit.

It's gonna be one of those days. Everyone's going to ask things of me. He shoved his phone under his hood to keep it dry and hunched forward a little. "Hello?"

"Hi, Noah. It's Jason. Miserable morning out there, isn't it?"

Out here, Noah thought but didn't comment. Some people still thought he was a bit weird for walking to work even though he only lived ten minutes' walk away. "Yeah, it is. April showers, right?"

"Bring May flowers? I hope you're right. So, about this little exhibition..."

Little exhibition? Noah bit back his annoyance. "Right?"

"The board is thinking of giving you half the space for the exhibition and reserving the other half for our permanent awards display."

No way. Jason had always been pretty straight-up with him, but there were bullshitters behind the scenes. "Why?"

Jason hummed. There was a story behind this. "Well, let's just say... someone with a particular attachment to the place thinks it's more important."

An ex-hockey player, then. Noah groaned. "I've commissioned stuff already – I've done a lot of work. Giving me half the space at the last moment? That wasn't our agreement.."

"I know," Jason said. "I'm sorry. I can understand that frustration."

No, you can't. "I'd politely disagree with this person," Noah continued. He straightened up despite the mist of rain that blew into his face. His speech was precise and crisp now. He'd practiced the non-accent to be taken seriously in his grad school classes. "Awards can be shown anytime, and they have been for years. I want to do something new."

"Well..." Jason drawled. He sounded like he wanted to agree. "I know, but there's some resistance to change. If you can appease them on the board, I'm sure I could try to have a chat with them."

Noah wracked his brain. "Why do they want the awards? Because of the local connection?"

"Yeah, they're all for local players."

Noah pressed a crosswalk button, gazing ahead to his art gallery. "Um, how about something custom? I already have two commissioned pieces, but I could possibly add more. I have enough room in my budget for a few more works."

"A contingency fund. Well done. I think that might do it. Email me with specifics and I can approach the people who make decisions over here," Jason promised. "No guarantees, but I'll do my best."

What about some original drawings or paintings? I have the painted pucks and the steel sculpture, but not traditional pieces yet... Noah was already thinking about local artists. "I'll get back to you as soon as I can. Thanks, Jason."

"Thanks. Talk to you later."

Noah shoved his phone back into his pocket. Fuck, this

town was sometimes so resistant to anything new. People wanted to be recognized, and saw anything new as an attack on them. It wasn't like he was demanding the awards be taken down. He'd planned carefully to work the artwork around them.

Time to check in on my commissions. He unlocked the side door with his pass card and shook off his coat like a dog as he walked into the building. The unpleasant day had ruined his hair and dampened his trousers already. He was going to have to sit in front of the heater in his office for a while as he made these calls.

While his computer booted up, Noah leaned back in his chair and wheeled closer to the heater, the phone against his ear ringing.

"Hello?" the gruff voice on the other end answered.

"Hey, Jackson, it's Noah. Just wondering how things are coming along."

"I'll be ready in good time, don't worry. I built in a week of wiggle room, just in case."

Noah loved Jackson. "Oh, God. Thank you," he groaned.

Jackson laughed. "That bad, huh?"

"Oh, you don't want to know. Things are changing on me," Noah admitted. "But don't worry – there *will* be room for everything, especially your piece and the other commission. I'll arrange the loans around that."

"Good," Jackson approved. "Good on you for doing all this. It's not easy to get people to agree to new things around here."

"I enjoy it," Noah fibbed. He *did*, just not this particular second. "And it'll be great."

"I know it will. I should get back to it, then. I'm about ready to have you come by and check on it... maybe this weekend?"

"That'll be great," Noah agreed, settling on a date and time. "Thanks a bunch, Jackson."

"Thank you," Jackson answered, polite as always. "See you."

At least someone around here kept his promises. Well, two someones... Cameron hadn't stood him up last night. And that had been an incredible date. Noah smiled to himself until he realized his name was being repeated from the doorway.

Noah was about ready to call it quits that day when another light knock sounded on his office door. He'd had to lead Sarah's guided tours since she was off sick that day. Then, a coworker and his boss had both checked in about that damn hockey exhibition. He'd assured them both it was all under control. Then, he'd gotten in touch with local artists about painting and sketch commissions.

And now it was the manager of the restaurant just down the street. Jay was a sweetie, about twenty years old and in their first managerial role ever. They were a bit of an anomaly here, even more so than Noah. Noah had liked them from the moment he first met them.

"Hey, Noah." From the way they said it, Noah knew they wanted to ask a favor.

"Hey. Join the line of requests," Noah teased, sitting up straight and gesturing for them to sit down.

"Actually, wanna come to the restaurant? I'll treat you to a drink and supper while I proposition you," Jay teased.

Noah laughed. The restaurant sometimes displayed art that the gallery had to sell after local exhibitions. It was a friendly working relationship, and he liked the sound of food and drink. "Sounds fair." It didn't take long for him to shut down his computer and close up his office.

"How's that hockey... league... going, then?"

"Oh, Jesus, I thought you were gonna ask about the hockey exhibit," Noah admitted in an undertone. Jay laughed. "The league's good, I think. Haven't had much time to think about it lately."

"I won't ask about the exhibit," Jay teased. "I saw both the ads in the paper. Nicely done."

Noah raised his eyebrow. "Did they run them next to each other?"

"You didn't buy a copy of the paper?"

"Oh, I was a bit jaded," Noah admitted. "I figured they'd make it sound boring."

"Come prepared to discuss symbolism at seven-thirty?" Jay grinned. "Yeah, that does sound a bit boring. Nah, both the write-ups were pretty good."

Noah ordered his usual without even thinking about it as they reached the restaurant bar. "So," Noah said, straightening up and turning on his stool once he had his cherry cocktail. "Hit me with it."

"We're planning this... charity event."

A smile tugged at Noah's lips. "Uh huh?"

"We've already got someone running it, don't worry. One of my good friends is the manager. But we need someone to help us source art and liaise with local artists. Since I took over, I haven't been in touch with a lot of the older painters. I only know the hip young zine-makers..."

Noah nodded. "Are we talking donations?"

"Maybe. We have a small budget. We're splitting the proceeds – a token artist's fee for each painting sold, with most of the proceeds to charity."

"They'll donate all the profits," Noah told Jay with a shake of his head, sipping his drink. "That's not a problem. If the charity's good."

"A new local homelessness initiative. We're fundraising over the summer, hoping to get a fund accumulated before the winter. Last winter was..."

"Nasty," Noah agreed, the corners of his lips falling. That *had* been a rough winter. "That's a good idea. It's a proper charity? Registered?"

"Yes."

"Then that shouldn't be a problem. We can do tax rebates, but even without that, they'll do it for good exposure. It has to be good, though. A brochure with addresses to everyone's website and portfolio is a start."

"Does that help a lot?"

"Oh, yeah. Our statistics tell us sixty percent of art buyers we track end up buying more artwork in that style. Twenty percent look for that artist again."

Jay blinked a few times. "Oh. That's – that's precise."

Noah grinned as his food arrived. "It's my job." As he ate, he delved into the details, making sure Jay had a good idea what to expect from the exhibition.

By the time he was on his way home, Noah's heart was light. In the five months since moving here, he hadn't felt like he'd made many friends who appreciated who he was. The hockey guys were great, but so straight. Jay had always been friendly, though. With the possibility of dating Cameron, things were looking up.

Even the light misty rain couldn't dampen Noah's spirits. He threw back his hood to let it cool his face as he strode home.

CHAPTER
Thirteen

CAMERON

"Hello? Is this Cameron Riley?"

From the moment Cameron answered his cellphone, he was suspicious. The man's voice sounded even and crisp, just like a reporter or a telemarketer. There was something not quite right. "It is," Cam agreed.

"This is Lyle Newman from the..."

Oh, no. The journalists have a hold of me. How the fuck did he get my number?

"...I have a few questions. First of all--"

It's a pressure tactic. You don't have to say yes. Cameron went over his media training again. "What's the question?"

"Your absence is noticeable on the ice. Everyone's wondering: are you joining another team instead of Toronto?"

"You should talk to Coach Walker about this. I'm not sure how you got my number, but I won't have much insight for you." Coach Walker was great at stonewalling. Cam's announcement would happen once the team's season officially ended.

"We're more interested in getting the whole story from you."

"Sorry, I can't help you with your story."

"What do you think of your team's chance of success on Thursday given your absence? We all know you're the star--"

"Call Coach Walker. He'll let me know if he wants me to set up an interview." Cameron hung up on him.

"Journalists?" Jackson asked from the kitchen and Cameron sighed.

"Yeah."

"That was quick. Do they usually bug you?"

"No. I don't know how they found me or why they're calling," Cameron admitted. "Coach Walker will shut them down though. What are your plans today? It's the big day... they have to get back to us by five," he added.

"Yeah. I'm thinking they'll wait as long as they can. I'm going to the workshop until lunch and then I'll head back here and wait around with you. Poor Thomas, having to go to work," Jackson laughed.

Cameron shook his head. "At least he should be off by the time we find out. Well, what is it, three-thirty?"

"Yeah, he took the early shift today to be home by four. And he's discussing the transfer today, too..."

"Man, I hope that goes well." Cameron was full of restless energy. He wanted to be out moving, pumping his legs, lifting weights... doing *something* to fill his day.

"We should hear about it on his lunch break. At least, if it doesn't go well, we'll know. I'm assuming it'll take some time to set up if they accept it."

Cameron nodded. "You'd better get to work," he told Jackson. "I'll keep you company." He liked hanging around the metalworking shop. The atmosphere was intense: sparks flying, the forge roaring, his brother focusing on drawing out the right bits and hammering down the others.

"Oh, no. Nah, it's boring. Just boring work today. You take it easy today."

Maybe Jackson was on edge with nerves like Cam and didn't want to show it. He'd let him keep his dignity. It would be a long day, but he'd find some way to fill it. Make a to-do list of utilities to contact, stuff to pack and sell, maybe get a quote from U-Haul.

As Jackson left, Cameron's skin crawled with energy. He'd been off the ice and out of the gym for long enough that it was starting to get to him. This was going to be the worst part of his new phase of life: learning how *not* to push himself to his limits every day.

Considering the scale of the news he was waiting for via Jackson, today was going to be the hardest easy day he'd ever had.

***

"Dude, you're not gonna believe this."

As Jackson burst through the door, Cameron spilled the bag of chips that had been under his arm. They crunched underfoot as he scrambled to his feet from Jackson's couch, his heart pounding.

There was a bit of dizziness, but he tried to breathe deeply and not let his anxiety rise. "We've got an answer? Why didn't you text me?" The disbelieving laugh that echoed from Jackson and the openness of his face told Cameron. "A yes from the realtor?"

Jackson strode forward to crush him in a hug. "Thomas called five minutes before her. The transfer's approved. Before I hung up with Mom and Dad, the realtor called..."

"*And?*" They'd gone in a few thousand lower than the listed price, sensing a lack of competition. If it paid off, it would cover their closing costs. If not... they could have lost the houses. But not with the way Jackson was grinning. "Spit it out!"

"The offer's been approved."

Cameron's chest was tight, but he took a few more deep breaths and sank down to sit on the couch again. "No way."

"Yeah." Jackson sat next to him, making a face at the floor and spilled chips. He shifted his feet to avoid further crushing them into the carpet. "As soon as we sign the papers, the houses are all ours. One month closing like we asked for."

"Thomas is taking tomorrow off and driving out tonight to get the papers signed first thing and meet his new branch. The realtor's fine with that. The offer's been accepted, they can't back out now."

The room shifted around him and his fingers twitched. "Holy shit."

It was impossible to process the simultaneously crushing and thrilling reality of this change. He'd have the weight of a mortgage but freedom from his rent payments, the joys of seeing his family every week, maybe every day...

"Stay calm," Jackson added after a moment, realization flashing over his face. "Shit. I forgot. Sorry."

"I'm okay." He could still talk and breathe, after all.

"I forgot..."

Cameron was sharper than he meant as he answered, "I know." Then, he felt bad. *I can't become a cranky dick about this.*

After a moment, he let out his breath and offered his brother a smile instead, then rose to his feet and hauled Jackson up to hug him.

Jackson laughed his surprise, then clapped Cameron's back and hugged him hard. "Let's call Thomas." He pulled back, his arm still around Cam's shoulders, and dialed Thomas's number. When Thomas picked up, he held his phone out at arms-length.

Several rings later, a grainy video feed popped into view: Thomas in the car, pulled over on the side of the road. "Hey, guys! Did you tell him?"

"Yeah!" Jackson exclaimed. "He nearly fainted."

"But I'm fine," Cameron added, shoving Jackson. "No thanks to you, asshole."

"Holy shit." Thomas laughed, disbelief and relief flooding his expression. "Careful, man. I told you not to stress him out."

"I forgot!" Jackson defended himself. "But holy shit, can you believe it?"

"Are you on your way here?"

"I'm stopping by home first," Thomas told him. "Then I'll drive straight out. I'll get there..." He rubbed his face and glanced off-screen. "Around ten? Depends where I stop for food."

"Too late for our celebration dinner with Mom and Dad. They'll stay up, but restaurants will be closed by then..." Cameron frowned, counting the hours on his fingers. "If you made it by nine-thirty..."

"No, don't worry about it," Thomas waved a hand. The camera wobbled as he shifted the phone. "Go celebrate and I'll join in tomorrow, huh?"

The atmosphere around the dinner table that evening was

bittersweet, though. It was ironic that they were making the move to be closer, yet Thomas couldn't celebrate it because he was too far away.

Cameron shook himself back to focusing on his dad's stories. *Soon, it'll all change.*

CHAPTER
Fourteen

NOAH

IN HIS LAST GUIDED TOUR ON WEDNESDAY, NOAH WAS HARDLY focused. It was a group of older retired folks, tourists, and two university students and he was showing them the exhibit on the cod moratorium in Newfoundland.

Nobody took much note of the photograph that was *his* favorite – an old black-and-white photo taken in the 90s. Two fishermen were leaning across the edges of their boats. One man braced his chapped, rough hands on the edge of his boat, watching and worrying. The other twisted the net away to reveal the bright, wide eyes of a scarce few small cod caught in the huge net.

After the tour, Noah came back to the photo to admire the details. Even in black and white, it was potent. Every time he saw it, he sensed the stress and the grief of the fishing life.

Before his life as a beekeeper, his uncle Bill had once spent his days fishing on a Newfoundland boat. Back in the late eighties, before Noah's birth, life had been good for him. He'd heard the story dozens of times: fish from shore to shore, good hauls, rough work that paid, and then less and less, and then the moratorium. Plants closing, docks shutting down, boats rotting, communities emptying out.

Bill had gotten sick of it and moved back to New Brunswick where Noah's dad's parents had lived briefly. He'd stumbled into beekeeping, and it was an industry that paid better each year.

It was the barest of connections between Noah and the piece, but it was enough that he stared at the men and wondered if his uncle would have known them. He'd only come to the art gallery a couple times, and never to this exhibit. He said it was too hard on him.

The gentle announcement from the front desk ushered visitors out. Noah snapped back to attention, a smile spreading across his face. Time to do a walk of the exhibit, answering questions while guiding visitors to the cloakroom.

And then... a shiver of anticipation ran down Noah's spine. Supper, a shower, and a date with the man who had been on his mind all day.

***

This time, Noah was the first to spot Cameron. The broad-shouldered man had a smooth way of walking, like he was gliding wherever he went. He had a certain graceful awareness of his body despite his broad, yet lean physicality. It was smoking hot.

"Hey," Noah called out to get Cameron's attention as he crossed the street toward the wine bar.

Cameron's head snapped up as he scanned his field of vision in one swift motion. He quickly made eye contact with Noah. The lazy, easy smile made Noah tingle. Cam's full, narrow lips pursed in almost a heart shape before his face cracked into a winning smile.

It was so easy to smile along with him, and Noah did.

"Hi," Cameron greeted as he joined Noah, reaching out to brush his hand down Noah's arm. Noah sizzled with pleasure.

"How are you? You made it," Noah commented, then kicked himself for stating the obvious. "Uh, I'm glad."

"I'm glad you did, too."

Already, there was heat between them. Noah resisted the urge to sway into Cameron and give him a hello kiss. "Come on in," he invited and waved at the wine bar. "Wine and cheese?"

"Great plan," Cameron agreed. "I have to warn you, I don't know a lot about wine. I usually go for beer."

"Tonight will be your education, then," Noah teased and winked. He knew that could be taken multiple ways.

Cameron caught on. His voice was sultry as he leaned in behind Noah to open the door for him. He murmured right into his ear, "I like being taught new things."

His breath on Noah's neck was warm. The quick brush of Cameron's front against Noah's ass, plus the innuendo... it all raced straight to Noah's cock. He knew he was blushing as he gave Cameron a quick wink, then headed into the restaurant. *He's gonna kill me before we even get to bed. Argh...* "Table for two, please."

Once they were seated with the wine and cheese menu, Noah dared to make eye contact again. Even then, Cameron was gazing right at him with those smoldering eyes. "Fuck," Noah laughed under his breath, glancing back down to his menu.

"Sorry," Cameron apologized with another easy laugh, but

he didn't sound apologetic. "You're just handsome today. Again."

"Thanks." Noah wore a tank top under a black pull-over cardigan with intricate crochet patterns. It was almost lacy with holes across his shoulders but a solid front and back. The tank top shoulders were perfectly hidden under a solid section around his neck, which made it look like he was shirtless. It was one of his favorite outfits for that very reason. The thin sweater fabric clung to his body, and his jeans were tight and black. He'd caught Cameron having a quick glance already.

Cameron looked good: a light blue collared shirt with the top few buttons undone and a zip-up black sweater with pressed trousers. Noah approved of the effort he'd put into it, even if he itched to try a few brighter colors on him. Cameron definitely pulled them off. His hair was short and looked touchable the way it was brushed neatly back.

The waiter came to collect their drink order before Noah got himself into trouble by leaning across the table to indulge his desire to touch.

"So, how's the hockey exhibition going?" Cameron asked once Noah had chosen their glasses of wine and a matching cheese plate. "Not to stress you out or anything..."

Noah laughed. "Oh, things were hairy for a bit, but it's gonna be good. There's a few custom pieces I'm excited about, and I think all the loans I wanted are solid. I'm commissioning several more to appease people who don't think it's local enough. Then everyone should be happy. Please, God," he mock-prayed, rolling his eyes and flourishing with a hand.

Cameron laughed. "It sounds like it'll be good."

"Which reminds me – did you want to come with me to the opening night? It's not for a while, of course, but..." Noah fidgeted with the menu against the table.

"Yeah." Cameron reached across the table to press his hand over Noah's. His palm was broad, callused, wonderfully warm... "I'd like that."

"You like hockey?" Noah asked, glancing down at their hands with a smile. He turned his palm over to touch each other's fingers. The first few dates were supposed to be full of unresolved chemistry, but he'd be happy to climb into bed with Cam tonight.

Cameron's fingertips hesitated where they rested on his palm, close to the gaps between his fingers. Then, he trailed his fingers down into those gaps, lacing their hands together. "Yes."

"Well, I've got a ball hockey league... it's only casual. I'm sort of the co-organizer. We're doing an intercity game with some other guys we know running casual clubs this summer."

For the first time, Cameron's confidence turned into a nervous expression as his lips pinched together.

Does he get performance anxiety? Noah tried not to giggle at the thought. "Hey, you don't have to... but it wouldn't be a big deal. We're casual. We all go out for beer afterward, win or lose. And you'd get some new buddies out of it..."

Still, Cameron hesitated, his gaze rising to pierce Noah's again. Those dark eyes pinned Noah to the spot, but long seconds later, Cameron smiled. "Sure. As long as they're as low-key as you promise. I could use buddies out here. But if it's at all stressful, I can't do it. I don't want it to be a big deal, you know?"

"Yeah, you've got enough on the go," Noah nodded. "It's not, I promise. Just a bit of running around and sweating. We did it briefly over the winter indoors, but then we got kicked out of the arena."

"That's a shame."

"Yeah," Noah nodded, sliding his fingers out from between Cameron's to pick up his wine glass and sip. "Oh, hey... I told my uncle about you."

Cameron's eyes widened comically. "Which bit?"

"*Not* what an amazing kisser you are, don't worry." Noah gave a flirtatious smile to Cameron.

The tough guy's cheeks flushed, and he sat back and averted his gaze a little like he couldn't accept the compliment.

Noah laughed and added, "About being interested in helping him with carpentry or beekeeping."

"Oh. That's great. Thanks," Cameron nodded, glancing back at him and swirling his wine glass around. His eyes scrunched a little each time he sipped the glass of wine, like he was trying to get used to it. He ate cheese between each sip.

Noah tried not to laugh at Cameron's palate adjusting. "He wants to see you this weekend if you're back in time."

"I'll... barely be back," Cameron nodded, his shoulders sinking in relief. The stress from moments ago was gone, replaced with a hopeful glow. "But yeah, I'll be driving back before then. That'd be fantastic. I mean, the new mortgage will take time..."

"You guys got the houses? Oh, man, congratulations," Noah smiled. "You like them?"

"Yeah. They'll need a bit of work, but they're in decent shape already. Just gotta live with my brother until the deal closes."

Noah nodded, then reached out to choose a piece of blue cheese Cameron had been avoiding. "You should try this."

Cameron looked suspicious.

Noah leaned forward to pop it between Cameron's lips, and Cameron was so startled he parted his lips. Then, Cameron's eyes crinkled with amusement as he chewed.

When he hesitated, Noah held his breath, but Cameron kept going and swallowed. "Actually, that's not bad."

"Told you so," Noah teased. "I know a thing or two."

"I know... a different thing or two."

"Mm. I'd love to skill-share," Noah winked, letting his gaze flick down to Cameron's chest. It rippled with muscles under the collared shirt and Noah itched to see it.

Cameron licked his lower lip, then bit it as he gazed at Noah. After a moment, he nodded. "It can't hurt."

Noah hesitated, trying to read that response. "If it's too new for you--"

"No," Cameron said firmly. "I didn't want *you* thinking it was weird. I don't want you feeling like you're a rebound."

Noah sat back as he swirled his wine glass, then shook his head. "I dated someone in high school who was terrible for me. By the time we'd broken up, we'd... been broken up for months." Cameron looked relived, his shoulders sinking as he nodded. "I get it."

"Oh. Great. Phew."

"A man of many words, all of them multi-syllabic," Noah pretended to swoon, finishing his glass of wine and the last piece of cheese from the tray.

"I'm sure you have some single-syllable words I'll find." Cameron said it in a meaningful purr, his voice catching in a slight growl, and Noah lost his breath for a moment. "Shall I walk you home?"

"Please," Noah agreed. His breathing was heavy as he signaled the waiter to request the bill, but Cameron nabbed it. "No, you don't have to--"

"My pleasure, in exchange for the education I've already gotten on... *blue* cheese," Cameron answered, grinning at the waiter. "It was surprisingly good."

"Good on you for trying it," the waiter answered, swiping Cameron's credit card. "A lot of our first-time guests don't."

"I made him," Noah smirked. "It only looks gnarly. The gnarlier something looks, the better it tastes."

Cameron's head was still down as he watched the screen, but his head turned slightly toward Noah. He gave Noah a meaningful sideways glance.

Noah nearly burst out laughing. *No. Not in front of the waiter.*

The transaction went through swiftly, and less than a minute later they were out in the cold again. "You know," Noah shook his head, "you're a handful."

Cameron's rich laugh echoed down the street. He slid his arm around Noah's shoulders, keeping his hand carefully on Noah's other shoulder. Those extra few inches made it feel like Cameron was tucking him into his side as they walked down the street.

Noah didn't hesitate to slide his arm around Cameron's waist in response. As they waited for the "walk" signal, he leaned up to press a kiss against Cameron's lips.

I could get used to this.

The ten-minute walk to his apartment took fifteen at their slow pace, but pressing close to Cameron for an extra few minutes was nothing to complain about. Cameron was warm against him, warding off the spring chill. More than that, heat had been simmering under Noah's skin since they'd said hello.

Noah kept his arm around Cameron's waist as he led him up to the front door. He fumbled to hold open the screen door while unlocking it.

Still close behind him, Cameron chuckled quietly and let his arm drop from around Noah's shoulders to hold it.

"Thanks."

As the door swung open, Noah stepped inside and kicked off his shoes. He toed them into the corner and stepped out of the way for Cameron to follow him inside. As Noah leaned in the living room doorway, he shrugged off his coat and hung it up, then waited for Cameron to slip his shoes and jacket off.

"You live by yourself?"

"Yep," Noah chuckled. "No awkward roommate moments ever again. Want something to drink?"

Cameron nodded. "A glass of water would be great," he agreed. As Noah led him to the kitchen through his cozy living room, Cameron followed. "Cute room."

Noah glowed with pride but tried to downplay it. "Oh, I've been slowly decorating it." In reality, he didn't have much more room for art. He'd chosen paintings proportionate to the space they took up, matched frames and furniture, and exploited thematic similarities. All in all, his living room was soothing, the dining room energetic, and the kitchen very simple. It just had one old hand-drawn map of Fredericton hanging behind glass.

Cameron paused to examine it, then came to lean next to the sink and checked his phone. Noah smiled to himself at the moment of distraction and the way his lashes dipped over his eyes.

When Noah offered it, Cameron took the glass of water, his lips downturned. Instead of sipping, he leaned in to press their lips together in a proper kiss. Warm, moist lips against his own made Noah shiver and turn his body into Cameron's. He fumbled to turn off the tap and avoid wasting water.

After a moment of probing his lips, making Noah melt with

the slow deliberation of his moves, Cameron chuckled and pulled back. "Get yourself a drink, too," he murmured. "I don't want to keep you from proper hydration."

"Everything okay?" Noah asked, staying close for now.

Cameron's eyes flickered to the phone and his frown lines deepened. Something was definitely wrong, but it was probably too personal for him to tell Noah.

"Just a friend... got bad news. Some friends, plural, actually," Cameron answered, his thumb tapping across the phone keyboard.

"I'm sorry."

Cam shook his head, then ducked it to type a text at blinding speed.

Noah swallowed and turned his attention to gulping a few sips of water, giving him a moment's privacy. Their tension was on pause but not killed.

When he looked back, Cam's phone was back in his pocket. The man leaning back against the counter was... fucking beautiful.

Cameron's back was to the counter, one foot propped up on a drawer handle. His trousers clung to strong thighs. His face tilted back, Cam slowly drank from the glass of water. His other hand was braced behind himself against the edge of the counter.

The evening light poured through the dining room window and struck him sideways. A sharp line of light skirted a slightly crooked nose and danced along the curves of his lips...

"I'd tell you to take a picture, but I'm enjoying it too much," Cameron drawled. He'd finished his glass of water and was gazing at Noah with both heavy-lidded seduction and amusement.

Noah finished sipping from his glass and took Cameron's,

placing both in the sink. Cameron stayed where he was, so Noah shifted to press up close to him against the counter.

Noah had been waiting for this moment, and it didn't disappoint. Warm, solid thighs pressed against his, their knees bumping. Their chests rose and fell against each other as Cameron leaned down and kissed him hard.

Now was no time for sweet.

Noah's body, already burning for contact, only ached more for the sensation of skin on skin. He cupped Cameron's cheek in his own, his thumb rubbing along Cameron's strong cheekbone to his hair as he pressed forward and demanded more.

Cameron's tongue slipped between his lips and played at the tip of his own, stealing Noah's breath. His cock hardened against his jeans, a distinctive firmness pressing into his hipbone too.

Noah ground slowly against Cam, slotting their thighs together to press his cock harder into Cam's inner thigh. Cameron kissed like a fucking tease, slowly catching Noah's lower lip and sucking. He flicked his tongue along the flesh, let go, teased again, and turned his attention to his top lip...

Noah whimpered his protest under his breath, already seeing stars. He was fucking desperate now – desperate enough to rut against Cameron until the man carried him to bed. His stomach was taut with arousal while his chest heaved. He couldn't catch his breath. Cameron tantalized his lips and tongue, then moved his kisses around to his jaw and behind his ear.

Somehow, the fucker instinctively sought out the spot right below his ear. It made him physically jolt and moan again, much louder than before.

Then, Cameron chuckled and kissed it again, gentler this time, and Noah swatted him away. "Goddamn tease," Noah breathed out. He rubbed a hand up along Cameron's chest and down again, under his hem, and his eyes widened.

Washboard abs rippled under his hand all the way up to unmistakably defined pecs. There was a faint, burning graze of shaved hair growing out on his chest.

Jesus, Cameron was hot.

Noah wasted no time unbuttoning his shirt, ducking his head to kiss at Cameron's neck. It was his turn to treat the man and get his mouth on every inch of this hot body. Noah wanted Cameron moaning and grunting and thrusting into his mouth with the same desperation he, too, felt.

He sucked on Cameron's neck, but not hard enough to leave a mark. As he finished fumbling to pull open the last few buttons, Noah shifted to kiss a slow trail along the smooth skin to his collarbone, then down to his chest.

Cameron had a few healing bruises. One was splashed across his chest, another near his hipbone.

Noah pulled back for a moment, quickly glancing up at Cameron. *That looked painful.*

"It's nothing," Cameron assured him with a smile. "I play rough, that's all."

Noah's fingers darted around the outside of the bruise as he ran his hand down to Cameron's waistband. "It won't hurt too much?"

"I grew up with two brothers," Cameron snorted. "You can slap it and I'll cope."

Noah burst out laughing. "I won't slap it."

Cameron winked. "Thanks."

Noah kissed Cameron's collarbone instead, his hand running down to cup the bulge in his trousers. Fuck, Cameron was big. A shaft strained at his underwear and trousers, and

Noah was hungry to taste it. He wanted to see if something as big and gnarly did taste better.

"Mm," Cameron whispered.

Even this quiet sound of fulfillment was gorgeous, but Noah wanted it to be a cry of pleasure.

Noah licked at Cameron's nipples a few times and kissed his upper chest, then sank to his knees, pressing his lips hard against Cameron's stomach near his hipbones.

Cameron laughed and shifted on his feet with a sudden twitch as Noah kissed near his belly button. He raised a hand to cover his mouth, his body twitching.

By the third twitch, Noah's eyes gleamed with amusement. He trailed his lips back down to the waistband, licking that gorgeous line that disappeared into his trousers. He loved a man with a good V in his trousers. "Ticklish?"

"Maybe," Cameron admitted in a mumble, dropping his hand to Noah's shoulders. "Just when you go too light."

"I'll be firm," Noah promised, darting his tongue for badness and licking along the waistband.

"Jesus. When you're ready, of course."

Noah popped open the trouser button, and dragged down the zipper. He relished the sound, and Cameron's breath caught at the same moment.

Noah kissed a few more times near the center of the waistband as he hooked his fingertips into the garment. Once the trousers pooled on the floor around Cameron's ankles, Cam stepped out of them.

Cameron's hands brushed across Noah's sweater before he poked his finger through the sweater holes. He tickled Noah's shoulders and plucked at the garment.

"Patience," Noah chided with a grin, but it was easier said

than done even for him. His gaze fell to the bulge pressing at Cameron's tight briefs.

Poor guy. He'd take care of that.

Noah caught the opening in a finger and dragged it to the side, parting the fabric to tug out that cock.

Oh, fuck, he's big.

Noah licked his lips instinctively as the flushed red length bobbed free. The head was pinker than the rest, and the shaft was straight and thick. The foreskin gleamed with a drop of moisture.

His breathing was shallow as Noah curled his fingers around the smooth shaft, pulling the skin down as he went and then back up again. God, it was velvety and heavy, and... it just *looked* delicious.

He leaned in to press his lips to the side of Cameron's shaft, mouthing at it a little while he slid his hand down to cup Cameron's balls.

"Nnh, fuck," Cameron whispered, his voice already hoarse.

Noah kissed the base of the shaft, then pressed open-mouthed kisses all the way up the thick length to the very tip before kneeling up straight. It was standing straight already, demanding more attention, and who was he to say no?

"You're fuckin' hot," Cameron murmured.

"Pretty hot yourself, there, Cam," Noah grinned. He gazed up the length of Cam's body, running the tip of his tongue around the head. The shaft gripped in his hand was about ready for anything.

Cam's hips twitched like he wanted to thrust but was keeping himself back against the counter. One hand wrapped around Noah's shoulder, the other around the edge of the counter as his nails dug in.

Noah closed his lips around the tip of Cam's cock, turning

his gaze demurely down to the length he was sucking into his mouth an inch at a time. He shifted on his knees a little, getting closer to angle his head a bit further down and better take the length of it.

Fuck, he was salty and musky and... *manly.* The masculine taste and the velvety weight of Cam against his tongue made Noah shudder. He felt Cameron's eyes on him as he reached down to rub himself through his jeans.

He sucked slowly, dipping his head toward the base and back up again a few times. Then, he set into a faster rhythm and closed his lips a little harder. All the way, he cast quick glances at Cameron now and then, letting him get better glimpses at the pink flesh sliding back and forth between his lips and the sultry expression in his eyes as he sucked Cameron's cock.

Cameron caught his breath a minute later and squeezed Noah's shoulder. "Get up."

That voice was a low command that Noah didn't hesitate to obey. He sucked one last time, bobbing his head all the way down until Cameron pressed at his throat. Then, he pulled his head back up and let the thick cock pop free.

He *really* hoped this meant what he thought.

"Where's your bedroom?"

Noah grinned. "Upstairs," he purred, pressing close and leaning in to press his lips to Cameron's jaw and neck a few times.

He expected Cameron's hands at his ass, but not those hands squeezing and pulling, hoisting him up into Cameron's arms.

Noah's eyes widened as he threw his arms around Cameron's shoulders. Cam crushed him to the counter and kissed him until he couldn't think straight.

His thought felt loud: *take me to bed.*

While moaning through the quick, fierce kisses and the demands of teeth and lips against his own, he managed to lift his legs. One at a time, he wrapped himself around Cameron's waist. Cameron was fucking *strong.* He didn't even feel a wobble as Cameron kept pushing close. His damp, hard, needy cock ground against Noah's stomach while Noah's throbbed in its tight trap.

"Take me to bed," Noah finally managed when Cameron came up for air and kissed his chin and neck. He rolled his head back, his whole body pulsing with need and pleasure. He *had* to be naked; he *had* to have that body blanketing him, pushing his legs up by his ears; he *had* to have that thick, swollen cock plunging deep into him.

He hadn't been this desperate in *years.* He was going to go fucking crazy without Cameron.

"With pleasure," Cameron whispered. Noah caught his breath and held tight as Cameron spun them and carried him – unwavering the whole way – around the corner and upstairs.

"Oh, Jesus," Noah moaned as Cameron shouldered through his bedroom door. He was almost shaking with adrenaline after the flight of stairs. He'd felt safe in those strong arms the whole time, but he'd never had a man show off like *this* before. "You're fuckin' ripped."

"I lift now and then," Cameron teased. "You're the most fun of anything I've lifted, though."

Noah's cheeks were flushed. Exhilaration raced through him as they tumbled onto the bed together. He untangled his legs from Cameron's, squirming his way up to the head of the bed.

Cameron followed him the whole time, crawling across him with the eyes of a predator and the body of a Greek god.

He grabbed the bottom hem of Noah's sweater and yanked it up and over his head, then ran a hand slowly down across his tank top. His fingertips teased and grazed Noah's nipples. "Too many layers," he teased.

"Two is too many?" Noah grinned, already reaching down to push off Cameron's shirt and leave him almost naked.

"Far too many."

Noah arched off the bed to let Cameron pull off the plain white shirt.

Cameron leaned down to kiss Noah's chest just as he'd had done to him in the kitchen, and Noah squirmed into the bed. "Mmmph," he whimpered, his thighs clenching as he almost held his breath. "Hnnh, I can't-- fuck, don't tease me anymore."

"Sorry," Cameron whispered across the moist nipple once he let go of it, but he still darted his head over to lick the other one.

"Fucker."

Cameron laughed, his eyes bright as he knelt back enough to unbutton Noah's jeans. He worked swiftly to pull them down as Noah squirmed out of them.

"Ooh, naughty," Cameron purred. Noah's bulge strained at his skimpy briefs. "And hot."

"Sucking your cock was hot, what can I say? But you know what'll make me hotter?" Noah breathed out, kicking off his jeans and shivering as bare skin finally grazed his legs and stomach and chest. Every spot Cameron brushed with nothing remaining between them tingled and burned.

"I can take a wild guess," Cameron whispered, and then he pulled down Noah's underwear.

Noah kicked it off as his cock bobbed free. The second it was free from pressure, despite the near-pain of confinement, it ached to be touched once again.

Cameron unthreaded himself from his underwear as he yanked that down, too, and twisted to kick it off. "Way too many layers. Too much work."

"Naked morning sex is the easiest," Noah murmured, winking at Cameron. "Just get it up and go..."

Cameron laughed and pressed their lips together again with such affection it made Noah blush. Then, he murmured, "You got condoms? My trousers being... downstairs..."

Noah laughed. "Bedside table," he promised. "And K-Y."

"Perfect," Cameron murmured, leaving him with one more teasing kiss by his ear before leaning over to search the bedside table drawer. Noah thanked his past self for having had the foresight to clean that out this morning.

Cameron knelt up between Noah's legs and Noah grabbed his knees to pull them up, his heart pounding with anticipation.

"You want me to fuck you?" Cameron grinned, twiddling a condom between his fingers while holding lube in the other hand.

"Only more than *anything else*," Noah moaned, and he knew that had been a lisp but he didn't give a fuck. Cameron found it cute.

Cameron's fingers were already slicked before Noah finished the sentence. By the time Noah had caught his breath, wet fingers pressed against his opening. Noah gave a full-body twitch, but the cool slickness rapidly warmed.

"I wonder how sensitive you are."

"Pretty fucking."

Cameron grinned. "This will be fun."

Penetration didn't come easy for the first few seconds, but then the fingers slid into him as a welcome relief from his craving. It wasn't what he was truly aching for, but it was a close second.

Noah caught his breath as Cameron crooked his fingers, slowly rubbing back and forth inside him until he found it. He squirmed, losing his breath even with the first few strokes of Cameron's fingers. Even two fingers were so thick it was a little *too* satisfying. "Oh, Jesus, you don't wanna do that too much."

Cameron laughed, leaning down again to kiss him. He was already sensually sliding his fingers in and out in a motion that Noah thrust his hips with. The bed creaked and Cameron whispered against his lips, "Maybe I do."

"I'd rather you fucked me than let me blow my load before we even get started." Noah wasn't shy about asking for what he wanted. The way Cameron's eyes widened and darkened made him shiver with pleasure. *That got him going.*

Cameron's cock had to be throbbing now. After Cameron pulled his fingers out and wiped them off, he rolled a condom on in one smooth swoop of his hand.

"Come on," Noah whispered, pulling his legs even further up and apart until he was bent in two. Cameron draped his body across Noah's, pinning him down to the bed and tangling his left hand in Noah's hair while his right guided himself inside.

Noah clutched at Cameron's back. Firm, thick pressure pushed at the opening. Then, it pushed *past*, and slowly slid further and further in.

Jesus, he's big!

The more he slid in, the more Noah wanted of him until they were pressed together about as tight as they could manage.

And then, Cameron pulled back and thrust his body into Noah's, his cock riding up inside him like a fuckin' *animal*.

"Yes!" Noah grunted, not caring that his voice was sharp and loud. His body craved a hard, fast pace, and his orgasm was going to be blinding. "Enough teasing. Hard."

Cameron obeyed, tangling his hand in Noah's hair as Noah moaned his approval. Cameron pulled Noah's head back and kissed along the exposed line of his throat. The cock inside him, rubbing hard against his prostate with each quick thrust, made his muscles pulse and flutter with pleasure.

He was so fucking turned on already – from dinner, making out in the kitchen, sucking Cameron's cock... It wouldn't be long, but it would be *incredible*.

"Tell me how you like it," Cameron encouraged in a whisper, his voice dripping filthy hot in Noah's ear.

Noah's nerves sparked over and over again. He was dull to everything except the cock in him, the hot body pressed up against him, the hand in his hair and the lips kissing up and down his neck and ear until he frantically squirmed into the duvet.

"Yes...! Oh, fuck, Cam, you're good. It's so fuckin' good. Hard and fast."

"You're gorgeous," Cam praised breathlessly. The bed creaked with each hard thrust of body into and across body. His skin shone with sweat as he focused completely on Noah's face like he was memorizing every moment of Noah's pleasure.

Noah closed his eyes but leaned up to invite a kiss on his lips again, and Cameron indulged.

As Cameron sucked on Noah's lips, Noah's legs dropped from between them. He spread them wide so Cameron better pressed against him. That gave fucking excellent friction between them as Noah's cock was squeezed tightly between their bodies.

"Jesus...! Cam!"

Now it wouldn't be long.

Cameron was already out of breath, but he kissed for all he was worth. Grunts and moans of pleasure were stifled against their lips.

Noah turned his face away for a moment just to force them to spill out into open air, and they sounded *incredible*. Every sharp, unrestrained sound between them made him clench tight with pleasure. Cameron's hips stuttered and breathing sped up. That spot deep in Noah's cock lit up with burning and swelling pleasure...

And then Noah was gone.

He lost himself to blackness for a moment. Every muscle drew tight and released in unpredictable patterns. His legs shook and he desperately rutted against those washboard abs.

Jesus Christ, he actually *felt* that most sensitive spot right on the underside of the head of his cock rub against the ridge of one of Cameron's abs! As he sprayed his pleasure across them both, he cried out Cameron's name.

Maybe a few curse words, too.

And "*yes!*"... several times.

Cameron's body slammed into his own as Cameron grunted, then caught his breath in quick, purposeful exhalations.

"N-Noah...!"

Holy shit. That was *hot*. Cam was coming inside him. Noah burned with the desire to be fucking *filled* and owned by this sex god who had landed in his town and his bed.

I want to be his.

His whole body pulsed and pounded with pleasure as

Cameron gave a few last grunts, his hips shoving up against Noah.

Then, his body finally went limp and blanketed Noah's. They sprawled together, their stomachs both wet from Noah's pleasure as limbs tingled to life again and awareness crept back.

Noah already knew he didn't want Cam to go, but he probably had to. "You have to go?" he asked, pitching his voice up in a question and trying not to sound too desperate. "I mean, your friends..."

Cameron's eyes flickered closed for a moment before he reopened them. "Yeah. I'm sorry. I should... call a few people, you know?"

"No, it's okay," Noah murmured, but he didn't move to get up yet. Cameron's cock slid out of him, and Noah lay back with a dopey little smile while Cameron peeled off the condom. "I had... so much fun. We're doing this again once you get back, right?" He smirked. "Well, you know, a date. Not necessarily *this*... but that too."

Cameron smiled with relief, like he hadn't expected Noah to want him back in the house again. "Yeah! I mean, yeah, whenever we can. I'll be back pretty soon."

Was he used to assholes? Probably. That ex didn't sound like a nice piece of work, and Noah just hoped Cam wasn't too bruised. But he seemed emotionally healthy on the whole.

"Good," Noah murmured, reaching up to cup Cameron's cheek in his hand. He liked the burn of five-o'clock-shadow across his palm. "God, that was good."

Cameron grinned. "My name's Cam," he teased.

Noah laughed and patted his cheek in not quite a slap, but a teasing reprimand. "Oh, don't be that guy with the massive ego. Your dick doesn't need competition."

Cameron's jaw dropped.

Noah burst out laughing at the expression on his face. "What? I tell it like it is."

"You're…" Cameron trailed off, but he was laughing. "You can say that again. All of it."

Noah laughed again, making his fingers tingle. In fact, his whole body was still buzzing with pleasure. He could hardly get up, but he should see Cam out.

As Cam collected his clothing and put it on, Noah stole moments to glimpse until Cameron laughed and told him off for being a voyeur.

"Guilty," Noah grinned, watching him step into his jeans in the kitchen. "I can't help it. Hot guy in my house, I'm gonna fuckin' watch him all day."

"You don't have many contractors comin' over, do you?"

"Not anymore," Noah mock-seriously joked, pulling his lips down in an exaggerated frown. "The last one couldn't take the heat. I've been without a bedroom door since."

It looked like Cameron was about to go grab his tool box. "I can help. That's not ri-- Oh."

A delighted laugh escaped Noah's throat. Cameron had taken him seriously, and the guy was a fuckin' sweetheart. "You softie."

Cameron blushed. "Well, I know a thing or two, and… you're a trickster, you know?" he scolded, patting his pockets to make sure he had everything.

"Mmhmm."

Noah was still naked, so he stayed back as he followed Cameron to the front door. "Good luck moving out of Toronto."

Cameron turned to face him when he reached the front door, then beckoned him over to lean down for a simple, sweet kiss. It was just a brush of lips on lips, but Noah knew it meant more than any kiss up in the bedroom had. "Thank you," he murmured. "At least I've got a couple good things waiting..."

That last sentence had just a hint of an uptick at the end to make it a question, and Noah knew what it was. He nodded firmly at Cameron. "You do. A third date, and that's when you're supposed to get lucky... I mean, if you're straight. Maybe that's a rumor. I don't know how straight people work," he confessed.

Cameron was grinning affectionately. It made Noah's heart hurt to think about waiting days to see him again.

Their goodbye kiss was sweet this time before Cam let himself out. "See you soon," Cam murmured, and that was a promise if Noah had ever heard one.

"Bye," Noah smiled.

Once Noah locked the door, it was time to get to bed and let that pleasant buzz in his body lull him to sleep.

CHAPTER

Fifteen

CAMERON

CAMERON SIGHED AS HE STEPPED INTO HIS TORONTO apartment. His legs were still woozy from turbulence. With a flight into the city center airport and no luggage, he'd made it here in record time, but somehow, it didn't feel like home.

The windows in this place were floor-to-ceiling along the lake side of the building. It was all hardwood and sleek design... and cold. The first time Nathan had walked in, he'd complimented the modern aesthetic while bending over the kitchen counter.

Jesus. How could I forget? He could still be around. "Nate?" Cameron called out, sighing with relief when he didn't get an answer.

When he rounded the corner to the kitchen, he found a set of keys on the counter. They sat on a note in Nathan's handwriting.

Not again.

"What do you have to say for yourself now?" Cameron muttered.

A glance around the place told him exactly what he'd done:

the stupid antique chair Nathan had bought was gone, the lamps Nathan liked were gone, the cabinet was gone...

"Asshole." He glanced at the note.

Dear Cam--

Can't handle this anymore. Like I said, it's all too childish. You look back at every guy who looks at you. I need something mature and if it's not one thing it's another with you. Last straw was the hospital for your "heart problem". You want my pity? You've got it. There's enough admirers to choose from in hospital I bet. Seek your attention there. Maybe they can help you grow enough balls to come out, properly.

Bye.

N.

"What the fuck?"

Cameron bent over, bracing his elbows on the counter. He *knew* Nathan was a manipulative bastard he shouldn't listen to, but Nathan had ripped off the gloves.

And it was so fucking *untrue*. Some of the other guys had girlfriends and a few were married. Others slept with every woman who smiled at them. That didn't mean shit about them as long as they were solid guys he'd trust his life with – and they were, every one of them.

Even when he and Nathan were off-again, Cam hadn't slept with every guy who offered. And if he had, so what? It wouldn't make him childish.

He straightened up and crumpled up the note, then shoved it into his jacket pocket. If he had to call the cops on Nate someday, this would be exhibit A.

"You're trash," Cameron muttered. "Okay. Boxes and the trailer rental." He grabbed his car keys, praying that dick hadn't fucked up his car. If he had... Cameron would make him pay.

Cameron's entire body ached by the time he finished shoving what Nathan hadn't taken into U-Haul boxes and loading up the trailer. Nathan hadn't scratched up his car, at least.

He'd sold his furniture on Kijiji for cheap, letting people in to buy and take away stuff while he packed. Box by box, he loaded up the trailer and the back of his SUV, thanking God he was a minimalist and Nathan a hoarder. Nathan must have worked for days to find every little fucking thing he could take. Cameron didn't care. It was worth the stuff to see him gone.

There was just enough room left at the top of the trailer for his mattress tomorrow morning. Moving it down single-handed would be a bitch, but he was too proud to ask his teammates for help. They were probably feeling worse than him after last night's loss. More boxes were loaded in the back of his SUV, including his box of trophies and awards.

"Oh, Jesus," he moaned once he collapsed on the mattress. He stared at the bedroom ceiling, then around at the dust patches. His apartment had been half-empty but still livable when he'd arrived just ten hours ago. Now, it was empty and dusty and echoed whenever he spoke or ripped the tape to seal a box. He couldn't even vacuum before he left: Nate had taken the fucking vacuum.

Cameron laughed at how goddamn weird this was – a breakup without any of the actual breaking up.

No time to dwell, though. He had to leave for the arena.

Having anticipated being sweaty and exhausted, Cam had kept out a box of shower supplies and a few changes of clothes. He scrubbed himself clean, dried off, and changed.

By the time he was en route, the U-Haul trailer safely underground, his stomach growled. His energy was back up again at the prospect of seeing everyone... and there was always pizza. And goodbyes for the guys who didn't make it to the party afterward.

Fuck. He *hated* goodbyes.

"Cam!"

"Cameron! Hey, Cam!"

"Hey, he's here! Bro! How you doin', bro?"

"Cam, the man, you're up on your feet."

The sudden chorus of deep voices greeting Cameron as he walked through the side door of the arena made him almost jump back. "Jesus, guys!" he laughed, but he had no complaints as Fisher, Matty, and Chris almost barreled toward him.

These guys were the forwards from his line, and fuck, he'd missed them.

He grabbed each of them in a back-slapping hug as the others crowded around to ruffle his hair and slap his shoulder.

Lenses turned toward him, so Cameron smiled for them and waved, then turned his attention back to the guys.

"God, it's good to see you all again. I'm fuckin' sorry about last night."

"No, man, we played a great game. Did you see?"

"I watched it on the plane this morning. Shit, when Freddy nailed that guy and he cross-checked--"

"--and the fuckin' ref didn't even blink!" Matty exclaimed, punching him in the shoulder. "I *still* can't believe that."

"C'mon, guys." That was Coach Walker's deep voice, and Cameron smiled. The coach looked the same as ever, but perhaps a little more tired. "We've had the talk."

"Yeah, yeah, sorry." Chris was a rookie – it had been his

first season, and Cam knew how much winning the Cup would have meant to him. The coach was right, though. It wasn't sportsmanlike to blame losing on the ref, and doing that would give them a bad name as a player and as a team.

Cam reached out to half-hug him. "You did great though. Two assists in one playoff game's not bad."

"They want you for a season-end interview," Coach Walker addressed him. "We just finished with twenty questions segments with Rich and Gus. Then we need to talk about your contract, if you're planning on leaving town tomorrow."

Cameron nodded sharply. "Yes, Coach." He jogged down into the locker room to pull on his team jersey.

God, this was going to be hard.

As the meshed material settled over his chest, Cameron took a moment to glance around at steel cubbies and broad benches.

This was the last time he'd walk out into the media pen and face the cameras. The last time he'd answer questions about his season's performance and what next year held. Next year, some other guy would get his locker and the team would move on without him. He'd been expecting that – but he'd also been expecting to step up.

Don't dwell, he told himself. *It'll only make it harder.*

"Cameron, over here." Mike, the assistant coach, was a godsend in the way he handled the media. He had his own ways of keeping them from getting too nosy.

"Hi," Cam grinned at him as he came up to clap Mike on the shoulder and mutually shake hands. Walker had only been coaching for two years, but he'd known Mike for a year longer. Mike had been there when he was signed straight out of university. Mike had always had his back, and no doubt their coach had told him not to let the journalists pressure him.

"Ready for your post-season interview?"

"Ready as I'll ever be."

Mike nodded at the journalists, most of whom Cam already knew. "All right, guys, you can roll."

The hours flew by: press meetings, interviews, meetings with his agent and coach and manager to sort out his contract, and the actual locker clean-out. Cameron lost track of the number of times he said, "a medical condition" and assured the camera it wasn't a grave illness.

Officially, he wasn't retiring permanently. To the media, he was stepping back until a diagnosis and treatment plan were found. There was a possibility he'd come back, in other words. To him, unless there was a miracle surgery, he was done. He'd been told not to expect a miracle, so he didn't.

None of the guys gave him time to mope. He drove in convoy with the others, giving Matty and Fisher a ride to the mansion for their season-end party. Owned by a famous player, the house was a private place for them all to get trashed and see out the season.

Training camp would begin in three days' time for the lucky few. Tonight, they'd toast the guys leaving their ranks for next season's major league lineup.

Being knocked out in the first round of the playoffs wasn't a small achievement, but it wasn't something to crow about either. There'd be a lot of locker room discussions during training camp that summer. Coach Walker was going to be relentless.

Speaking of whom, the coach had gotten there first. He approached Cam to pull him aside. "Hey, kid. A word?"

"Of course." Cameron followed the coach up the staircase to the landing overlooking the entrance hall. They both watched the guys pile inside, clapping each other's backs and handing out beers.

Coach Walker leaned against the railing. "You did good today, kid. Stuck to the party line."

"What, about being on the injured roster and not the quitters'?" Cam answered, his jaw twitching as he cut a quick glance across the empty space over the front hall.

"Kid..."

"Sorry, Coach," Cam added with a jerky nod, sipping his plastic cup. "I'm not begging for sympathy. It's just... weird to wrap my head 'round."

"I know you're not. There's something you should know. Are you moving back to Fredericton?" Coach Walker knew all his guys – where they got their start, who mattered to them, what they dreamed about. Definitely where they were from.

"Yeah."

"There's talks about a team forming in New Brunswick again."

Cam snorted. Hell would freeze over first. There hadn't been a professional team there for a decade. The province had cycled through half a dozen teams in the eighties and nineties and thousands. None lasted more than a few years before getting bought out and moved to another city.

"No, Cam. For real this time."

Cameron's eyebrows shot up. "...Oh."

"There's a few teams talking about it. Montreal. Florida."

"No shit." Cameron straightened up, his mind spinning. They'd be looking for some big names to sign for the first season.

Fuck. No.

"They're gonna want you, and they won't take no for an answer. No matter who winds up buying the franchise and moving it there – and that is happening this time."

Cameron rubbed a hand over his face. "If they can get some miracle surgery... but otherwise, no."

"Even we couldn't get anyone to do it, Cam, and believe me, I *tried*. But they think you're being secretly groomed for success, some star player a team can pull out of its sleeve in September."

"Shit," Cam muttered. "I just wanted to get out of this."

Coach Walker half-smiled. "Did you? Have you been planning your next time on the ice yet? Or concrete?"

"No," Cameron defended himself, then winced. *I **did** agree to play on Noah's team. Shit.* "Not professionally."

"Be careful," Coach Walker murmured, reaching out to squeeze Cam's arm. "You've got talent to flush out anyone's roster, and you're hungry to play. It'll get worse. Stay off your skates. Heart problems are *not* something you wanna fuck around about." It was rare for him to curse – even while coaching – and it made Cam stand up and pay attention.

"I'll be careful," Cam promised. "Nothing stressful. I just bought a house out there anyway." *And Noah... I want to give Noah a chance.*

"All the more reason they'll want you. They'll say you can stick around home while you play. Best of both worlds. That's not something I could ever have offered, but..."

"No, I was happy here," Cam defended the coach with a firm shake of his head. "Am." His shoulders were heavy with the knowledge that he had to go tell his buddies he was done. "But I'll move on."

"Give it a year or two off skates, without flying and busing all over the damn continent and barely seeing home. You might find something else to keep you home." Coach Walker was watching him like he read Cam's mind. Cam's cheeks flushed as he glanced out over the railing again.

"Anyway, kid, the night's short. Go tell 'em what you gotta tell 'em."

Cam reached out for a strong one-armed hug, clapping his coach's back. Coach Walker always had his back.

So did the guys down here. Now, to hope they'd take it all right.

His heart thudded dangerously by the time he reached the bottom of the stairs. There was no way he could put off the announcement all night and let the stress build up. He might end up fucking passing out *again,* and that would be the ulti-mate humiliation.

Everyone was here. No better time.

"Hey, guys."

It was like they'd been waiting for the word. Conversations went quiet as his teammates and friends – dozens of guys who had run alongside, pushed up with, slapped pucks past, and slammed into him all season – turned to look at him.

Cam managed a smile. *Don't fuckin' cry.* "I'm, uh... I'm sick, you know that. Heart problem. They can't diagnose it." There were murmurs of agreement. "And I'm fuckin' sorry I couldn't be there yesterday, or the games before."

They all protested – "No, man, you were sick," and, "It's not your fault."

Cam smiled and waved off the comments, but shook his head. "Let me get through this without fuckin' embarrassing myself, already," he laughed.

After a quiet murmur of laughter, silence fell.

"I lied to the papers. It's not temporary. I, uh, packed up my place today."

"No way. The docs can't help you?" That was Matty, and he was shouldering his way past Chris and Gustav and Heinrich to get to him. He was... crushed. Everyone else barely breathed.

Cameron cleared his throat and shook his head. "Gotta wait in line with the rest of the public. I might as well do that in New Brunswick, back home."

"What about the team--"

"No specialists felt confident in taking him on as a risk." That was Coach Walker. "We tried. A... sister team... was willing to help."

Coach Walker was trying to spare his feelings, but everyone knew who he meant. *They **were** going to make me an offer.*

Cameron bit his lip hard for a moment, then shook his head, pretending he was just talking to Matty and Chris and Fisher. "So I'm out, and I don't think I'll get back."

"I'm a decade older than you and I'm here," Fisher told him with a frown, reaching out to slap his back. "Never say never."

Cameron shook his head. "Then I won't say never. Just... not for the next couple seasons. Best case scenario, I see a doctor in a couple months, get surgery around November. And I can't properly train until then. All I can do is pickup games, you know?"

There was a world of difference between a basement gym and what Coach Walker would have had him doing this summer. "Then I spend a year catching up to where I am now. After that point, who knows? If they'll have me back, if I'm safe to play..."

Coach Walker was watching him hard.

"They can't even guarantee I won't have a heart attack at home in bed, let alone on the ice. I don't think it'll happen. But if it did... it'd be an honor to play with you guys again. I mean that."

Matty silently hugged him while someone else reached out to crush his shoulder and tug him back and forth a little. His friends stepped forward to surround him while the others came up to punch his shoulder or shake his hands.

Cameron waved a hand after a minute of this. "Get the fuck off me, I'm gonna spend the summer lying around doing nothing. You guys deserve the party. Someone put the music on," he ordered them with a laugh, and that finally broke the tension.

Laughter, music, beer.

A couple more beers for good measure as the hours passed.

His buddies, always there near him, recounting his best moments like he was the guest of honor.

The announcements of who got pulled over to the big league roster. Matty was one of them. He clapped harder than anyone for Matty and crushed Matty in a hug. Matty fucking deserved it. He'd been working his ass off all season and in the games Cam was off, he'd caught up in points.

He let his body metabolize the drinks he'd already had so he could drive.

They managed to give Coach Walker a round of applause and a toast before he escaped.

Music, laughter, the pool opening up, the greatest hits of team video highlights from the year playing on the big-screen above the pool. A fair number of manly tears hidden in the darkness outside. Girls arriving, more partying, louder laughter.

Time to go.

A sobriety test administered like it was a joke, and it made him smile. They did it to each other to be assholes, but because they cared, too. He walked the line just fine. He desperately wanted to drown his sorrows in beer like the rest of them, but he had to drive out early.

He couldn't get away without crushing hugs from Matty, Fisher, Chris, Gustav, K., Tom, – okay, this was getting fucking ridiculous. "I'm not dead, just two provinces over," he teased them as he waved goodbye to everyone else. "I'm driving out early."

"Don't you dare fuckin' disappear on us," Matty warned him. "You're turning up for parties when and where we say." The other guys laughed, but they agreed.

"Okay. Give me some notice and I'll be there," Cam promised. He'd promise anything to these guys, and he intended to follow through. "And I'll be watching for you next season, superstar."

Matty gave a bashful but pleased laugh and one of those broad sheepish grins. Just like last October, when he'd slapped the puck into Cam's fuckin' shoulder so hard it had bruised. Cam had nearly punched the grin off him, but they'd bonded afterward.

"Bye for now," Cam said so his heart would stop thudding. The music faded as he ducked out the door and his footsteps crunched down the path. He headed toward the driveway where cars were parked tight to each other.

The assholes. They'd painted a giant maple leaf in white silly string across the side of his car. He turned to the door and saw it open again, a bunch of shit-eating grins on their faces as they pointed his reactions out to each other, and someone hollered, "Show your pride!"

Cameron turned to them with a broad grin and gave them two middle fingers to another uproar of laughter. He collapsed into the driver's seat to drive himself back to the apartment. It was his final night there before he hit the road for New Brunswick.

He glanced in the rear view mirror at the guys clustered in

the doorway. Matty was right there in the middle, holding up his beer bottle like a toast.

Cam swallowed hard and leaned on the horn to honk a few times before pulling out of the driveway for the quiet, late-night road.

What was he doing moving back home after one little setback like this?

He was regaining his blood family, but there were thirty guys in his hockey family he'd miss so hard. He'd probably cry like a bitch on the road tomorrow, or even tonight. If he did, he'd never tell a soul.

CHAPTER

Sixteen

NOAH

"If there's any room at all here, I could split the exhibit into two parts, and--"

Noah already knew what answer he was going to get, but he had to try.

"--I could put the commissioned pieces and local themes there, and put the rental series here..."

"It's ambitious, but it won't work," Greg told him. His fellow curator was a bit of a hard-ass, but he was a realist as well. Noah needed that reality check right now.

The arena had come back and said it wanted to see the local commissioned pieces before it agreed to give him the full space. When he checked the contract, it had specified that they'd rent him "one half or more of the lobby space" with only a verbal agreement on it being the whole lobby.

"There's the Picasso in two weeks..."

"Oh, right," Noah groaned. Greg had been in charge of that, and Noah didn't envy him. Anything world-famous came with insurance up the yin-yang and thousands of people who came just because it was famous. Greg's job was to try to convince visitors to come see the other exhibits, too.

"It feels a bit like... ghettoization," Noah shook his head.

Greg blinked. "Hm?"

Sarah was quiet, but she watched him.

Noah bit his lip, not sure if he should share it. Greg and Sarah were fantastic to work with, but they couldn't change the museum layout. Didn't stop him wondering why the higher-ups had decided to accept a loan on the Picasso a month *after* his hockey exhibit was finalized.

They're just humoring the queer doing the exhibit about hot butch men.

Sarah reached out to squeeze Noah's arm. "You'll get a bit more say in things when you've been here long enough," she promised. "They stopped stepping on my toes after the pottery thing went wrong last year, before you got here."

"Oh?"

Sarah winced. "I'll tell you about it later," she promised.

"Oh, it was bad," Greg murmured.

Noah nodded. "Sorry. All right. I'll figure out how to make it work no matter what happens, I guess. They just *have* to like the local pieces. I gotta see Jackson and Chase soon..."

"I'd better get back out to the floor," Greg told him. "My tour starts in ten minutes."

"Right." Noah waved him off, then rubbed his face. He still had stupid grant paperwork to fill out, too, but he was supposed to be circulating the second floor today. *Oh, God.* He hated the modern art exhibit, but it was Jaclyn's pet project and she was off today.

Suck it up, he told himself. Nobody had to like all the art – they just had to know the history behind it. This was still a cushy job by comparison to many.

Noah's date yesterday was still on his mind, but he tried to ignore it. For some reason, knowing that Cam expected to go with him to the opening night made the pressure far worse. He wanted everything to be perfect.

The day was long, and he hadn't heard back from Cameron in hours. Noah expected that much, but it still made him sad not to have a comment or thought from Cam to tide him over. The unexpected text had been sweet, but since his response, radio silence.

The grad student exhibition was a big event. Noah tried to stay focused on socializing and helping the students feel comfortable presenting their work. Cam wasn't even due back in town for a couple days, so he had no excuses for distraction.

He almost bumped into someone who'd been standing behind him to admire a painting. "Oh, sorry…"

The words trailed off on his lips. It was Russell. The asshole who'd asked Noah out to the bar last weekend and no-showed on him. In a way, Noah was grateful because he'd arranged for his first date with Cam, but he was still pissed at Russell.

"Hey, Noah. I'm so glad I bumped into you." Russell was dressed for work, his office swipe card dangling from his belt as he swished his wine glass in his hand.

He wasn't looking at Noah the way Cam did. His eyes were locked on Noah's instead, his hand on his hip in a stand-offish way. "We should make up for the weekend. I ran late and you were gone by the time I got there, but I'm free this weekend."

"Er, wait," Noah shook his head. "Are you asking me out again?"

"Well, it's still the same date, just a different day," Russell smiled.

No. Fuck you.

"You were at least forty minutes late, and you haven't been in touch since to apologize. I don't think you did just now, either." Noah kept his voice soft and a pleasant smile on his face so they weren't overheard. "I assumed you weren't interested."

"Oh, don't be so hard on yourself."

Noah took a deep breath while counting to six, then let it hiss out through pursed lips, counting back down to zero. Then, he licked his lips and smiled again. "No, thank you."

Russell looked confused and stopped swirling his wine. "No to what?"

"No to going out again."

Then, that familiar ugly expression crossed Russell's face. He turned away, but not in time for Noah not to hear, "Bitter bitch," under Russell's breath.

I'm at work. I. Am. At. Work. That was all that stopped Noah from following Russell and demanding he repeat that a little louder. *Let it go.*

If Cam were here, he'd have punched Russell.

True or not – Noah wasn't sure yet how Cam handled these situations – the thought made Noah smile. He wouldn't mind having a guy like Cam on his side... or on his arm.

By the time he was home in bed, Noah's energy was gone and he was praying that Friday was easier on him. He barely changed and washed up before crashing. Once he plugged his phone in to charge, he saw a text.

Packed up the house, great party with my friends, driving back tomorrow.

It was Cam.

Noah's heart sang. He unlocked his phone and locking the orientation while lying on his side to answer without sitting up. *Glad you had fun tonight. Are you in your place or a hotel?*

Mine. They let me finish vacating by noon tmrw.

The 1st? Nice of them. All packed?

Everything but my mattress and tomorrows clothes.

Noah knew that feeling. *Wow. Empty place feelings?*

Lol. Yeah.

Noah wondered how Cam was doing right now. Should he call? Nah... that might seem a bit stifling. They were only waiting for their third date. Instead, he texted, *Can't wait to see you but drive careful. Could be late ice.*

Aww xx. Thank you. I will.

Noah smiled. *You're welcome.* His eyes were getting heavy.

How was work?

Long. Gotta get commission progress reports for the arena, long story. Also that asshole who stood me up showed up.

No way. Did you kick him out?

Noah chuckled. *I'm not allowed unless they're abusive. But I turned him down & he stormed out.*

Good job. I'm going to sleep now.

Noah bit his lip, imagining what it would be like to snuggle up to Cam. Was he a furnace at night? He was a big, solid guy, so probably... He answered, *Sleep tight. Stay in touch tomorrow & text when you arrive.*

Will do. Good night. Sleep well xo.

The habit of adding kisses and hugs to his text was the cutest thing Noah could imagine, but he didn't want to embarrass Cam. He just sent back, *Xoxo.*

Sleep came fast, accompanied by the memory of Cameron's lips on his.

Seventeen

CAMERON

THE ROAD STRETCHED BEFORE CAMERON AND ONTARIO BECAME Quebec, the signs French, and the drivers angrier.

He kept his energy up by changing the radio station and trying to understand French talk radio. He'd skipped French class because he was an athlete, but whenever he was in Quebec he regretted it.

His drive had started at seven after a quick A&W run, and he was still tired despite it being just after one. He wasn't quite halfway home, but he'd gotten through the snarl of Montreal traffic. He kept a sharp eye out for diners. By the time Cameron spotted one, he was in Trois-Rivières and his stomach growled.

Mindful of his extra momentum with a trailer attached, he changed lanes and signaled to exit. He was already tingling with anticipation. He wanted a warm cup of coffee and something filling for lunch. Maybe not too filling, though... soup and bread? God, that sounded nice.

The highway had been bare and sandy, great conditions for

this time of spring, all the way out here. Once he crossed into New Brunswick, all bets would be off. The province was too fuckin' broke to fill in their potholes.

Cam pulled in near the back of the parking lot with the larger vehicles. He took a look around at the wooded area and restrooms powered by solar panels. Sketchy. He wasn't out to get his dick sucked; he'd wait for a bathroom in the diner.

Once the trailer was backed up against the woods so tightly only a team of professional lifters could jack it, he hopped out of his truck and locked it up. Then, he strode for the diner to pursue his daydreams of coffee.

"Hello-bonjour."

"Afternoon," Cameron greeted the waitress who met him at the front of the diner. She guided him to a table near the window. There were a few couples and groups of friends, but mostly single guys – truckers and the likes. None of them were even hot enough to risk watching.

It was a good menu: simple, hearty road food, with the names of the dishes in English and French. The descriptions were only French, but "tomato soup" was self-explanatory. There was something about bread in the description, and he was pretty sure *beurre* was butter.

Did Noah know French? Growing up in Ottawa, there was as good a chance he did as Cameron. Maybe he'd been a French immersion kid. He seemed like the classy type. And was he working for the government, or was that a private art gallery? If it was a government job, he'd know it.

He smiled, pulling his phone out of his pocket as he waited for the waitress to bring coffee. He sent a quick text to Noah. '*In Trois*'-- He made a face at his phone and guessed.

Trois Riviers.

It didn't bother auto-correcting and he muttered under his breath, "Useless thing." Before sending it, he added one more sentence.

Hope your day is great :)

He hesitated, then pressed send. The waitress delivered coffee first. Before he'd even finished the first cup, he had his soup with bread and butter. Her French accent was thick as she wished him "bon appetit" with a wink and bustled off to take care of another table.

She thought he was straight? Or was that a friendly wink because she'd guessed he wasn't? Either way, Cameron smiled to himself, glad for the human contact in his long day of road noise. His hands still vibrated a little from the wheel.

When he finished his soup, bread, and coffee, he left a couple bills for the meal and a tip. He went to use the restroom inside since it was cleaner than he guessed the one outside would be.

On his way back down the hallway toward the restaurant, a young guy with a shock of dyed-blue hair approached. Cam didn't even need to pay attention to his gaydar. Cam wanted to give him a smile of camaraderie, but the other guy kept his eyes down. He made a wide berth around him, his shoulders rising defensively.

Oh, shit. I do come off straight.

Cameron headed out of the restaurant, zipping up his jacket against the spring chill. He'd been planning to stick around and stretch his legs, but now he just wanted to drive.

It was weird: it wasn't like he was out to the world, but he wasn't closeted, either. As he merged back onto the highway, Cameron wondered for the first time if everyone on his team *had* known.

Maybe Nathan was right. Maybe people hadn't known about them and he'd been accidentally inviting attention from others. Or was there something wrong with *him* that Nathan hadn't wanted to show him off? It had been a mutual decision not to discuss their relationship status...

Cameron turned up the music.

CHAPTER
Eighteen

JACKSON

THE MOMENT A PURR OF AN ENGINE STOPPED OUTSIDE HIS house, Jackson switched off the TV and jumped to his feet. He'd been waiting all evening, drinking a few beers and watching a Storage Wars marathon. That could only be the person he'd been waiting for: his little brother.

He pushed aside the curtains to glance out into the dark evening. Yep, Cameron's SUV was parked on the curb in front of the house, hitched to an orange and white trailer.

A grin spread over Jackson's face. He strode to the foyer and shoved on his shoes just in time to hear footsteps on the porch. He yanked open the front door before Cam knocked.

"Welcome home, little brother." He pulled open the screen door and stepped outside to hug him, then help him get his stuff inside.

Fuck, Cam looked exhausted. He had dark circles beneath his eyes, a shock of hair pushed up at the back of his head from the car headrest. It wasn't as bad as at the hospital, but it was a close second.

"Thanks," Cam chuckled, his voice hoarse. He cleared his

throat. "Just gotta bring in a box from the car with the important shit. Everything else can wait. I'll load them inside... next week, while you're at work. I've got the rental 'til Monday."

"I'll get it," Jackson told him, walking down his driveway with Cam. "How was the drive?"

"Can't complain. Long, though. Remind me never to do that again."

Jackson laughed. He'd never driven straight through to Ontario before. He'd gone there with buddies now and then, and to Montreal, but they'd always taken turns driving. Cam must have had a real fire under his ass to take it all in one day like this.

"I can get the box," Cam grumbled. Jackson grabbed it from the SUV anyway while Cam slammed the back hatch and led the way back up to the step. "I hope you have beer. I could use one."

"Yeah, of course. I picked up a case yesterday."

"That's my brother," Cameron approved.

Jackson laughed. He thought his brother had gone through his partying phase by now, but maybe not. In any case, there was reason to celebrate tonight. Speaking of which... "Did you have your season end party?"

Cameron winced and Jackson frowned, then kicked himself. Of course it would be touchy. "Yeah. Lively as always. Matty got picked."

"Holy shit, no way." Jackson had only met Matty a couple times, but the guy seemed decent. According to Cam, his agility was second to none, but he'd still scored fewer points that season than Cam. Which meant...

"They were gonna draft me," Cam added, his voice carefully neutral.

Jackson didn't quite know what to say. He set the box down

in his living room while Cam shut the door, then hauled Cam in for a tight hug.

Cam clapped his back a few times and squeezed Jackson before letting go and jutting his chin out. He threw his coat near the closet and kicked off his shoes while Jackson kicked his off, too. "Where's that beer?"

Jackson took the hint: don't mention the fucking team for a day or two. "Lemme grab them. Want anything to eat?"

"I'm starved. Something quick would be awesome."

"A couple sandwiches?" Cam always had two. His appetite... well, he had to feed an athlete's body, like Jackson had to feed a blacksmith's muscles.

"Thanks, man."

As Cam browsed his phone, Jackson put together two sandwiches just the way their mom had made them for school. Two slices of ham, thick slices of cheddar cheese, a slice of lettuce, and a slice of tomato. Extra mayo and butter on the bread. Cut into halves. Served with a cold beer. Well, that was a new addition.

He shoved them both onto a plate and handed them over as Cam put away his phone and wolfed them down.

Once Cam had eaten and finished half his beer, they moved back to crash on the living room couch. "So everything got packed up fine? Utilities canceled?"

"Yeah, I took care of most of that by phone," Cam told him. "The landlord's walking through today and I'd better get most of my deposit back. I didn't wash the walls or anything."

"You slob." Jackson smirked and swigged his beer.

Cam groaned. "Get off my back," he bantered, jabbing an elbow into Jackson's arm. "But yeah, it all went fine. Nate was already in to pick up his shit so I had half the work."

"Oh... Good?"

"Yeah. I didn't have to look the prick in the eye."

Jackson let out a breath he didn't know he'd been holding. Cam *was* over him, at last. "I worried about that."

Cam nodded. "Don't. He's gone. I dunno how great New Brunswick will be for dating, but... I want to have a family of my own, and that was never gonna happen in Ontario with everything I had going on. Especially not with him."

Kids? Or just a husband? Jackson watched his little brother with a smile. "Yeah?"

"Yeah. What about you?"

Jackson shifted, unsure how to answer. It wasn't like he wasn't interested in dating, but... things just came up. His art show project, staircase posts, snowstorms... He knew it was all excuses, but he hadn't met anyone who was worth getting over those excuses.

"I'm happy for now," he finally answered. "I *do* wanna meet someone, but... it'd take someone to put up with me."

"Yeah, it would," Cam teased, finishing off his beer bottle and setting it aside on the coffee table.

Jackson kicked him. "You little brat."

"Glad your little brother's home?" Cameron rose to his feet, eying the staircase up to the guest bedroom.

Jackson stood up, too, to gather up the empties in the living room. He gave Cam a sincere smile. "Very."

Cam turned a little red and punched Jackson in the shoulder as he passed by. "Me too. I gotta crash. Night, man."

"Night," Jackson said, bringing the bottles to the kitchen to rinse out and slide into the case of empties.

He grimaced at Cam's coat on the floor and picked it up to at least hang it on the hooks that were *right there*... Living together wasn't easy, but his brother needed a place until the houses closed.

A crumpled piece of paper left on the floor caught his eye. He stooped down to pick it up, and though he hadn't meant to read it, he scanned it to see if it was his or Cam's.

The answer was clear: Cam's. He scanned the last line twice, not sure he'd read it correctly.

Maybe they can help you grow enough balls to come out, properly.

Jackson's jaw dropped. "That asshole," he whispered, the blood heating up in his veins. He wasn't one for fighting unless he had a good reason, but this was a *great* reason to kick the shit out of Nathan.

He had to fight to calm himself down, patting Cam's jacket down for a pocket to shove the note into.

The worst part was that he suspected Nathan might be in touch again, and Cam might not say no. Cam was the type to need someone around. Not for his ego, but because he got lonelier than even he knew.

His heart heavy, Jackson climbed the stairs for bed.

CHAPTER
Nineteen
CAMERON

As the pillow rustled under his ear, Cameron groaned. It had to be no later than six-thirty.

Fuck his body's routine. He didn't *need* to wake up early... but once he opened his eyes, it was too late.

He rubbed a hand across his eyes to wipe the sleep away, then rolled out of bed. He crept downstairs and brought his box of essentials up to the guest bedroom. Once he found a t-shirt and jeans, he headed for the shower and changed into them, then dug out a hoodie for warmth.

The drive had exhausted him enough that he eyed the bed as he dressed, wondering if he could make a rare exception and climb back in.

No... I've got somewhere to be.

He glanced out the living room windows to make sure his SUV and trailer were still parked there. They were, of course. He was in his hometown, not Toronto, where they'd knock him over the head to unload the trailer behind his back.

After coffee, cereal, and peanut butter toast, Cam grabbed his phone and wallet and he was ready to go.

He even skipped the jacket that morning. The brisk early May air was refreshing, but as soon as the sun peeked over the tops of the trees that lined Jackson's street, he overheated. Sunshine on his face made him smile with anticipation for the summer ahead. Renovations, backyard barbecues, and more awaited.

He unzipped his hoodie, then caught his breath. It was one of his Toronto team shirts.

Oh, crap. Noah better not notice it...

It wasn't that he was hiding it, exactly. He just didn't want to get into a full explanation of all the shit of the last month. Even Jackson's question last night had made his gut twist. That little voice in the back of his mind shouted, *Come on, Riley, push through it. Don't be a coward. Why fear?*

Cameron turned his face toward the sun as he ambled. It didn't take long to smell the distinctive mix of cinnamon, samosas, and hot dogs that heralded the Saturday market. He smiled as he strolled through the light crowds of people with canvas totes full of veggies.

He tried to remember where Noah's uncle's honey stand was. It took him a while to work his way over until he spotted the yellow signs. An older man stood behind the stall, his hair up in a cowlick. He had wide brown eyes like Noah's. The similarities ended there, but it was enough to convince Cam that this was the right guy.

Unlike the last time he'd visited the market, it was quiet enough to approach the stall right away. "Hello, sir. Do you have a minute?"

The beekeeper seemed startled to be approached so directly. "Well, hello. I do." He scanned Cameron's face as if trying to place it.

"I'm Cameron. I met your nephew, Noah..."

"Oh, you're his Toronto boy! I'm Bill." The man's face warmed up immediately as he reached out to shake hands.

His Toronto boy. Cameron's heart lurched, but he tried to move past the excitement the phrase instilled. Noah had been talking about him. "Pleased to meet you."

"I understand you're interested in an apprenticeship this summer, and possibly carpentry?"

"Yes, sir. I'm just looking for any kind of work right now. I grew up here but I'm moving back to town, so I'm job-hunting, you could say."

Bill nodded. "You look strong enough to lift fifty pounds at a time."

Cameron bit back his amusement and licked his lips. Coach Walker would have laughed in his face. "Yes, sir."

"Oh, it's just Bill."

"I'll try to remember that. It's a hard habit to break," Cameron admitted. He "sir"-ed everyone from the ref to his coaches and the docs. It opened doors that even talent didn't.

Bill laughed. "Toronto fan, eh?"

Cameron glanced down at his shirt and smiled. There wasn't a good way to admit he was more than a fan... but shit, now he *was* just a fan. "Uh huh. You follow the minor leagues?"

"Oh, yes. Best way to spot talent."

It's not like I'm hiding...

"Any draft picks?"

"Um... I haven't decided yet," Cameron admitted. Shit... if he knew the team that well, he might recognize him. He had to tell Noah before Bill did, but he was the failure who'd blown their best shot at the Cup in years. He hadn't even been on Twitter or any of the fan sites, too worried about what he might see there.

"Well, I'll be watching. Season's over for them, now, eh?"

"Yep." Cameron offered another smile. "Shame."

"It is. They had a great run. Anyway, how about dropping by tomorrow to help build some supers? We can talk more there and I can show you one of the yards."

Cam wasn't sure what a super was, but if it would get him an in with Bill, he'd do it. "Of course. What's your address?" He pulled out his phone to take note of it.

"One p.m. work for you?"

"Yes, sir—Bill." Cameron reached out to shake hands again. "It's a pleasure to meet you. I'll let you get to it," he nodded at a couple people in his peripheral vision waiting for a chance to talk to Bill.

From hockey player to beekeeper: who the fuck made these kinds of life decisions? It definitely wasn't to get closer to Noah.

He smiled, taking out his phone to see if Noah had responded to his texts from last night.

"YES, YOUR GROUP COUNTS AS A COMMUNITY GROUP, SO THE rentals will be free for your intercity club games, provided no other sports groups need the space at the same time."

Noah rolled his head back with relief. "Oh, thank God. And thanks, Jason."

"But there's one catch. It's... not related to your club, actually. It's about--"

"--the art exhibition," Noah finished at the same time as Jason. Oh, God. This thing was gonna kill him. "What's wrong now?"

"The specs you sent for the commissions were good. They're just looking for something a little less... informal."

Noah wracked his brain. He'd thought the proposal was amazing – a rough sketch of kids skating on the frozen-over river. How much more Canadian and local could you get?

"Well, it's not like we have a local professional team anymore. Not even Moncton or Saint John. Closest one would be St. John's, right?"

"There's still a history. A lot of players here were drafted for pro teams – some kids have gone on to big things. That's what they're proud of."

Noah rubbed his face. "All right. So paintings of them? Are any of them on the board?"

"There's a few..."

I knew it. The same guys who made their names two decades ago when hockey didn't even need helmets. "Look," Noah said, keeping his voice calm. "How about the up-and-coming? Jo does good, fast work. She can paint a series based on a variety of local teams. And I still want to get the river painting. They'd all be in that same style."

"Okay. You go ahead with that," Jason agreed. "That should be good."

Finally, a breakthrough. Noah was itching to call Jo that instant, but he nodded. "I'll get to it," he promised and clapped Jason on the shoulder, then strode out of the office. He had a mission on his mind.

When he closed his hand around his phone, it vibrated and rang.

His first thought was, *Oh, crap. Cameron.*

Cam had sent him a sweet good night text last night. He'd found it that morning, but in his haste to meet with Jason and confirm the arena rental, he'd forgotten to answer.

The call wasn't Cam, though; it was his uncle. *Not another swarm.* "Hello?"

"Noah, hi. It's your uncle Bill."

Noah rolled his eyes but smiled, glancing down the street for the bus. *Faster to walk.* "I know. How can I help? Is it a swarm?"

"No, no. It's nothing like that. I just met your friend Cameron."

"Oh. All right." A little shiver ran down Noah's spine as he heard Cam's name aloud. He'd told Bill about a strong, honest, hard worker who needed a job. He'd also hinted that they might have gone out.

"How'd you like to come by tomorrow around one, help me build boxes with him? Don't worry, we won't make you do any heavy lifting. Your boy there looks like he can handle it."

"Ha ha," Noah groaned, but smirked to himself. Cameron *could* handle the heavy lifting. "Okay, I'll be there."

"All right. I gotta go. See you tomorrow, Noah."

Noah knew more than ever that he wanted to see Cameron without family around.

He texted Cam. *Welcome to town. I heard you're helping build stuff tomorrow :) I'll be there too. Wanna have dinner tonight?*

Before he got home, he had an answer. *Thanks :) Sorry, I can't. Already told my brother and parents we can have supper. You're invited too though if you want.*

Oh, God, he couldn't meet his family yet. He hardly knew Cameron, and they might have... expectations. Sure, there were expectations Noah wanted to fill, but...

Maybe after another few dates? It feels weird to be introduced so early, he answered.

Cameron responded, *OMG. Yeah that would be weird sorry. I'm getting ahead of us.*

Noah grinned. *Not that far ahead. ;) Date tomorrow after carpentry then?*

Sure :) Can't wait.

Me too. See you soon xx, Noah texted back, his heart downright skipping a beat.

The answer made him blush. *xox. I was gonna one up you and respond with three xs but that might be getting ahead of us too.*

Noah licked his lips and answered, *xxx ;).*

He got a single word back: *yum.*

Noah laughed as he fumbled to unlock his door. *You do taste great. ;) See you tomorrow.*

I'm sure you do too. Soon... xxx.

Noah tossed his phone on the side table and made a beeline for the bathroom. He'd much rather have Cam's mouth than his own hand, but he'd take what he could get for now.

Twenty-One

CAMERON

Gravel crunched on the driveway as Cameron pulled into the driveway of Bill's house. He lived on a large property near the edge of town, along a winding road. When he hopped out of his car, the garage door opened and Cameron waved at Bill and Noah emerging from the building.

"Hi," Noah greeted, walking ahead of Bill to meet him. Already Noah's eyes fixed on him like he was the most interesting man in the world.

Cameron had to resist the urge to get flustered. *This is work,* he reminded himself. "Hi, Noah. Hi, Bill."

"Good to see you," Bill greeted, reaching out to shake hands while Noah stood by his side. "Come on in. I've got the pieces ready, so the assembly shouldn't take long. And I'll pay you for the day – this isn't an unpaid internship."

Noah laughed and looked at Cameron.

"No, that's fine. I'll get an idea what the work's like," Cameron told Bill.

"I'm paying you one way or another," Bill promised with a vaguely threatening grin. "What's your rate like?"

Cameron laughed. "I don't know the going rates around here." His agent would have killed him for that, but this was different. "I haven't done this kind of work in a long time."

"A hundred bucks? I guarantee I'd wind up paying college students to do this job otherwise."

Cameron nodded. "Okay. If it'll make you feel square."

"It will."

They shook hands again with mutual shoulder-claps.

Cameron noticed the way Noah's eyebrows raised slightly at the move. *Yeah, I speak straight man.*

"So, Noah can show you how the boxes are put together. Once they're assembled and dried, I'm painting them on the driveway. I'm working on yesterday's built boxes right now out back."

"Great," Cam agreed, clapping his hands together. He'd worn a plaid work shirt over a plain gray t-shirt and jeans in anticipation of rough and dirty work.

Bill nodded and walked off to rows of square wooden boxes. Some were unpainted and others were glistening in wet, bright colors under the sun. The breeze caught the distinct smell of paint and wafted it past Cameron's nose and he coughed.

"Yeah, let's head into the garage. It's not much better there, though. Fuckin' glue."

Cameron laughed with surprise. "You've been sniffing glue?" he teased.

"Oh, I promise I haven't," Noah shivered, his expression serious.

Cameron reached out to squeeze Noah's arm and nodded. *Small towns like this, some kids do.* "So, show me these boxes."

It took just a few minutes to explain how the boxes worked. Wooden tabs slotted together when the pieces were placed into a rotating jig, glued, and stapled together. As soon as Cameron wrapped his mind around how the jig worked, he got it.

Noah took charge of handing over pieces, glue, and the air stapler as they worked out a system for working together on the boxes.

"Hope you're not getting paid in dinner tonight," Cameron teased once he had enough of a rhythm to risk distractions.

"Nope, my calendar is clear for you," Noah smiled back. "How was Toronto?"

Cameron laughed. "Shitty as always. Glad to be back."

"That was all your stuff moved out now?"

"Yep. I shouldn't have to go back, except when--" *When the heart specialist gets in touch. Shit.*

Noah quirked an eyebrow.

"--When I wanna visit, but that's unlikely," Cameron snorted, pretending to focus on turning the jig around. He reached for the air stapler and Noah handed it over.

Their skin brushed in a small electric jolt and Cameron shuddered. Noah gasped just before the air stapler fired.

Oh, crap. This was only the first box of... fifty? Eighty? There were stacks of pieces everywhere. He couldn't get turned on yet.

Noah flinched so hard Cameron stopped before the second staple went in. "Loud, eh?"

"It just startles me," Noah laughed. "I'm fine."

Cameron smiled. "Want me to warn you?"

"Nah. I just assume whenever you're holding it, there's going to be bangs."

"Lots of bangs," Cameron teased, keeping his voice down.

Noah blushed and laughed, reaching out for the box once he loosened the jig and slid the box out. "Excellent. Yeah, this is a solid one. I'll stack them over here. So you said Toronto was okay?"

"Yeah, nothing eventful. Except saying goodbye to my buddies and packing up and selling all my furniture..."

"The rest of my week was boring compared to that," Noah laughed. "Uh, I'm getting approval for the full exhibition space as long as I make it as 'local' as possible," he air-quoted, rolling his eyes.

Cameron grimaced, squeezing glue into a line across the third board and sliding in the fourth. "That's ridiculous. Just being here makes it local."

"Oh, I've had those discussions," Noah laughed. "But I'm gonna get some commissions done – probably of the..." He trailed off as he handed over the air stapler and cringed.

Cameron reached out to squeeze Noah's shoulder as he pressed the tip to the wood and fired it twice, rotated it, and repeated. With each *bang*, Noah flinched. By the time he finished the fourth one, Cam figured Noah had lost his train of thought. "Commissions done?"

"Of the local hockey teams," Noah continued as if nothing had happened. "University teams, maybe our ball hockey team, local kids on the river, that kind of stuff."

Cameron saw a chance to distract Noah from his stress by asking more about the artist. That turned into a discussion of the exhibit in general. Noah was excited about several loans and the commissioned local pieces, but he talked more about the overall vision for the exhibit.

Box by box, Noah relaxed while Cameron got into the routine of light manual labor. He liked hammering boards into place, gluing, stapling, and pulling at the sides to make sure they didn't come apart. It was easy work.

Bill came to check on them a couple times as the stack of

boxes grew, and he seemed impressed by their progress. For the most part, he let Cameron be once he saw the quality of his work, and Cameron's chest glowed with pride.

By the time they reached the bottom of the stack of pieces, Noah was getting restless. "Oh, thank God," Noah breathed out as he handed over the last few pieces. "This is it."

"That was it?"

Time had flown by with Noah's easy company and a little hard work. This was the kind of work Cameron would lose himself in for days.

"You wanna see the hives? This is the good bit," Noah promised with a grin.

Cameron's heart raced. He'd never been up close to a swarm of bees and had that end well. "Without protection? I don't think they like me."

Noah's lips quivered and Cameron's cheeks flushed. *Oh, you know what I mean.* Noah went on without commenting. "Yeah. They're gentle, I promise. It's wasps that are nasty bastards. And hornets, and pretty much everything else. Honeybees are a little tougher than bumblebees, but they don't sting unless you're threatening them."

"Can they smell fear?" Cameron rubbed his glue- and sawdust-covered palms together to try to clean them off a little.

"Nah. You'll live. Here, wash your hands first." Noah led him over to the industrial steel sink along the edge of the workshop, leaning over to turn on the water for him.

Cameron smiled, glanced behind to the door, then leaned in for a brief kiss. Noah's lips were soft and sweet, and Noah rose up onto his toes to press into the kiss.

When Noah pulled back, his eyes were wide and his lips were wet. He was *so* fucking kissable that Cameron had to resist the urge to do more than give one more peck on the lips.

Noah laughed at that little gesture and nudged him. "Come on, don't waste water."

Cameron scrubbed off his hands, doing his best to get the glue off with soap powder. When his palms and nails were finally clean and his hands were dry, Cameron asked where the hives were.

Noah answered by taking him by a newly-dried hand. The touch of Noah's palm against his own made Cameron shiver with delight. Noah led him out of the workshop toward the tarps where Bill painted the last few plain wooden boxes.

With drying boxes everywhere, Bill was the king of a miniature city, surrounded by skyscrapers in cheerful colors.

"Already done? Oh, lord. It's coming on five," Bill shook his head as he glanced at his wristwatch, holding his paintbrush. His eyes flickered down to their joined hands, but he didn't show any hint of surprise or disapproval. "That's nearly eighty in four hours. Great work." He seemed sincere, and Cameron smiled. "I left your money in the car," Bill nodded toward Cameron's SUV.

"It was nothing," Cameron assured Bill. "Really." He almost felt guilty taking the cash, but he knew his work would be rock-solid and it made Bill feel better.

"I'm taking him to see the hives you just unwrapped on the corner lot," Noah said.

"All right. Watch out, there's a nasty one by the back corner. I'm checking them next week to see if there are queen problems... once I unwrap the rest."

"Will do," Noah promised, raising a hand in a little wave. "Then we'll be off, unless you need anything else?"

"No, that's great for a day's work. Thanks again for coming

by, Cameron. I'm gonna be busy building gear and unwrapping the rest of the hives for the next couple weeks. I should be all right for that on my own, but I'll need a lot of help checking on them once they're all opened up."

"Okay."

"Tell you what: I'll call you in a week or two to start work. We'll work out a pay rate once I call a couple apiaries and find out the going rates. It'll be eighty hours a week for the next couple months. Get settled in town while you can," Bill instructed Cameron. "You'll be shit beat soon."

Noah squeezed his hand and Cameron laughed. "Okay. Sounds fair, sir. Thanks for the heads-up."

"See you soon."

"Good luck with them." Noah led them down the driveway to the road where Cameron had parked, then beyond. "So, I guess I got the job."

"I knew you would," Noah grinned, squeezing his hand. He waited until they were halfway down the driveway before leaning up to peck Cameron's lips.

The little playfulness between them was impossible to resist. Cameron gently hip-checked Noah, grinning when Noah smacked into his shoulder. He let Noah knock him off a straight course and feigned injury.

The corner lot was easy to identify: a bright yellow electric fence protecting painted boxes scattered around in clusters. "Is all this your uncle's land?"

"Yep, he owns this whole farm. Well, it used to be a farm. He's got it as an apiary now. That's his house, a processing building, an old warehouse, and the garage for carpentry."

"Nice," Cameron whistled. "He's doing all right, then."

"Yeah. That's why he needs help. I think it's getting kinda overwhelming now that he has hundreds of hives. And he insists on running the market stand, too," Noah clicked his tongue. "Stubborn."

"I don't know anyone who's stubborn like that," Cameron teased. Noah shoved him with his hip and Cameron, caught off-guard, nearly stumbled into a ditch. "Hey!"

Noah laughed and hauled him closer again, making sure he had his balance before letting go of his hand. "Sorry." He strode ahead to the gate. Cameron's nerves tingled at the fact that he was just inches away from the fence, reaching up to switch it off.

When Noah reached for the fence, Cameron flinched.

"Aha. City boy," Noah teased, winking as he unhooked the gate. "I turned it off."

"Still, I keep expecting... a shock," Cameron laughed. "I'm not a city boy, shut up."

"What part of Fredericton did you grow up in?"

"...The downtown part," Cameron grumbled, rolling his head back for a moment. He couldn't match Noah's natural dramatic flair. "Fine."

Noah laughed, then beckoned. "Come on. They won't sting. Probably. Don't act like a bear."

Cameron eyed Noah skeptically. "I'm built like a bear."

"Come on," Noah laughed. "You don't look like one."

"Thank God, I hate playoff beards," Cameron murmured under his breath. He walked through the long grass until he reached the fence.

Large dots flitted into and out of a couple dozen beehives. "Are the ones stacked up all the same hive, too?"

"Oh, boy. You *are* a rookie," Noah laughed. He took Cameron's hand. "Yeah. Normally, they are, but over the winter they can be stacked for warmth. There's about fifteen here. That's a lot for one place."

Cameron caught his breath as a small bee, just the size of his nail, dove for his head before diverting course with a buzz just past his ear. "Whoa." It was only Noah's grip on his hand that kept him from swatting at it.

"Don't worry. If they're going for you, you'll know it," Noah promised.

"That's... not as reassuring as you might think."

Noah laughed, approaching one pallet with a two-box-high hive. "Here, this one's a nice hive."

"How do you know that?"

"All the hives here are nice, except that back one. The yellow one."

"Is that why it's on its own pallet over there?" Cameron laughed, squinting at the hive in question. It was a good five feet away from any other hive.

Noah nodded. "And the other hives next to it didn't make it."

"Through the winter?" When Noah nodded, Cameron winced. "Ouch. That's gotta be hard."

"Uncle Bill takes it a bit harder than he lets on. The first few winters were roughest. Now he's more used to it, but... you know."

Cameron nodded, his gaze drawn back to the hive closest to him. He let go of Noah's hand and crouched a few feet away from the hive. There were lots of lumps in the grass under the hive entrance, and he squinted at them, then stared. "Shit, are those dead bees?"

"You thought they buried them?" Noah teased, but he squeezed Cameron's shoulder as he stood next to him.

Cameron winced and glanced down, then shuddered, trying not to think about stepping on dead bees. "Harsh."

"Sorry," Noah chuckled gently. He leaned down to kiss the

top of his head in an affectionate move that made Cameron's heart soar.

Cameron leaned his head against Noah, his temple touching Noah's thigh. He grew entranced by the little creatures swooping into the hive, crawling inside and back out again. "Are they gathering?"

"Something like that," Noah agreed. "Bringing back water, pollen, and nectar. Uncle Bill will tell you their life stages, but they all have jobs."

"How responsible," Cameron marveled with a light laugh. "I can... I think I can hear them." Noah was silent for a moment, and Cameron became certain of it: there was a low buzz coming from the hive. It was almost a deep purr of an engine. "Wow," he whispered.

Noah murmured, "Often on warm summer days, the whole yard hums."

Cameron's heart fluttered. Now that he was up close to them and they were ignoring him, his curiosity was overcoming him. Some flew to water buckets that were set up with rocks piled into them for places for them to sit. Others were flitting around looking for flowers, and every one seemed to know where it was going.

As he sidled closer to the hive entrance, he saw their fuzzy bodies and alert eyes watching him.

"Don't get closer," Noah warned with a quiet chuckle.

"Oh, *now* they're dangerous?"

Noah flicked the side of Cameron's head and Cameron laughed under his breath. "Spring's when they're most vulnerable. They get defensive."

"Coulda told me that earlier."

Noah reached down to cup Cameron's cheek. "You're doing fine."

God, that view up Noah's body was sexy. Cameron had been resisting touching or ogling him for hours now. It was hard now – especially when Noah stood beside Cameron, his groin right at face level.

Cameron reached behind Noah, his eye caught by something on the back of his thigh. "I think you have a bee..."

"Just brush her a little and she'll move," Noah murmured, shivering at the touch.

Cameron brushed the insect away, and Noah's thigh twitched under his touch. "There she goes. She?"

"I'll explain later." Noah gripped Cameron's arm to pull him to his feet, his gaze locked with Cameron's. "I think we should... get going."

A smile spread across Cameron's lips. "I don't think I wanna get to second base in the middle of a bunch of angry spring bees..." He leaned in to kiss Noah again.

Noah laughed against Cameron's lips and pulled him in with a hand on each cheek, pressing up to him. "I missed you."

"Even in those couple days?" Cameron teased, but he knew exactly what Noah meant. It was only Sunday and they'd slept together on Wednesday, but it felt like forever since Noah's hands had last caressed him.

And that goodbye kiss...

In mutual agreement, they walked together out of the yard, their hands hardly leaving each other. Noah kept stopping to press kisses to Cameron's lips. The heat built deep in his stomach and Cameron barely knew where he was going by the time they reached his car.

"Let me check you," Noah murmured. His hands ghosted down Cameron's body, across his t-shirt and jeans. They wandered slowly down his thighs and around to his ass. Then, Cameron felt a sudden squeeze.

"That's not a bee sting," Cameron teased.

Noah winked. "Turn around so I can make sure."

Cameron shivered and turned on the spot, letting Noah's hands run down his back and sides. Noah sidled up to his back and whispered into his ear, "You're clear. Am I?"

Cameron had to fight to turn around in Noah's hold and inspect him quickly. "Yep." He wasted no time climbing into the driver's seat.

Noah had him on edge. One touch of Noah's hand to his cheek, to his ass, to his back, and he couldn't fuckin' think straight. For better or for worse, Cameron didn't want to.

CHAPTER
Twenty~Two
CAMERON

"Christ, you're a good kisser."

Cameron blushed, pausing in the foyer of Noah's house to give Noah one more lingering kiss. He'd driven home without incident, but Noah's hand on his thigh hadn't helped. "Thanks. I appreciate your feedback."

Noah laughed. "Smart-ass, too."

"You thought I had a smart ass when you stung it, didn't you?"

"Your brain's just as smart, but yeah." Noah laughed as he pushed his way past Cameron.

Cameron winked. "Full of compliments today, aren't you? I wonder what you want from me?" he teased.

Noah smirked, looking Cameron up and down before shooting him a come-hither expression.

Cameron couldn't resist those narrowed eyes and sultry, pouting lips. He stepped out of the entrance into the living room, his hands going for Noah's waist. Cameron loved to pull him in and up for a good, deep kiss.

They didn't pull away this time even for breath. Cameron

kept sucking on Noah's lips while Noah gasped for breath. When it was Cameron's turn to breathe deeply and ground himself, Noah pressed feather-light kisses along his jaw.

Cameron gasped as Noah tugged him by the wrist toward the staircase. "Oh, yes."

Noah laughed against Cameron's lips. "I love how enthusiastic you are," he whispered. "Catch me if you can." He bolted up the stairs, taking them two at a time with a broad grin flashed over his shoulder.

Oh, it's on. Cameron sprang into action, thundering up after Noah. Noah didn't know he'd just challenged the best sprinter in camp.

He wrapped an arm around Noah's waist on the last stair to catch him and swing him around into his arms. Noah's feet nearly slipped off the top stair, but his weight was secure in Cameron's arms. He grabbed Cam's shoulders hard nonetheless. "Oh!"

"Mine," Cameron teased with a wink. He pulled him into the master bedroom, Noah's hands running up along his chest.

Then, Noah pushed against his chest to knock him flat onto the bed. His feisty partner crawled over him, running his hands up his shoulders and over his cheeks. Noah's lips pressed against his and Cameron's gaze softened. He was so affectionate.

Cameron rolled them over in a swift motion, the bed sheets rustling under them and the mattress creaking. He grabbed Noah's waist to haul him up until his head rested on the pillows so he'd be a little more comfortable.

"Jesus, you must work out every day. You could bench me."

Cameron laughed. "Yeah. I do."

"That's the manhandling I was talkin' about." Noah leaned up to kiss Cameron's jaw and again just by his ear.

A shiver wracked Cameron's body as a line of heat burned straight down to the base of his cock. He was swelling in response to the touch, like there was a direct link. *Christ.* "And I was just saying last night how delicious I bet you are..."

He yanked Noah's t-shirt up and off in a swift motion. As he fumbled to pull off his own unbuttoned plaid shirt, he crushed their mouths together. Noah's hands came to his waist, each brush of skin on bare skin electrifying Cameron's nerves with pure physical chemistry. He'd never felt anything quite like it, and he was hooked.

Noah yanked off his t-shirt and Cameron closed his eyes as the neck caught on his nose. He tilted his head up, and then his torso was bare and Noah's eyes and hands were raking along it.

Noah's fingers pinched one of his nipples and twisted gently.

Cameron's whole body arched into Noah. "O-Oh, Christ..."

"Too hard?"

"No," Cameron whispered. The sting of white-hot pain melted into bone-deep pleasure that made his cock throb with desire.

Noah licked his fingertips, his tongue tip circling them in a way that made Cameron remember the warm wet of it against his cock. He reached out to tweak and pull at the other nipple, flicking his fingers in a tease across it.

In response, Cameron ground against Noah, his cock painfully tight in his jeans and underwear. The friction helped, but he ached even more desperately to be bare, too. Every little tweak of his nipples built up the heat under his skin. When Noah leaned up to brace an elbow behind himself and close his mouth around one nipple, Cameron rolled his head back. "Ohhhh..."

Noah moaned, pinching the nub with his lips as his tongue

drew rapid circles. Cameron was on edge, his breath coming in harsh pants. He rolled his hips forward against Noah's, noting the bulge that slotted against his own.

He only gave Noah a few seconds of this before pushing down on his chest to flatten him to the bed again. Cameron scooted down, pressing his lips to the middle of Noah's stomach. He licked a trail down to his waistband, unzipped his jeans and unbuttoned them, and pulled them off along with the underwear beneath.

As the last of Noah's clothes hit the floor, Cameron kissed up to his stomach and back down his thigh. He teased him with his lips in a straight line past curly hairs to the base of his cock.

"Nnh-- Nnh, Cam," Noah panted, his back already rippling and thighs twitching. "Yes, Jesus..."

"Mm?" Cameron licked a slow, wide stripe from the base of Noah's flushed cock to the tip. Along the way, he admired the veined length and beautiful blunt tip up close.

Noah drew in a sharp breath as Cameron's tongue tip lingered around the slit, then licked slowly around the head. "Please..."

Cameron wrapped his lips tightly around the velvety shaft and pulled them back across his teeth. He cupped the head with his tongue before letting it slide across to the back of his throat as he bobbed his head down. He took in the shaft in a smooth movement, his eyes flickering up in rapt fascination to Noah's face.

God, Noah was beautiful. His eyes were wide, his cheeks a cute pink, his teeth sparkling white as his lips opened for gulping breaths.

Cameron pulled his head back up with a quiet moan and sucked his cheeks in around the gorgeous cock. Then, he set into a slow, steady rhythm. Minutes passed with just breathy gasps, whimpers, and moans from Noah. Cameron's breathing was harsh, and he gave quiet moans around Noah's cock now and then.

"That's good," Noah breathed out at last, and Cameron sucked his mouth off the wet, throbbing rod. Noah's arm was flung up above his head. His other hand reaching out to squeeze Cameron's shoulder and caress his hair. "Jesus."

"You *do* taste excellent," Cameron teased, just to see Noah's cheeks red with embarrassment.

"I'm... glad," Noah managed with a quiet laugh, then squirmed over the bed to open the bedside drawer. "Need a condom again?"

"I brought my own, but I think *you'll* be wanting this..." Cameron leaned over Noah with a peck of his lips to grab the lubricant. Before he opened it, though, he settled back on his heels over Noah's stomach to unzip his own jeans.

"Oh, fuckin' finally," Noah breathed out. Cameron laughed, letting his jeans drop to reveal his jock strap.

Noah's reaction was priceless: his jaw dropped, his gaze fixed on the bulging package. Cameron shifted onto one knee at a time to pull his jeans off leg by leg. When they were off, he fished out a condom from his wallet and tossed aside the garment.

Meanwhile, a soft kiss pressed to the stubble on the inside of his thigh where he trimmed a little to keep pinches and zipper mistakes to a minimum. By the time Cameron glanced down at Noah, both of Noah's hands were squeezing his ass. Noah pressed him down against him hard, forcing him to grind against Noah's hip.

Then, Noah reached between them to pull aside the jock strap so Cam's hard cock finally popped free from the cloth prison. Cameron gave a sigh of relief as the dull ache faded into pleasure, his stiff cock poking into Noah's thigh as he slid down between his legs.

"That's so fuckin' hot," Noah whispered. "You have no idea."

"I have a bunch of these." Cameron's slick fingers pressed at his entrance and inside.

"Oh, the world is a better place now," Noah groaned.

Noah was just fuckin' *fun* to finger. The way his back arched and lips parted into a quick "o" shape before he tried to exhale and calm himself... The way he moaned in little whimpers near the back of his throat... The way his cock stiffened and twitched further when Cameron rubbed his prostate...

Noah slapped Cameron's wrist after a minute. "Don't waste any more time."

"Foreplay is a dead art." Cameron winked, slid his fingers free, and wiped them clean.

"Good."

Cameron laughed, ripping open the condom package and rolling it down his shaft with a few skillful strokes.

Then, he was pressing against Noah. Noah's feet rose to his thighs and arms wrapped around his shoulders. Cameron sank into the tightness and intimacy of Noah, and he never wanted to leave.

As Noah enveloped him, Cameron let a quiet grunt of pleasure escape at the squeeze of his body. He pushed further and further in, until he couldn't go any more.

Noah pulled his hips back at the same moment as Cameron, then pushed up into him. His back flexed as he worked with Cameron to drive Cam good and deep into him. With each thrust, a small grunt or moan of pleasure escaped him, and Cameron marveled at how fucking vocal he was.

"Cam...!"

Noah was overwhelmed, so Cam leaned in to kiss him until he whimpered again.

Thrust by thrust, their bodies worked together. Deep intimacy thrummed through Cameron's bones. Cameron watched the pleasure work its way across Noah's face, and he loved it.

Noah pulled him in for a deep kiss, and Cameron knew the edge was close. He couldn't keep it slow anymore.

He grabbed Noah's hip and curled his fingers around it hard, pushing into the tight perfection of his body faster and deeper. Noah grunted, still pushing up into him, but his thighs were quivering against him. His stomach tensed each time Cameron thrust across that one spot inside.

Noah reached between them to stroke his cock. Cameron grunted, pushing his face into Noah's neck to kiss at his shoulder while keeping his breathing slow and steady.

The doctor's warnings still echoed in his mind: prolonged elevated heart rates or brief extra-elevated heart rates could be – no, *would* be dangerous for him.

But he couldn't fuckin' freeze this sex life. Not now that he'd found the most intimate moments of his life in this man's bed just a week after meeting him.

Fuck. I fell hard.

Still, Cameron grinned as he watched Noah's back arch and ripple, his hips push up... Then, his cock squirted out every drop of passion between their bodies. The extra clenching milked Cam's pleasure until he stumbled over the edge. He had barely enough time to gasp, "Noah...!" as his balls tightened.

Then Cameron was coming, too, plunging off the edge and clinging half-desperately to Noah like a life preserver. His heart pounded, his thighs quivered, his muscles drew tight and released in spasms of ecstasy...

Noah pulled him in to kiss him as soon as his cock slipped

free. They shared a long, slow kiss or two against each other's lips before Cameron pulled back to breathe, still grinding their bodies together for the extra sparks of warmth.

"Christ," Cameron whispered.

Noah giggled, and the sound became a throaty chuckle, then a deep laugh. "Y-You're saying that a lot lately," he teased. "My name's Noah."

Cameron swatted Noah's thigh. "Get your own line."

"Sometimes, the classics work." Noah rubbed Cameron's back slowly as they cooled down together, limbs still tangled. He kept pressing sweet kisses to Cameron's lips, and then to his jaw and up to his temple and behind his ear – everywhere he could reach.

It was almost overstimulating, but Cameron liked it.

"I – I hate to be the one to bring this up, but... I don't want this to just be about sex," Cameron murmured. "You?"

Noah pulled back enough to lock eyes again. His expression was sincere as he nodded. "Me neither. But even if it were, I wouldn't care as long as you treat me well."

"Do I treat you well?"

Noah smiled. In answer, he leaned in to press a slow, aimless kiss against Cameron's lips, then sucked on Cam's lower lip. When Cameron could hardly breathe again, Noah murmured, "Damn near perfect."

Twenty~Three

NOAH

"So, the date for the art show is August eleventh. Noah, will that give you enough time?"

Noah was distracted enough to need a nudge from Jay. August eleventh. It was the end of the summer, months away, but he knew something was happening that day. What the hell was it? It wasn't his exhibition, that was much sooner.

Oh, Christ. The Moncton hockey game. He'd just been to see Jason a couple days ago about getting the arena for the big intercity match – that was why it was stuck in his brain.

But he couldn't back out of Jay's art show for career, charity, and friendship reasons. Likewise, he couldn't back out of the hockey game. The guys were counting on him, weren't they?

"Er, no, that's okay," Noah told them, rubbing his chin as he took out his phone. "The eleventh? What time?"

"Seven to ten-thirty."

The game's at seven, too. Oh, boy.

Noah wished he were back in bed with that gorgeous, affectionate hunk. Somehow, his life had become complicated enough that he'd be letting people down any which way.

It wasn't life or death to attend the art show, but as the curator, he'd be practically required to be there. Likewise, as one of the leaders of the hockey club, he was supposed to be there, too. Then again, he wasn't the team captain – that was Kevin, an enthusiastic, young, yet experienced university player.

Something would have to give, and the match couldn't be rearranged; Moncton had already booked their bus.

Maybe he'd just run away with Cam that day... Except Cam was joining the team, too.

Can he play in my stead?

He tried to shake off the thoughts. He had all summer to figure this one out.

"Behind you-- oh, Art!" Noah groaned as his friend completely missed the ball skidding along the pavement behind him. Ray hooked the ball around his blade and was off down the pavement.

They were the only three there yet, but as guys showed up, they joined in. The game began once they had enough to form teams.

"That your new friend?" Ray asked, pausing long enough to gesture with his stick toward the ball field entrance.

Noah glanced toward the gate, then nodded. "That's Cam." He hadn't been specific about how he knew Cameron, just said another guy was interested in joining. He hoped Cameron wouldn't be questioned any more than the other guys he'd recruited.

And he hoped Cameron was some good. They weren't a serious club by any stretch of the imagination, but a few of the guys here were competitive.

"Hey, Cam," Noah called out, jogging to the edge of the concrete pad and through the fence gate. "We always bring a couple extra sticks. We don't have any other gear right now, but they want us to have some safety gear when we're in the arena."

"All right," Cameron agreed easily. He was dressed in loose shorts and a t-shirt, both of which still managed to cling to his fuckin' hot body.

Noah saw a few other guys approaching, so he offered Cam his choice of sticks and waited while Cam picked them up and eyed them. "I'll introduce you to the rest of them."

Cam chose one, squinting with one eye down the length of the stick and balancing it on a finger. It slipped sideways, but he caught it and hefted it, testing the weight. "Okay. This one. Thanks."

He introduced each of the guys as they approached. It was easy since Cam bantered with them no problem and asked them about the club, giving Kevin the chance to brag a little. When Kevin mentioned the Moncton game, Cameron's expression flickered and he nodded without commenting, then asked how many guys there were.

Noah kept his distance, letting them all bond a little before gesturing. "Come on, the day's getting old."

"Kevin – we got positions?" Cameron asked, glancing up and down the court to assess it. He sensed that Kevin was the captain, then.

Kevin nodded. "But we play in all of them. You better at anything?"

"Rotating, wow. Keep me on my toes. I'm used to forward... right-winger, if I can. Do we have that many players?"

"Depends who shows up," Kevin told him and Cameron nodded.

Noah laughed under his breath. "You've played before, then."

"Yeah, for a while," Cameron answered, shaking out his shoulders. "Who's got the puck? Er, ball."

As more guys showed up, they joined in, fleshing out the teams. Noah was thankful that Kevin put Cam on his team; while Cameron got the right-winger position he'd asked for, Noah took right defense. That gave him a great view of Cameron's muscled thighs and ass. Not just that, but the way his shirt pulled tight over his shoulder blades and his head moved as he kept watch on the ball and everyone else.

The way he ran was fluid, like he was expecting skates under his feet. Noah had to laugh a little – most kids in Canada had played ice hockey at some point, but ball hockey was different without the momentum of ice.

Cameron was *good*, too. Despite his casual attitude and laughter, he kept getting into focus. He was competitive, then, too. Noah jogged forward as Cameron pirouetted to avoid Ray's defense and turned left, looking for someone to pass to. With nobody there, he backed up a pace and Kevin snuck his stick in to steal the ball.

"Fu-- oh, you little," Cameron grumbled as the guys laughed. He jogged backward while Noah had to shift his focus from Cameron's body to the game to try to challenge Kevin.

They didn't push themselves to the limit that day, leaving Noah the chance to look around sometimes and gauge who was there. Just about everyone had shown up, which was a great sign.

There was someone in the parking lot, too, watching them. Maybe someone waiting to use the court for their own practice... or someone who wanted to join in? He squinted, but he couldn't see much more than a guy sitting in the driver's seat.

A little creepy.

"Hey!" Cameron's sharp call snapped Noah out of it and he sprinted left to back up Jonathon.

"Over here!"

The second Noah caught the ball with his stick and turned to pass up the court to Cameron, Cameron was exactly where he needed him to be.

Cameron was watching him just as closely, anticipating his every need.

The thought made Noah shiver before he slapped the ball up to Cameron. Cameron rolled it down the blade to the back to spin it around Kevin's blade once, then twice. He hip-checked him out of the way and passed it.

Every contact Cameron made with a guy on the other team made Noah's jealousy flare up, even though he knew it was ridiculous. Cam was there for and with him.

When they called the game quits an hour later, Cameron was sweaty but breathing easier than the rest of them as he approached. "Cool."

"You *do* work out a lot," Noah complained. He was flushed with heat and resisting the urge to double up for breath. He leaned heavily on his stick instead. "Fuck your composure."

Cameron laughed with shock and shoved Noah lightly. "Hey, don't hate. We won."

"True." Noah straightened up and wiped his forehead. "So you in for the game versus Moncton? You could be the secret weapon. You're pretty good."

Amusement flashed through Cameron's expression, then a

wary moment. "Maybe. I gotta... watch my back with this," Cameron admitted, walking down the court to drop off his stick as Noah followed.

"Oh." Noah had no idea what that meant. Cameron *had* been worried that it would be too serious. Maybe he had stress management issues. "Yeah, no problem. Nobody's forced to. Well, you know, me and Kevin and Rick – the guys who organize it – are... but other than that..."

Cameron flashed him a little smile. "We'll see."

Noah remembered the guy he'd seen in the parking lot earlier and glanced up to scan the lot, but that car was gone now.

Huh. Must have given up.

Something niggled at the back of his mind, but he set it aside. "Going out for beers with us?"

Cameron relaxed and clapped Noah's shoulder, rubbing with his thumb before letting go. "Hell, yeah."

CHAPTER

Twenty~Four

JACKSON

JACKSON HAD TO GET AWAY. HE'D COME HOME ONLY TO TRIP over Cam's shit in the front hall and then make them both supper. He and his friends were out for drinks at the local bar, and his temper was cooling off as fast as it heated up. Close quarters weren't easy for anyone.

As Jackson leaned back and told his friends about forging a hockey stick, there was Cam: walking by the window of the bar.

And Cam wasn't alone.

Of all the fuckin' people, he was with Noah, the art director of the very show Jackson's piece was appearing in.

The very openly gay Noah, who'd come here this winter with his lisp and tight clothes and an ever-bright smile.

It didn't take a brainiac to put two and two together.

Crap. I guess that's why he hasn't been moving his boxes or tidying up. Jackson's eyes followed them as they strode past the window.

Cameron brushed a hand down Noah's arm, and Noah was enraptured. A game smile lingered on his lips as he listened to whatever Cameron was saying. Noah laughed and bumped his shoulder against Cameron's to point up to the cocktail bar across the street.

They crossed the street hand-in-hand, jaywalking as Cameron boldly led them. Noah lingered reluctantly, making Cam tug his hand to get him to jog across the road.

Before Ashley and Ryan followed his gaze and outed Cam, Jackson hastily snapped back to the conversation.

Even in those ten seconds, that was more chemistry than he'd ever seen between Cam and Nathan. And Noah was sweet, from what he knew – maybe a little fussy, but sincere and honest. He knew his shit about art. He was a curator or director or something at the local gallery.

Jackson bit his lip and signaled the waitress for another round of beers. "My turn."

CHAPTER

Twenty-Five

CAMERON

CAMERON COULDN'T BLAME JACKSON FOR HIS ANNOYANCE. Jackson was a bachelor used to living alone in a small house. Now he was boxed in by Cam's clutter and his own, and he'd always had a low tolerance for clutter.

That was just one of the reasons Cam looked forward to the houses closing. Also, besides having the biggest financial decision of his life hanging over him, he wanted a nice place to bring Noah.

He scanned the living room for messy spots, then tidied up a few of them. Once the place looked a little better, he hauled up a few storage tubs to the guest bedroom and found a spot to stack them.

"Good enough for now."

Something more urgent called him.

Cam shoved on his shoes, he fished his phone out of his pocket and dialed Noah's number. They'd parted ways after hockey and beer last night with a quiet kiss outside the bar. They hadn't been right within sight of Noah's buddies, but they weren't exactly hiding it, either.

"Hey, Noah. What's up tonight? Working?"

"No, I'm off. Why?"

"I'd like to see you."

"Sure. Wanna come over?"

"I was thinking I'd take you out for a cocktail..." Cameron trailed off with a meaningful smile. He moved his phone to his other ear and locked up Jackson's house. Jackson was long gone, probably to walk off his temper and have a drink.

"Oh," Noah murmured, and Cameron pictured the smile accompanying the surprised sound. "Yeah, that'd be great."

Cameron kept his voice down as he trotted down the steps to the sidewalk. "I mean, unless you *really* wanted to spend every date in your bed..."

"Cam!" Noah laughed. "Not that I'd say no. Okay, are you on your way over?"

"Mmhmm. There in fifteen. Be ready to drink and dance," Cam teased. "I'm assuming you like to dance."

"I love to dance. See you."

Cameron smiled, pocketing his phone again as he strode down the sidewalk with a mission in his step. He wanted to have Noah on his arm every night. It was becoming obvious that they had to talk about their relationship.

Maybe not tonight, though. They could have another fun date first – not that Cam thought there was much he was waiting to find out about Noah. Noah had been honest and forthright from the beginning about his intentions and who he was, and Cam loved that bravery.

Braver than me.

Cam had to tell the truth about at *least* the heart problem. He'd hide the "former professional hockey player" bit for a little longer so Noah didn't get starstruck like Cam had had happen before. It was only fair to tell the guy he was seeing that he couldn't have sex *too* much or play hockey *too* hard or even get into a stressful argument.

Cameron smiled when Noah clattered down the porch steps in tight black jeans, silver shoes, and a strappy silver top under a stunning blue sweater with art screen-printed on the silk. Noah's coat was half-closed so he didn't know what painting it was.

"A masterpiece," he gestured toward Noah. "And the sweater's cute, too."

Noah blushed and came to hook his arm around Cameron's. "You flatter me too much. My ego will explode."

Cameron bumped their hips together. "It's not flattery if it's the truth."

"It is too," Noah laughed, leaning up to peck his lips. "How was your day?"

"Quiet," Cameron admitted. "Made a few calls and recovered from yesterday, pretty much."

"Oh, God, I felt it when I woke up," Noah groaned, tipping his head back to gaze up at the evening sky. The sleek line of his throat, only broken by his Adam's apple, made Cameron lick his lips. "I barely got up."

Cameron fought the urge to laugh. In truth, that had been part of a morning's workout for him, but he didn't want to make Noah feel bad. "It was intense," he agreed. "You didn't play last year?"

"I only moved here six months ago--"

"Oh, right, right. Sorry," Cameron chuckled. "I forgot. No ice hockey over the winter?"

"No. God, no. I'd freeze," Noah exclaimed. "And get crushed. Do I look like I'm built to be smashed into boards?"

Cameron's lips twitched and he glanced over to let his eyes flicker down Noah's slender body. "You're built to be smashed into walls, and doors, and staircase landings..." He freed his arm to run his hand down Noah's back. Cam hooked his arm around Noah's waist to pull him against him with a quick, playful jerk. "And mattresses..."

The sun hadn't set enough to hide the fact that Noah was blushing hard. Nonetheless, he was bantering right back, his arm sliding around Cameron's shoulders. "I like the way you think."

"And fuck," Cameron whispered, leaning in to press a kiss against the corner of Noah's jaw. A shiver ran down Noah's spine. Cam smirked, loosening his hold a little as he raised his voice again. "But that's for later."

"Yeah," Noah murmured, nearly tripping over a crack in the sidewalk from his inability to tear his eyes away from Cameron's.

"Eyes on the road," Cameron teased. He appreciated that he had that effect, but he didn't want Noah to smack into a telephone pole or something.

Noah pulled away a little and touched his face as if regaining his composure. Cameron's ego swelled even more. "What bar were you thinking?"

"Skylight? It's new since I moved away but it looks like the kind of place we could go... Are they open Wednesdays?"

"Yep. Good choice. It's not the gay bar. Fuck, the single gay bar here and all the straight students in it..." Noah rolled his eyes.

Cameron laughed. "Hey, you don't know they're straight. You would've thought I was," he teased.

"Nah," Noah said. He smirked as they waited at a red light. "I could have sussed you out in a few seconds."

"How?" Cameron laughed. Noah sounded so confident in himself.

"A little dirty dancing in just the right spot... eye contact..." Noah ground against his side, then took his hand to lead him across the road, his steps light and grin playful. "Get you to buy me a drink or two..."

"You were bold in Ottawa."

"Not usually," Noah laughed. "But with a hunk like you on the line... Everyone's gotta play dirty to get the one they want to go home with."

Cameron squeezed Noah's hand, then laced their fingers as they approached the lights of downtown. "I'm impressed."

Noah let go of his hand and drew away a little, giving him a moment's glance up and down. "Then you just pull back a little and see if they follow..."

Even though he registered Noah's words, Cameron didn't process them until it was too late. He was zig-zagging to follow Noah and get closer to him. "Oh." He brushed a hand down Noah's arm. "You're a lot cleverer than I was back in university. When I was here, I just sort of hung out and waited for guys to choose me..."

Noah laughed, then pointed up. "There's the Skylight. Let's cross the street over there." Their bodies brushed as Noah leaned into Cameron's shoulder.

Cameron snorted and reached out to grab Noah's hand. "We can cross here. Traffic's light." He stepped off the sidewalk.

"And if we get caught jaywalking?" Noah rooted his feet for a moment, making Cameron glance back and tug him.

"I'll flutter my lashes," Cameron deadpanned. "I can unbutton my shirt, if that'll help."

Noah laughed and shook his head but followed as Cameron led him across the road to the bar Noah had pointed out.

They hadn't had a sip of alcohol yet, but Cameron's heart soared and his hands tingled every time he looked at Noah.

Over the first few cocktails, they chatted about their days. Cameron shared his frustration at waiting another three weeks for the houses to close, and Noah vented about the flaky arena board of directors.

Noah perked up, dragged out of his funk by a sudden thought. "You know, I know a lot of local artists... How were you thinking of decorating your new place?"

Cameron raised his eyebrow. "I thought with local art. Is that the right answer?"

"Is it true?" Noah was eager yet tentative.

Cameron smiled. "Yeah."

"Okay. Well, I can get some deals. And there's some auctions and charity nights and stuff so I can bring you to those and get an idea of your style... Um, assuming you want to."

"That'd be amazing," Cameron said, and he meant it. Even his fancy-ass Toronto loft hadn't been very personal. "An expert touch. The only thing that I know that I want, for sure, is my brother's work. He does steel art."

Noah got a funny look and Cameron hoped he wasn't biased against blacksmiths somehow. Some people thought blacksmiths only made medieval armor or swords. Yeah, his brother *did* make swords for local fencing clubs, but there was so much more to it.

Then, Noah asked, "Is your brother... Jackson Riley? Actually, is *your* last name Riley? I don't even know that yet!"

His brother's name made Cameron blink with surprise. "Yeah, it is. And yeah! That's my brother. What's your surname?"

"Clark." Noah laughed. "I know your brother."

*Oh, boy. He'd better not mean he **knows** him.* Cameron shook his head. "Small town."

He'd felt this claustrophobia before. Everyone knew at least one of his brothers, and there was nowhere he could go without seeing someone he knew. Even the bartender here had been in his university class years ago.

"Yeah. He's doing a piece for the art show, actually," Noah told him. "Has he mentioned it?"

"Not much. He doesn't like to show off until he's done a piece, so I'm waiting," Cameron shrugged. Now that he was worrying about how many degrees of separation there were between him and Noah, he couldn't get it off his mind. "You met him before?"

Noah paused, scanning Cameron's face His eyes narrowed, and then a smile burst over his face. "Oh, shit, no. I know what you're think-- no," he laughed. "No, he's not my type."

Cameron let out a breath of relief and nudged Noah with his toe. "Dude, don't scare me like that."

Noah laughed and reached over the table to squeeze his hand. "Sorry! So, Cameron Riley... Are you a blacksmith, too?"

Cameron made a face. "No. My brothers and I are all pretty different. I mean, I've helped him out before, too, but... that was never my thing."

"Ah," Noah nodded. He was eying Cameron like he was trying to remember something.

Cameron had seen the exact expression before among hockey fans and guys he was dating, and sometimes those groups were one and the same. He'd made a policy of not sleeping with fans, just in case.

To distract Noah, he nudged him gently. "Hey, you up for dancing? Or are you going through the Yellow Pages in your brain?"

Noah snapped out of it and laughed. "Sorry. Yeah, I'd like to dance. I know a place close by."

"Perfect."

They finished their cocktails and headed to the club Noah chose, holding hands the whole way. This was a hell of a way to come out: on the arm of a hot little guy with a lightning-fast wit and a deep local knowledge.

And, thank God, not too deep a knowledge of the locals.

The blinking lights bounced off their bodies as they rotated, swishing up and down through the air and sometimes blinding Cameron.

Cameron's heart rate was a little up, but he was safe: he'd counted while Noah used the bathroom half an hour ago.

It wasn't his heart, but his legs telling him to stop dancing now.

"God, you gotta be tired out," he laughed as one singer's voice faded into another.

Noah's face gleamed with sweat, but his eyes were sparkling and he had a gorgeous, healthy flush to his skin. Cameron had stayed close all night, not wanting anyone else to muscle in on this territory.

"Come home with me," Noah invited him, sliding his arms around Cameron's neck. "Assuming you're not too straight for me, of course..."

Cameron laughed. "You caught me," he teased, leaning in to kiss Noah. "Detective Clark."

Noah winked and pulled him off the dance floor. They stumbled together, neither of them drunk but both high on each other and three hours of dancing. Pulsing music and flashing lights and sometimes singing along – Cameron off-key, Noah with sweet, melodic tones... The walk back to Noah's place was chillier than earlier that evening but it didn't take long. They were too busy swaying into each other. They hummed and laughed over nothing at all.

Noah fumbled to unlock the door and Cameron wrapped his arms around him from behind, kissing his shoulder and pushing the door open for him.

"Thank you," Noah laughed and they almost tangled up as they stepped together into the house. They pulled off and discarded shoes and jackets. "Want some water?"

"No, that's okay," Cameron assured him. "I haven't had that much."

Noah nodded. "I should be all right, too." He took Cameron by the hand to lead him straight upstairs to the bedroom.

They stripped off together, still grinding and kissing playfully. Nonetheless, Cameron didn't feel Noah pressuring him to fuck. It seemed they were both contented to just... be together that night.

Cameron crawled into bed and raised the covers for Noah, pulling his bare body in against him and spooning around him. After dancing for so long, the bed seemed almost too still. The room didn't spin around him, so he was safe from hangovers.

"Good night," Noah murmured, snuggling back into Cameron and resting his arm along Cam's. Cam found a spot under Noah's head to slide his other arm. "I had a lot of fun. Thank you."

"Thank you," Cameron countered, smiling to himself. "You're wonderful to be with."

"You, too," Noah murmured, twisting in Cameron's hold to kiss him one more time.

This kiss was slow and sweet, with no pressure to be

anywhere or do anything. Their lips gently parted, tongue tips playing at each other's lower lips before they pulled apart with a slight smack.

Noah gave a contented sigh and settled back down onto Cameron's arm and against his back.

With Noah, even a night without sex was one of the best Cam could remember. *This is exactly what I want.* The thought made Cameron smile. He breathed along with Noah's deep, steady breathing and he was asleep.

Twenty~Six

NOAH

Bubbles rose through the batter and Noah stood at the ready with his flipper. The edges of the pancake hadn't quite firmed up enough, but they were close.

When it was ready, he flipped the pancake and allowed himself a self-indulgent grin. He was *great* at pancakes. He'd already got bacon done and warming in the oven, and he'd wait to do eggs until he heard Cameron get up. This was the second-to-last pancake anyway.

And, speak of the devil, he heard water running in the bathroom upstairs.

He turned on the heat for the eggs, then dumped the mixed-up eggs and milk into the pan. He hummed under his breath, scrambling the eggs while finishing the last pancake.

"Good morning," Cameron greeted. "Oh my God, you even cook breakfast."

Noah grinned at Cam and glanced back over his shoulder at him. "Morning, sleepyhead. Did I tire you out with all that dancing?"

Cameron laughed and leaned against the counter, staying

out of his way. "A little. Wow, that looks good. Pancakes and eggs?"

"Bacon's in the oven already, with the rest of the pancakes."

"Music to my ears."

"Go sit at the table," Noah directed him, pointing over to the kitchen table with his wooden egg spatula. It was draped with a yellow sunflower tablecloth and set with condiments. He'd chosen maple syrup, ketchup, butter, and whipped cream... canned, not freshly-made. He wasn't *that* prepared.

Cameron laughed. "Yes, sir," he teased and leaned in to steal a quick kiss before seating himself.

Noah brought their plates to the table a minute later. He slid Cameron's plate in front of him first and then his own. When he dropped into his chair, it was with a contented smile. Then, he remembered his apron and stood up to take it off.

"Aw, it's cute," Cameron teased. It was the usual cheesy *kiss the cook* apron, but it had a little rainbow over the words.

"My old roomie got it for me in university, and I never quite grew out of it," Noah admitted with a laugh. He tossed it onto the counter and sat down to enjoy breakfast.

Only a few minutes in, though, Cameron drew a breath and squared his shoulders.

Uh oh. A conversation. I hope it's a good one.

"I've got something to tell you."

Noah winced. "Well, now that I've discovered all my deep-seated anxieties..."

"Sorry," Cameron laughed. "Don't worry, it's not – I don't think it's *that* bad. I should have said something earlier, but... I've got a couple medical things going on."

Noah blinked, then fidgeted. "Not..."

"No, I mean, a heart problem."

Oh. Ohhh. "Like... exercise-aggravated?" Noah instantly felt guilty. They'd danced for hours, and played hockey, and he was always walking over to see him...

"Yes, but it's not constant," Cameron assured him. "It's not formally diagnosed right now. The doctors tell me I can't do... pro-level sports. No sustained, elevated levels of stress, long periods of exercise, that kind of thing. A casual pickup game every week won't kill me."

"Okay." Noah put down his fork to gulp orange juice and cleared his throat. "Even stress?"

"Yeah. High levels, that is."

"What about beekeeping?" Did Uncle Bill know yet? Probably not. "I can tell my uncle about it--"

"No, that's fine," Cameron assured him, reaching over the table to touch his hand. "I didn't want you to freak out about it or anything. I know my limits. Beekeeping will be okay as long as I'm not running two miles and vaulting fences to get away from angry bees..."

That broke Noah's tension, and he laughed. "Okay. Sorry, I don't want to make you feel weird about it," he apologized. It was startling to hear this after several dates, but there hadn't been a good time to bring it up earlier. "And I can still tell Uncle Bill--"

"No, I'll handle it. I'll let him know beforehand, but like I said, I doubt it'll be an issue," Cameron assured him. "Everything I've been reading says you're supposed to stay calm and... zen around them, you know? So that'll be perfect for me."

Noah nodded. "So, why tell me? I mean, I'm glad you did, but..." he trailed off, finishing the last few bites of his food and setting down his utensils.

Cameron had already polished off his plate and he was leaning back, watching Noah. "I just need to make sure there's not much stress between us, too. I'd... If you're up for it, I wanna have that conversation."

"I thought we were about to until you started this one," Noah chuckled. "The relationship one?"

"That's the one." Cameron's expression was careful, yet he was smiling. "Do you want to date me?"

A shiver of delight coursed up Noah's spine. *"Fuck, yes."*

That might have come out a little louder than he'd meant it to, but Cameron just laughed. "Well, that leaves no doubt in my mind."

Noah laughed, too, and stood up from the table to take Cameron's hand and pull him to his feet. "Leave the dishes, I'll deal with them later. If I'd known I just had to cook you breakfast..."

Cameron chuckled, sliding his arm around Noah's waist and kissing him. He tasted like maple syrup, and Noah resisted the urge to suck on his lower lip.

When they pulled apart, Noah slapped Cameron's ass. "Go on, get upstairs. I've got spare toothbrushes for you. You can even choose your own color."

"You got a blue one?"

"I don't know. The package is in the middle drawer. I don't keep track," Noah laughed. He gathered the dishes and dumped them in the dishwasher as Cameron disappeared upstairs. Cameron's chuckle echoed in the stairwell.

When Cameron was out of sight, Noah took a moment to pump his fist in the air, then rubbed his face, trying to calm down. *Play it cool. Oh, God, you have a boyfriend. You're someone's boyfriend. No, calm down...*

He followed Cameron upstairs to brush his teeth, still beaming.

Cam squeezed Noah's hand as he stood outside the art gallery with him. Once they dropped hands, Noah tucked both his hands in his jacket pockets instead.

"You didn't have to walk me to work," Noah said for the fifth time that walk, but he was smiling hard. In fact, neither of them had stopped smiling since their conversation over breakfast.

"Of course I did. That's what boyfriends do. It's the honeymoon phase; enjoy it," Cam teased.

Noah laughed. "Until you get sick of me and send me on the bus?" he teased.

Cameron laughed. "Never."

"What are you up to today?"

"Sorting out boxes at my broth-- at Jackson's house, and tidying up. Still gotta live with him for three weeks... I want to be a good guest."

Noah's chest swelled with pride and he leaned up to kiss him goodbye. "Aww. Have fun."

After they kissed goodbye one more time and Cameron waved, they parted ways. Noah walked into the building sizzling with energy and ideas.

Today was going to be great.

CHAPTER
Twenty~Seven

CAMERON

The days passed in a blur as Cameron did spring yard work for his parents and tidied up Jackson's house. Cameron still expected to hear from Bill any time. He kept his phone on him, ready to race to his new apprenticeship as soon as Bill said the word.

He and Jackson decided against renting a storage locker. Jackson just wouldn't look for a buyer until the move was over. They'd work together to clean up, repaint, and do a few light renovations once the house was empty to increase the value.

To his surprise, Jackson showed up to the next pickup hockey game, along with another artist. Both of them lingered around the periphery of the fence, sketching what was going on. Cameron was a little self-conscious at first, but he forgot about them in the excitement and frustration of amateur hockey.

Holy shit, these guys were clueless, but he couldn't expect much more. Kevin was the exception, and fair enough since he was the only semi-pro player. He was just waiting to be drafted. Cameron still didn't push himself to his limits. He didn't want to stand out or seem like he thought he was too good for the rest of the guys.

He and Noah didn't get the chance to see each other after hockey since Noah had to meet the artists and discuss arrangements. By Saturday, he was getting anxious to see his new boyfriend.

The days were warming up. People were walking in light jackets or sweaters without a heavy winter coat over top. It was supposed to be clear with not a chance of rain, either.

It was perfect weather to walk to the art gallery.

Cameron trotted up the steps and inside to the front desk a little before noon, glancing around to spot Noah. There were a few spacious, bright gallery rooms on the main floor, but no signs of Noah.

"Hi," he greeted the clerk who was already reaching for the computer mouse. "Uh, I'm here to see Noah, if I can...?"

"Oh, of course. His office is through that way," the clerk pointed down a narrow hall.

"Thanks." Cameron slowed at each door to read the plaques. Some of the names he vaguely recognized from Noah's conversations about work, but none made him smile like seeing *Noah Clark* on the third door from the end.

He knocked on the open door and stepped inside.

Wow. A few deep green houseplants snaked out from between shelves and rows of books. Art snuck into every aspect of the office. Paintings hung from the walls while sculptures sat atop filing cabinets. A mixed media art piece shadowed the computer monitor.

"Welcome," Noah greeted him. Cameron's eyes were drawn back to his main interest in the room: his handsome lover. Noah was dressed in a gray waistcoat and dark blue collared shirt with the sleeves rolled up to his elbows.

God, he was gorgeous.

"Hi," Cameron answered, gesturing around the room. "Nice place here. It suits you."

The titles of the books, the decorative art, the bright window overlooking the street outside... It seemed like the kind of place Noah would hang out just for fun.

"Thanks," Noah laughed. "To what do I owe this pleasure?"

"When's your lunch break?"

"Right about now, I bet," Noah winked and glanced at his watch as he stood up. He grabbed a peacoat from the back of his chair to shrug on. "If you're asking, of course."

"I am. I don't know where's a good place for lunch around here, but I'll take you there," Cameron offered with a laugh. "There used to be a good lunch place that did sandwiches and stuff."

"A cafe? Yeah, there's a few good ones nearby."

"Let's do that," Cameron suggested, and he was met with a bright smile.

"Nice to see you again, by the way," Noah murmured. "I've been missing you." He left his coat unbuttoned as he stepped out from behind the desk and approached Cameron. Noah didn't hesitate to stretch up the inch or so that separated them and press a kiss to Cameron's lips.

Cameron cupped Noah's cheek to peck him on the lips, then put his hand on his shoulder. "How's your day going?"

"Oh, you know," Noah sighed with a touch of that amusing over-dramatic attitude. He led Cameron out of the office and down the hall, pausing at an open doorway. "Sarah? I'm going out for lunch."

"Okay," Sarah answered. The petite woman pushed her dyed red hair out of her eyes as she glanced up. She was clearly taken aback to see Cameron standing there with his hand still on Noah's shoulder. "Oh, hello."

"Hi. I'm Cam," Cameron introduced himself while Noah smiled at him.

Sarah's eyes lit up. "Ah, *you're* Cam... Nice to meet you," she winked. "Go on, Noah. Have a good lunch date."

"Thanks." Noah steered Cameron back down the hall and around the reception desk to the door.

When they walked down the steps together, Noah reached out to lace their fingers and swung their hands.

"Was it okay that I did that?" Cameron asked with a quick glance at Noah's expression.

"Did what? Oh, no, that's fine. She knew. Everyone knows," Noah laughed. "Remember, there was never a closet for me."

"Right," Cameron laughed under his breath. Noah was so expressive that he almost took it for granted now. "So, what have you been up to that's so stressful?"

Noah laughed. "Well, when you put it that way... Just arranging a charity show in my off-time, and a few of the artists are more... flaky than others. But for charity, you can't complain."

"You're always arranging shows. Is that typical for you? Or is this an unusually busy time?"

Noah led them to the crosswalk and paused with him. "Er, no... it is a bit unusual. I usually try to stick to one exhibition at a time, but the charity show is something I'm doing personally and the hockey show is for work."

"Ahh."

"Now I have to sign a bunch of loan paperwork and try to help Sarah untangle some... acquisition problems. There's a tour at three, too. And a members-only evening that I have to help with. Well, I shouldn't say *have to*. I like the members.

They're much more polite than the general public. Then again, I shouldn't malign the general public..."

"I get the idea," Cameron laughed. "People can't keep their hands off?"

"Oh, tell me about it. This one guy tried to touch this textured painting in gallery two – I need to take you through it so you know what I'm talking about, by the way. I *just* stopped him in time."

Cameron winced. "Even I know better."

"You like to play the uncultured bad boy, but you know a thing or two," Noah addressed him with a wink. "I've noticed."

Cameron's cheeks heated up and he squeezed Noah's hand. "Where's the cafe?"

"Just a few doors down," Noah grinned. "What about you? How was your day?"

Cam struggled to think of anything interesting that had happened. "I finished consolidating some of my boxes and helped Jackson pack some of his stuff in the basement."

"That's important."

"Mmm. The move's coming up soon, like it or not. We still have to talk about the details – which of us will move in first. Presumably me since I have less stuff, but..."

"Well, with three of you, you can all help each other. And I'll help," Noah offered.

Cameron grinned. He playfully squeezed Noah's bicep before pulling open the cafe door. "I wouldn't want to over-work you."

"Hey," Noah laughed. "I happen to lift weights at home sometimes."

"Sometimes?" Cameron teased.

Noah blushed. "When I remember."

"Ahhh."

Cameron chose a table with Noah near a window. A waitress approached to hand over menus, and they relaxed into light lunchtime conversation and flirtation.

This time, Cameron didn't let Noah escape back to work without promising him another date on Wednesday. The weather was supposed to be this great once again then.

"Texting alone just isn't enough," Cameron smiled as he and Noah ambled back toward the art gallery.

"No, it isn't," Noah agreed. "We should see each other every time the weather's this nice."

"That'll be every day in a few months' time," Cameron grinned. "Sounds perfect."

Noah laughed and leaned in to kiss Cameron. "Wednesday," he promised before pulling away. "Thank you for the lunch date."

"Thank *you*."

Cameron knew he couldn't get used to dropping his boyfriend off at work with a goodbye kiss. His own job would start up soon, and from the sounds of it, he wouldn't have much free time.

For now, he'd enjoy what he had.

Twenty~Eight

NOAH

For a Wednesday afternoon, there were a surprising number of people out and about. As they crossed the bridge to the heart of downtown, Noah leaned in to murmur to Cameron, "I think they're all skipping work today."

The weather was gorgeous enough, after all. They hardly needed their jackets, and the sun was bright on their faces.

"They could all be retail shift workers," Cameron retorted with a laugh. "Or students. Or just have the day off, like you."

Noah was off because he'd worked the last weekend, but he couldn't complain. The lunch date had broken up his weekend. "Right, right," he dismissed Cameron with a laugh. "I think they're all skiving."

"Skiving," Cameron repeated with a laugh. "What a word."

Noah's pocket buzzed with the distinctive ringtone he'd assigned to Uncle Bill. It had made him laugh when he'd done it, but now it seemed a little... on the nose. "Hold on, my phone's--"

"Tell me that isn't Bill."

"Uh... it might be." Noah fished out his phone, his cheeks

hot. "I thought it was clever." The buzzing sound stopped when he answered. "Hello?"

It was indeed his uncle, and his voice was dead serious. It melted the smile from Noah's face. "Noah, there's a problem at the yard."

"Shit. Which one?"

"The corner lot. A bear."

"No," Noah whispered, a chill running down his spine. He let go of Cameron's hand and adjusted the phone against his ear. "You need cleanup help?"

"Yeah. It must have been last night, when that bear report came in. I decided to check the yard this morning just in case. Good thing, too. Some of the hives haven't swarmed yet, but they'll be close."

"Did it go through the fence?"

Uncle Bill's voice was clipped. "Fence was off. Can you make it in?"

"Yeah, I'm off." Cameron was gesturing at himself. "Hold on." Noah covered the phone. "You want to help, too? Bear in the yard." He sped up his steps and Cameron kept pace.

"I heard," Cameron murmured and nodded. He was pale. "I'm coming, as long as I won't be in the way."

"No, you'll be helpful." Noah felt relieved to have one more pair of hands, even if Cameron might be a little shy at first. This would get him over *that*. Noah had only been to one destroyed yard before, but it had been a hell of an experience. "Hey, Uncle Bill, Cam's coming too. He'll give me a ride so we'll be there ASAP. You got gear for us?"

"Yep. See you."

Noah shoved his phone in his pocket and glanced at Cameron as they walked. His nervousness was in turn unnerving for Noah to see. "You sure you'll be okay?"

"Fine," Cameron answered, his voice tight. "Is that the yard we went to?"

"Yeah."

"Does he visit a lot?"

"Probably not, if he's been running around unwrapping other hives. Why?"

Cameron winced so hard Noah thought he must be in some physical pain. His steps sped up even more and Noah had to trot to keep pace with him. "Not since we were there?"

Noah drew breath to answer, then stopped in his tracks. Cameron grabbed his arm to pull him along. "Shit. Oh, no." Fuck. Cam was *right*.

They hadn't turned the fence on after he'd shown Cameron the yard.

Had they?

He searched his memory. He remembered hooking the gate back on, laughing with Cameron, walking to the car...

Not turning the fence on.

"Oh, fucking *shit*," Noah whispered and let Cameron pull him back into a half-jogging pace. "You're right."

"I'm sorry," Cameron murmured, his voice hoarse. "I must have distracted you..."

"No, it's my fault. That's a basic... that's so basic it's *stupid*," Noah groaned. Cameron led them across the road to the cafe where Cam had parked, and Noah circled to the driver's side. "I'm at fault."

Noah was glad Cameron was driving, since his hands shook.

Silence fell for a minute while Noah ripped himself apart for the stupid mistake. If the hives were all gone, that would be down to him. The gear was expensive, too, and that wasn't counting the loss of bees and honey. And the loss of life: bears ate bees, and many would have died attacking it.

And, shit, Cameron's heart!

"Oh, are you--" Noah wasn't quite sure how to ask this. He looked carefully at Cameron to make sure his paleness wasn't from his heart condition. "Are you okay with the stress?"

Cameron sensed his thoughts and reached out to squeeze his thigh. "Hey," he murmured to get Noah's attention. "I'm okay. What happened... happened. I can't be sheltered from everything. We just have to clean up and make amends now, right?"

"Yeah."

"As long as it's not playoff stress, I'm all right."

That got Noah to smile weakly, at least. Was Cam the type to not shave his beard until the playoffs ended? "The Moncton game won't be that bad," he promised.

Cameron paused, a frown line between his brows for a few moments before he nodded. "Oh, right. Yeah."

They hadn't been on the same page just then, but Noah didn't have time to worry about it. He had a huge mistake to make up for, and one that affected more than just his family.

Uncle Bill was going to be pissed, and please God let it be at him alone. Noah *really* hoped he hadn't gotten Cameron fired before he even began his apprenticeship.

CHAPTER
Twenty~Nine
CAMERON

WHEN THEY PULLED UP NEAR THE FIELD, GRAVEL CRUNCHING, Cameron parked in the same spot as before. There were a few open rubber tubs at the top of the driveway. He spotted white bee suits, some silver and bright blue things poking out of the tubs, and a bag of straw and grass.

Noah was over his brief moments of crushing guilt and into action mode. "Okay," Noah said, hopping out and slamming the car door. "We'll get suited up. He always has a few spare suits kicking around, so they must be in here."

Cameron smelled wood smoke from nearby. He'd been reading up on bee books in his spare time lately, but there was nothing like hands-on experience. "Is that--"

"The smokers, yeah," Noah nodded. "I'll show you how to use those, too." He was rummaging through bins. "Large?"

"Yeah."

"Here you go." Noah handed him a suit, and Cameron swallowed hard. *This is the trial by fire.* It unzipped, so he pulled down the zipper and pulled the hood back. Elastics around the ankles and... those must be sleeves...

"I just step in, right?"

"Oh, crap. Right." Noah was already halfway into his suit and Cam watched him kick off his shoes, to shove his legs through the suit legs "I'll help get it done up."

Cam imitated Noah's movements, leaning against the car to keep his balance when he pulled off one shoe at a time. He pulled the suit up around him, noticing the way the shoulders stretched out. The suit was almost a little small for his broad frame, but it would do its job. Thank God he'd worn his sneakers for the walk around town and over the bridge – he didn't mind them getting muddy.

When he was in with it zipped up, Cameron fidgeted with the hood, twisting to get a look at it. Noah had pulled it up and zipped it up in ten seconds flat.

"Look straight ahead," Noah coached, pulling the hood down and zipping it up. Cameron didn't even have the heart to acknowledge the tingle of chemistry between them as Noah's fingers brushed his chin.

"There."

"I'm safe?"

Noah circled around him and double-checked each zipper, then nodded. "With gloves, you will be. And better boots."

He rummaged through another tub and pulled out gumboots. "I hope you're around size nine or ten."

"Yeah, nine and a half."

"Jesus, there's a bit of luck. Nines or tens? I can do either."

"I'll take the tens."

Noah crouched near a box lighting piles of straw inside two silver tubular bellows while coaching him through pulling the suit ankles around the boots. Then, Noah handed one over to him. "Don't touch the metal. It'll take a couple minutes to really get burning."

"Right. You've... done this a lot?" Noah seemed to know his shit. Why hadn't *he* done an apprenticeship with his uncle?

"No. This isn't normal for bees," Noah assured him, handing over a pair of gloves. They walked down the road toward the corner lot. "They were calm before, but they'll be looking for every chance to attack now. Check your suit often."

Cameron swallowed hard and pulled the gloves on. Compared to his hockey gear, this thing was a suit of armor. It was clumsy and baggy in some spots. The hood obscured his vision and the boots gave him a clunky step.

It felt like he was in goal, only there were thousands of tiny opponents and he had no idea what to expect from them. Like every playoff nightmare ever, then.

Speaking of which, the moment in the car had been a little too close for comfort. He *had* to tell Noah the truth sometime soon.

As they reached the edge of the lot, Cameron heard a distinctive deep rumbling sound. It wasn't the same quiet hum he'd heard before. It was... angry, and it sent a chill down his spine.

"That's them," Noah confirmed. "Deep breaths. You ever meditate?"

"No. Someone tried to teach me before. I can visualize, though."

"Then do deep breathing like you're visualizing," Noah murmured, giving him a concerned frown. He was clearly worried for Cameron's health and the concern was sweet. Cameron was already pretty calm – or he had been until he'd heard that buzz, anyway.

He breathed in and out a few times until his shoulders sank and he slid into the zone. "Ready."

They stepped around the last grove of trees and Cameron almost choked on his deep breath.

Pallets were askew, wooden boxes scattered across the field, frames tossed across on the dirt and grass and mud. It looked like a thousand-pound toddler had thrown a tantrum.

Clusters of bees were forming on boxes – supers, Cameron reminded himself of their name – and frames. Some of the frames were ripped apart, one box shattered against rocks behind the pallet.

Noah moaned under his breath as he gazed around at the twenty-odd hives. The ones near the back of the field were fine, but the dozen closest hives had all been destroyed. Their contents were scattered everywhere.

Another man was already there in a suit – Bill, presumably – and crouched over a box, gathering scattered frames.

"Hey, Uncle Bill. Where should we start?"

Bill raised a hand but didn't look away yet. "Help look for queens. Those three need queens spotted. I think we're screwed, but if you can find one..."

Noah led Cameron over to the closest box and crouched by it. Cameron flinched at the harsh buzzing around the back of his head. Bees were circling both of them, landing on the hood near their ears and throat and crawling across the black masks. "Okay. Queen bees are much bigger than the others. See those there?"

"The big ones? Yeah."

"Those are drones. They're not the queen. Those are workers, those are drones. The queen's bigger than both of them. When you see her, you can't miss her. Help me out – look on one side of a frame while I check the other."

Cameron crouched opposite Noah as Noah pulled out a frame, then scooted up closer for a better look. He flinched, half-expecting stings from every bee crawling over the frame, but they stayed on it. A dozen or more bees were crawling over Noah – no, two or three dozen.

They can't get in.

Cameron focused his gaze on the frame, squinting at the masses of bees crawling across the frames. He shook his head slowly, scanning up and down and back and forth.

Then, Noah flipped the frame over to exchange sides.

"No?"

"No," Cameron confirmed.

The next frame was the same, though Cameron gave a few false alarms from thinking drones were queens. On the third frame, though, Cameron caught his breath. "Oh, shit. I think that's her."

Noah gently turned the frame around for a look and Cameron scooted close to point out the one he meant. She was larger and darker than the others surrounding her.

"Yes," Noah breathed out. Even through the hood, Cameron saw the smile of pleasure and relief crack his grim expression. "We've got one, Bill."

"Thank God. Seal them up, hopefully they'll stay put."

Cameron helped Noah get the frames arranged and the lid back on, following Noah's cues on what he needed next.

When the lid went back on, Cameron breathed out a sigh of relief. "So, same thing for the next two?"

"Yep."

Noah's uncle was approaching. "It's not good. We're going to lose a lot."

Noah rose to his feet and Cameron mirrored him. "Uncle Bill – it was us. I think we forgot to turn the fence on. I'm a stupid... I'm stupid. I'm sorry."

Cameron cleared his throat. "I'm sorry, too. I should have known better."

Bill waved a hand. "Doesn't matter," he cut off their apologies. It wasn't unkind, but he wasn't mincing words, either. "Shit happens. Right now, we just gotta work fast so we don't lose too many swarms. I was planning to unwrap the last big yard today so this is a setback, but we've gotta save these ones."

"We're here as long as you need us," Noah promised with a glance at Cameron.

Cameron nodded instantly.

For the first time, Bill relaxed a little. "Thanks, boys. All right, get searching for queens while I try to piece together that one."

They couldn't spot queens in the other two hives. Noah stacked up boxes and put plastic mesh between them to keep them separate in case they'd missed them. Noah told him if both had queens they would be kept apart from each other. Otherwise, they could raise a new queen of their own.

Cameron did his best to memorize every nugget of knowledge Noah or Bill passed along. Together, they gathered empty frames, shook other frames into hives, looked for queens, and reassembled hives.

An hour in, the first sharp sting flared in his wrist. "Oh, fuck--!"

Noah was by his side already. "First sting." He grabbed Cam's hand and pulled back the glove long enough to scrape his nail along Cameron's skin.

"Ow," Cameron groaned at the extra scrape to the stung skin.

Noah pulled the glove back down over his bare skin before the bees got in and squeezed his hand apologetically. "Gotta get the stinger out. You're not allergic, are you?"

"Now's a good time to ask," Bill laughed, but he was glancing at them with concern.

"No, no," Cameron assured them both. "I'm fine."

"I've got antihistamines in the car," Noah added. "You can take one now, if you want."

Cameron squeezed Noah's arm. "It's okay," he assured him. "I've had a lot worse. What's next?"

"We're just about there. You two want to bring the damaged stuff back to the property while I put the fence on?" Bill asked, and Cameron nodded. He squatted to pick up a few boxes from the stack, balancing the weight against himself. Noah grabbed the last two boxes and led him out of the field.

A twinge of guilt shuddered through Cam as they passed the fence control box. They walked across the ditch to the road, then around to a shed on the apiary property to drop everything off.

Once they'd placed their burdens in the shed and closed it up, Noah got Cameron to spin around and brushed bees off him. Cameron brushed two off Noah before nodding. "You're safe, too."

They unzipped their hoods and gasped fresh air, the light bright and the air open around them now.

"We made it," Noah smiled, walking back up the driveway to the boxes of gear. He paused and caught Cameron's hand. Their gloves sticky with wax and sap and honey, the gloves audibly cracked as he peeled his hand away, and they shared a laugh.

"Yeah," Cameron murmured. His wrist still stung from his single sting, and Noah had gotten two as well. Bill's five had happened before they'd gotten there.

Noah pulled off his gloves and tossed them into the gear boxes. Once Cameron followed suit, Noah leaned in for a strong hug. "It was half my fault, too," he murmured as a sort of reminder, then pulled back to unzip his suit and work his way out of it.

Cameron pulled off his glove, relieved to see his wrist wasn't too swollen. His fear was that Bill wouldn't see it that way, but part of him wanted to take full responsibility, too. He'd been deliberately distracting Noah a little in the yard... And vice versa. Six of one, half a dozen of the other.

Bill gave a tired nod of acknowledgment as he approached and they all fought their way out of the white protective suits. "Cameron, your job starts tomorrow and we'll call it square. I should have checked the fence. I usually check the hives weekly or more, too, but I was too focused on carpentry and unwrapping hives. It was my own damn fault."

Cameron shook his head slightly. "Still, it didn't have to happen."

"It didn't, but we all learn." Bill bundled his suit into a box before extinguishing the smokers with water. "It could have been anything else, too. Ten days is too long this time of year. They could've had disease, swarms, too little forage... I was sloppy. Kinda like driving. When you've been driving for years, you don't always use your turn signal. Teaching a kid – I taught Noah here – reminds you of all that."

Noah made a face. "I hate it when people don't signal," he muttered, and Cameron and Bill shared a chuckle.

"I'm sorry for my part in it, regardless," Cameron told Bill, approaching him to shake hands. Bill's grip was firm and his smile sincere. "And I'm glad you're still willing to offer me the job."

"Course I am. It was all of our faults," Bill told him and Noah, glancing between them. "I hope this doesn't put you off the job, though. Most days aren't like this."

"Not at all," Cameron promised. "Now that I've had the crash course, I'm looking forward to the easier bits."

Noah laughed. "Yeah, but one sting? You'll get a lot more than that."

"Just flick 'em out, like he did for you," Bill added, sitting on a closed bin to change shoes. Cam leaned against the car to do the same, returning the gumboots to the bin in favor of his regular sneakers. "It'll be good to have an extra pair of hands... and an extra brain to catch my mistakes."

"I'll do my best," Cameron promised, hoping that didn't sound too cheesy.

"Off you go home, then. Get some rest. You'll need it."

Cameron made himself focus on driving so he didn't make any errors in judgment from sluggishness. His hand hurt a little whenever he had to turn the wheel, but he pushed past that, too.

"Back to your place to change and treat those stings? Here, open wide."

Cameron pulled up at a stop sign and opened his lips to let Noah pop the pill into his mouth, then took a gulp of water from his car water bottle. "Thanks. Yeah, we'll stop by Jackson's first. Assuming you don't just wanna be dropped off at home."

"Not at all," Noah smiled. His gaze was half-lidded with exhaustion, but he was pleased.

Despite all they'd just seen and done, the silence was more contented than tense this time.

CHAPTER

Thirty

NOAH

"Sorry for the mess," Cameron apologized before they even climbed out of the car, and Noah smiled. He seemed self-conscious about bringing Noah here, but Noah knew they were moving. He couldn't judge them on their pre-move chaos.

When they entered the cute little house, though, Noah didn't see much to apologize for. Just boxes in neat stacks, and Jackson in a t-shirt with the sleeves pushed over his shoulders.

"Oh, hey, Cam," Jackson told Cam, his eyes on Noah. "Hi, Noah."

"Hey. Jackson, Noah – Noah, Jackson. I gather you know each other anyway."

Jackson laughed and nodded. "Through the art show, yeah. So you two...?"

Noah nodded.

"We're dating," Cameron confirmed.

"Wow, congrats." Jackson glanced at Cameron, then narrowed his eyes. "You're swollen. Did something happen?"

Then he noticed Noah raising a foot to pull down his sock from his ankle and inspect it. "So are you."

"The bees had an emergency. I went in to help," Cameron told Jackson. "Noah, do you mind if I change and grab some more antihistamines?"

"No, go ahead," Noah assured him.

"Sit down. Can I get you anything?" Jackson offered, dusting his hands off after taping a box shut.

Noah nodded. "Water would be amazing, thanks. Long day out there."

"Yeah? How about the art show – that coming along all right?"

Thank God we've got that in common already, Noah thought. He watched Cameron disappear upstairs while Jackson went to grab him a glass of water. "Yeah, really well. I think Jo's art will fix everything. They accepted the proposal and we've got the full space."

"Oh, awesome." Jackson came back with three glasses of water in his hands. He set two down by the couch, then leaned back in the armchair nearby with the third for himself. "So you're dating my little brother? He never said."

"He didn't?" Noah laughed under his breath.

"Nah, but he's always been quiet," Jackson grinned. "He hates being teased. But I'm glad for you both. He could use someone smart like you around to keep his head on straight."

Noah laughed again, his brief worry dissipating. "Ouch. Can't blame him."

"Nah, he's plenty smart on his own," Jackson chuckled. "He was up for team captain before, on his team."

"Yeah?" Noah wasn't sure what team Jackson meant, but he smiled regardless. "Where was that?"

"In Toronto. That's why I had to get sketches of him here, to finish my piece off."

Noah blinked a few times. "Sorry, I don't..."

Jackson's eyebrows raised. "The Toronto minor leagues. The hockey team he quit."

Oh. "...As in, pro hockey."

Jackson grimaced, worry clouding his expression as he glanced up to the stairs and then back to Noah. "So he didn't tell you he was a pro hockey player."

Noah fidgeted with his water glass. This was awkward. "Yeah, no." It was his turn to learn something new about the man. *A pro. Oh my god, and I invited him to play on our little team. He must think we all suck.*

"Don't take it too hard. He's going through a bit of a... rough transition, I think." Jackson cleared his throat. "So, how were the bees?"

The distraction worked: Noah explained that he and Cam hadn't turned on the bee yard fence and a bear had struck. Jackson sympathized as Noah described the cleanup.

When Cameron came back downstairs, he gulped down some water and then nodded. "Ready to go to yours?" he asked Noah. "Be back later," he added with a glance to Jackson.

"No rush," Jackson assured him. "I'm about at the limit of what I can pack up anyway. Enjoy your evening."

"You, too," Noah bade, standing up again while Cameron led him back to the door.

"See you around," Jackson answered.

Despite how well they'd gotten on, the surprising news left Noah glad he had the chance to talk privately with Cameron. But how was he gonna bring this up?

"Your brother's very different. He told me before he doesn't play hockey at all... and you said you can't do the forging stuff he does." It was a clumsy segue, but it was all he could think of.

"Different strokes," Cameron shrugged. "Why, you were recruiting?"

"Yeah. We can always use more good players on the team. You're good."

Cam tensed up a little and Noah wondered if he'd get the truth, but then he relaxed. Suddenly, the playoffs comment earlier made more sense – and lots of things did. "Thanks. But I've been thinking the stress might not be good. I can't push myself much, and... beekeeping might be more stressful than I was thinking."

"Of course. You can quit anytime," Noah reassured Cam, reaching out to squeeze his arm.

Cameron flinched and nodded. "I'll think about it." Cam didn't make eye contact for the rest of the short drive to Noah's place, and Noah didn't push him.

Noah just glanced out his window, watching familiar streets pass. His new boyfriend was a little more closed-off than he'd anticipated.

Why doesn't he want me to know such a big part of him?

"Pull out the staple, and then we can cut away the rest of the foam."

Cameron held the pliers tightly through his thick glove. He wiggled the metal left and right. Once it popped out of the side of the super, the foam draped around the box came free.

"That's it. Now just do that a billion more times," Bill told him with a laugh.

Cameron echoed his quiet laugh and nodded, dropping the staple into a small bucket. The hives were wrapped in pairs with thick black foam and black plastic wrap. Some were two or three boxes high. He was warier of those ones, since they sounded louder.

The day was warm, a perfect first day out in the fields with the bees.

Compared to yesterday's experience, they were quite calm. There were only one or two bees flying at him when he came too close to their entrances. These ones didn't buzz angrily past his ear every few seconds.

"This is pretty light work, but there's just a lot of it."

"Yeah, of course. I don't mind at all," Cameron assured Bill. "I won't have a lot to do in town until I get the house anyway."

"When's that?"

"Two weeks."

Bill nodded as he bundled foam into a pile and plastic into another. "What part of town are you living in? Got a backyard?"

"Downtown, about ten minutes' walk away from Noah's. We will have one, yeah."

"Any interest in a hive in your yard?" Bill said, grinning.

"Er... I might have to think about that."

Bill laughed. "It's legal and it's pretty easy. I'm always looking for spots to pawn off hives. If you put it facing a hedge and keep a water buckets nearby, they aren't nuisances."

Cameron didn't mind that idea, but he had to talk to Thomas and Jackson.

"I'll talk to my brothers about it first. We're buying houses together – three in a row." Cameron bundled his first set of wrappings into a pile.

"Oh, that's unusual." Bill brushed a bee off his hood and leaned in to look at his hives, then moved to the next pallet.

"Yeah, an investor who had them all wanted to sell them together, so we took it. It was a pretty good deal. Cheaper as a package than they each would've been on their own."

"And you didn't fight over houses?"

"Not like fighting over bedrooms, nah," Cameron grinned. "Each of us was drawn to a house. Theirs are more traditional and mine is a little weirder. Fitting."

Bill chuckled. "Come here and see this hive."

Cameron set down his pliers and approached, crouching next to Bill.

Bill pointed to the carpet of bees that blanketed the box around the entrance. "They're bearding."

"Is that good?"

"Yeah. They're heading out to forage. First good, clear day, and they have more entrance access now. You can lean in closer and take a good look. See the ones watching you?"

It was hard to miss them. They watched Cameron and reared up on their hind legs, their front legs waving in his direction. "Er, yeah. Definitely."

"They're guard bees. Each bee has a life cycle where she goes through a bunch of jobs according to her age. They start off cleaning out their own cell and so on. The last stage is foraging."

Cameron smiled as he watched the bee waving her front legs at him. "So that's a warning?"

"Yeah. Those guards look out for animals--"

Cameron winced and said nothing.

"--or other bees, invaders from other hives."

"They break in?"

"They'll try," Bill sighed. "So that's something else to watch out for – battles happening at the entrances. We'll see after we finish unwrapping whether they're in danger. Then we'll crack open a few hives and check them."

Cameron nodded, rising to his feet to resume ripping off the outer winter coverings of the hives. It was early days, but there was something satisfying about this job.

A quarter of the hives were dead. Cameron's heart fell, and even Bill was solemn. He better understood Noah's emotions yesterday – grief as well as guilt. The bees were somehow... vulnerable, despite how tough everyone seemed to think they were.

It made him want to protect them.

Much better were the ones where Bill cracked the top open and bees came up to peek up at them, raising their front legs in warning.

Cameron leaned in, smiling at a row of bees peeking up at him. "Hello," he greeted. "I'm new around here. Be nice to me." He didn't see Bill's smile, but he felt his approving glance.

"It's been a while since I've worked with anyone who cared about them as more than just money," Bill told him.

"Why didn't Noah stay around?"

"Oh, he was never interested," Bill told him. "In a job, anyway. He likes it as a hobby and he's a good man – he helps without complaint when I need it. But I can tell it isn't his passion."

"Art is."

"Art is," Bill echoed.

They smiled over their shared understanding of Bill's nephew, Cam's boyfriend.

Then, Bill settled the lid back on the hive and they rose to inspect the next one together.

The afternoon was long, the evening light lingering until late this time of year. Cam had just changed out of his bee suit and was climbing into his car.

His phone rang and he frowned, keeping his car running but not pulling away yet. "Yeah?" he answered.

"Cameron?"

"Yeah, that's me." Cameron raised his hand to wave to Bill as he pulled away past him in the opposite direction.

"This is Jonathon Field. I'd like to have a chat with you about the New Brunswick minor league team that's forming."

Cameron dragged a hand down his face. He hadn't gotten stings, but it was still rough physical work. He was hungry and he wasn't in the mood for fucking journalists. "I'm leaving hockey. I've left."

"Where are you going to live, then? I heard you're living in New Brunswick, and there's rumors that you can play at home now."

Cameron gave a huff of irritation. "Coach Walker gave a statement last week, didn't he? Saying I left hockey. That still applies."

"A lot of people wonder about that. I mean, it's terrible about your medical condition, but a lot of teams were vying for you before that happened. It's not unthinkable that one could privately fund treatment and training. They could make you the surprise star of the new team. Then draft you for the major leagues after the first season..."

"I'm out. Do you have an actual question?" Cameron snapped, more venomously than he'd meant.

"Are you going to quit your passion so easily? A lot of people think--"

"You know what? Fuck off." Cameron hung up and shoved his phone into the cup holder, then pulled away from the curb.

He wasn't usually one to swear at them, but there was nothing they could do to him anymore. Coach Walker said the story had already broken in the sports section of the papers. Cameron hadn't read them, and he didn't intend to.

"I'm gonna quit my passion whenever I fuckin' want, thanks," he muttered under his breath. He rumbled along the back country road, home and supper the only things on his mind.

CHAPTER

Thirty~Two

CAMERON

SATURDAY AFTERNOON WAS CLOUDY, BUT AT LEAST IT STAYED DRY and the hockey court was clear. Cameron appreciated not being soaked during practice. Even in field drills, he'd never learned to embrace the cooling rain.

"Cam, off for a bit," Kevin called out, gesturing for Justin to take his place instead. "Justin."

Cam frowned as he trotted off the court. More guys were here now – almost enough for proper lines – and Kevin had been swapping him back and forth all game. At first, Cameron thought Kevin wanted him to play hard or else get off the court. Now, as he crouched near the fence with the other two guys who were off, he realized that Noah was probably behind this.

Thursday, Friday, and even this morning had been filled with beekeeping. Cameron enjoyed working hard, but he hadn't seen Noah much since their talk about his heart condition. Noah might be worried for him.

He checked his watch. Only ten minutes left in the game.

When Kevin gestured for him to come back on the court

and replace an exhausted Lonnie five minutes later, Cameron was sharp and focused.

This was his chance to prove himself.

He ducked into the fray without hesitation. Straight away, he snaked his stick around the blade of a defense player and flicked the ball away to Kevin.

Kevin took the pass and dodged Noah while Cam spun around George and avoided his fierce stick work. When Kevin passed back to Cam, Cam was already waiting at a forty-degree angle to the net. Matt, the goalie, *always* left a gap there.

The ball barely grazed his blade before he flicked it into the corner of the net. Blue, who'd been reffing since he was sixteen, called the goal.

Easy as pie.

The second goal took a few minutes longer: he had to fight harder against George. The guy had a way of always being right where Cam needed to be. Still, Cam barely broke a sweat as he and Kevin drove through the defense line to score again.

Cam got the sense time was ticking down, so he kept his body and stick in the way of the best angle for Noah to pass up the court. Blue yelled, "Game over."

"Whoa. You two," Noah breathed out, glancing back and forth between Kevin and Cameron. The guys came up behind them to slap their backs and bump their chests.

"Great work--"

"Holy shit, you two were on fire--"

"Well done--"

Even Matt came up to fist-bump them both, especially Cameron. "Nice, man."

Cameron indulged himself for a moment in a smile, even if he knew it had hardly been a fair fight. With Kevin and him on the same team, they hadn't even stood a chance: 6-2.

"I'll have to put you on the other team from now on," Kevin teased Cam, new respect in his eyes. He looked almost suspicious. "You been practicing?"

Cameron shook his head. "Just stretching my legs."

"Yeah, yeah, showoff," Justin laughed from nearby, and even Noah chuckled.

Everyone piled off the court, dropping off sticks or carrying their gear to the car and bantering.

Noah came up next to Cameron and squeezed his arm. "You doing all right?"

"I'm not gonna pass out," Cameron told Noah. "I wanted to show you – my health's fine. Between bee yard work and field hockey, I can manage it. I can't, like, run marathons anymore... but I can do *this*. I'm sure of it."

He hadn't even had a dizzy spell, though the court wasn't large enough and the competition wasn't skilled enough to keep an "elevated heart rate" and put him in danger.

God, he was hating that phrase.

"I just... don't want to get the guys' hopes up," Cameron murmured, his voice lower as he slid both his and Noah's sticks into his backseat. He perched on the bumper for a moment and Noah stood in front of him.

"Why?"

Cameron's eye was drawn by a guy in a car just on the other side of the lot – sitting in the driver's seat, scribbling. "Hey, that one of your artists?"

Noah got a funny expression on his face. "No. Kevin, uh, just pulled me aside during the break to tell me he went up to the guy and make sure he wasn't some perv."

"Oh, God. Is he?"

"No, he's... he got a call the other day asking about our best players. And this guy asked if someone had been in touch yet to ask about players. We're thinking scouts."

Cameron's brows shot up. "Why didn't you tell me?" Noah gave him a pointed look: they'd been playing hockey, not sitting around gossiping. "Sorry."

Noah shrugged it off. "But yeah. There's some rumor of another team forming or whatever."

Cameron rubbed his chin and leaned down to get a proper sight of the guy. He didn't recognize him, but the interior of the car was dark on this gloomy day. The car was dark blue too, a station wagon of some kind.

He couldn't shake the suspicion that something wasn't as it seemed. Was this a reporter? "Well, I'm not gonna get scouted, don't worry," he snorted lightly, but Noah didn't seem as amused as he did.

"Right," Noah nodded.

If he finds out I quit the team, though... I don't want him thinking I'm some loser who runs away when the going gets tough. When the cup's on the line. Cameron licked his lips. *Which I am.*

It had been too long since he'd felt Noah's bare skin under his. Cameron let out a breath, trying to forget about everything. "Wanna go back to your place?"

Noah let out a breath, like he'd been waiting to be asked. "Sure. I'll just tell the guys I'm gone."

Cameron raised a hand to wave to the guys still milling around and climbed into the driver's seat. When he glanced to the left again for one more look, the dark blue station wagon was gone.

They barely made it in through Noah's front door, kissing all the way up the stairs. Both Cameron and Noah tumbled into bed together, limbs tangled and smiles on their lips.

Cameron rolled on top of Noah and kissed him hard, grinding against him as Noah grabbed his ass to pull him in closer. They both moaned through the kiss, and then Cameron pulled away to grab lubricant and a condom.

Noah tossed his head, his eyes wild as he stripped and then yanked Cameron's clothing off.

When they were naked together, Noah wrapped his hand around both of their cocks to stroke a few times. Cameron rolled his head back, thrusting lazily against the firm, stiff flesh. Noah squeezed his hand around the heads and Cameron groaned his appreciation.

"I want us to get tested soon," Noah murmured, pressing a kiss to Cameron's neck.

"So we can do it bareback?"

Noah nodded, pulling back to look at Cam. "That cool?"

Cameron didn't mind condoms as much as some guys, but having one less step before sex? That made him shiver with pleasure. "Yeah. Let me know when."

"A'ight," Noah murmured, his lips busy with Cameron's earlobe. His tongue and lips were doing things that made Cameron's thighs clench and quiver.

Cameron pulled back from Noah's hold on his cock and knelt between his legs, pouring lube over his fingers and pushing them in. He wanted to make Noah squirm with need. His own need for penetration was almost unbearable.

So gorgeous.

Noah's back arched, his stomach pushing into the air and chest heaving. His toes curled into the bed and fingers clenched around his own thighs as he pulled them apart...

In certain small moments, Cameron fell for Noah all over again.

He shook his head to clear it and slid his fingers out.

"Nnh," Noah moaned his complaint. "You're fuckin' good at that."

Cameron grinned. "You wanna come just from fingering? When you've got a cock right here?"

"Good point," Noah whispered, trying to catch his breath. He flattened against the bed again. "I just want it on record."

"Noted."

When he pushed the condom-covered tip into the warm tightness, Noah's spine arched again. Cameron slid one hand into the small of his back to support him, leaning over him to press their lips together. Inch by inch, he slid into Noah.

"I'm good," Noah whispered when Cameron's balls brushed Noah's warm skin. "Cam... Fuck me."

Cameron gripped Noah's shoulder hard and slid his other hand down to Noah's hip to hold him in place for the familiar rhythm of fast, desperate, hot sex. If Noah wanted him hard and deep, that was exactly what he'd give him.

Noah rolled his head into the pillow and groaned. He grabbed Cameron's ass to force him all the way in with each thrust.

Demanding little bastard today, Cameron thought with a grin. He leaned in to kiss around Noah's lips. He propped himself on his elbow to let his lips trail down Noah's neck and collarbone, then back up to his ear. Noah quivered as he sucked around his neck and shoulder.

With each pounding thrust of his hips, he squeezed into Noah and past his prostate. Noah trembled and squirmed – slightly, at first, then harder. Their bodies rubbed together, bare skin burning skin as Noah moaned.

"C-Cam--" Noah whispered, his voice hoarse.

Cameron pulled back enough to murmur, "Yeah?"

"You wanna jerk me off?"

I'd love to. Cameron grinned as he was entrusted with all of Noah's pleasure. He braced himself on his forearm and reached between their bodies to curl his fingers around the sensitive, stiff cock. The velvety weight in his hand twitched when he grabbed it, so he kept his first few strokes light before firming his grip.

Noah barely needed that adjustment time. "Yes...!" he groaned, clenching subconsciously around Cameron's cock. He shivered in a series of squeezes that milked Cameron's cock. Cameron barely hung on. His muscles burned for release, his head spinning and heart pounding.

Extended periods of elevated heart rates, my ass.

They rutted together and moaned each other's names with sexual desperation into the quiet air.

Seconds later, Noah's cock pulsed in Cameron's hand. He squirted his load across his own stomach, arching off the bed and pushing his hips into Cameron's cock. Noah fucked himself as deep as he could on Cameron.

Cameron kept stroking and pounding Noah for a few seconds before letting go of Noah's cock. He grabbed Noah's hip to push into him one or two last times. Then, blackness hit and he couldn't hold out a second longer: he came in a burst of heat. All that registered was utter focus on Noah's pleasure-twisted face and sweating, slender, gorgeous body.

Heat poured from deep within and pooled in his stomach, his muscles quivering and clenching. Noah pulled him off-balance and down against him to kiss him hard, and Cameron moaned against Noah's lips. He was so oversensitive, but Noah sucked on his lower lip and ran his nails down his bare back and he loved it.

"Holy fuck," Cameron whispered when he could pant for breath and his cock softened. He pulled out of Noah but Noah wouldn't let him get away until he'd kissed him thoroughly.

Cameron finally rolled onto his side and then his back to catch his breath. Noah stayed on his back next to him rather than following to cuddle into his side.

They were silent for a minute or two, Cameron's hand lightly tangled with Noah's as his body cooled off. When he rolled his head over to watch Noah, his gaze flickered along Noah's parted lips and half-closed eyes, noting the way he stared at the ceiling.

Something odd and distant was in his expression but Cam didn't think it was the moment to discuss it. It just... looked familiar in a way he didn't want to think about. But Noah was lying here with him, holding hands and sometimes squeezing Cameron's fingers... Nathan had only wanted to fuck fast and hard in a vicious cycle of whatever the fuck they'd had between them.

This was different in every way.

"I wanna do *that* again," Noah murmured at last.

Cameron chuckled. *As long as that's not all we do.* His stomach twisted with brief anxiety before he let it go. Cameron raised Noah's hand to his lips to brush his lips across his fingers.

Noah slid his hand onto Cameron's chest and closed his eyes. Cameron watched Noah's expression clear up as he grew sluggish and contented. *I want to make love to him.*

Thirty-Three

NOAH

"ALL WEEK, I'VE BEEN WAITING FOR THIS," NOAH SIGHED. HE tapped his foot as he leaned against the side door of the arena, raising a hand to squint across the parking lot. "And now look."

Jason was supposed to be here to give him the key to the arena lobby, open the Zamboni door to bring the steel sculpture in, and supervise its installation. Everything else could be carried by hand the day before the show.

Jason was infamously bad at keeping appointments. Now Jackson was going to be here any minute with his sculpture and equipment for moving it and no way to get it inside.

At the same time, Noah was fielding calls from artists who were interested in the August charity show. He'd stupidly put the word out on a local mailing list that morning before leaving the house. His phone rang again.

"Hi, Noah. It's Chase."

Chase...? Right: the tattoo artist who'd painted a series of ten hockey pucks and stuck them together with needles into a mural. God, Noah loved that piece. "Yeah, hi. What's up?"

"I forgot – is the opening next Saturday or Sunday?"

"The reception is Saturday evening. We're doing art installation and setup on Friday. Why?"

"Okay, phew. That works. Just making sure," Chase answered. "I've got appointments on Sunday and I about had a heart attack there."

Noah winced and swallowed. "Yeah. No problem. See you Friday, right?"

"Friday." Chase promised and hung up.

Jason's pickup truck crunched into the gravel side lot, then over to the paved section. Noah raised a hand to wave Jason over.

As he'd expected, Jason jumped out of the truck and practically sprinted over to him. "Sorry I'm late. Everything all right?"

"Good. Jackson's supposed to be here in – oh, I think that's him." Noah waved over to the pickup truck that was turning into the main lot, gesturing it over. The truck came around the side of the building toward them.

"Just in time, then," Jason declared and strode for the side door to unlock it. He stepped in to roll up the bay door.

Noah let himself glare at the door for a moment before he forced a pleasant expression again. He didn't mind Jason, but untimeliness was one of his pet peeves. It was disrespectful of both his time and Jackson's.

"There we are," Jason nodded as he waved Jackson's truck into the arena.

"Hey," Jackson greeted from his rolled-down window. He backed up past Noah, his eyes flickering between the mirrors.

"Hi. You got what you need?" The load was covered by a large tarp and a lot of bungee cords, so it was hard to tell.

"Yep." Jackson stopped once the back end of the pickup was

inside, then yanked the parking brake on and climbed out. He clapped Noah's shoulder. "Excited?"

"Very!" Noah grinned. "You didn't even let me see it past the halfway point."

"Yeah. It's – I'm happy with it." Jackson strode around to the back of the pickup truck, pulling down the gate. "Got the loader?"

"It's through this way," Jason told Jackson. They strode off for it while Noah waited by the pickup truck. He heard them talking about how their days were going, traffic, and football season, so he let them be.

A few minutes later, the small vehicle returned with a helmet-clad Jackson at the wheel. Jason walked behind it. "Either of you trained at this?"

Noah and Jason both shook their heads.

"No problem." Jackson opened the door and clambered down to the ground, then up into the bed of the pickup. "Just keep back, then."

Noah shifted anxiously as Jackson unfastened the bungee cords and straps, coiling everything up and tossing it all to the ground out of the way. Then, the tarp came off.

The steel sculpture glistened from inside its wood crate, and Noah rose onto his tiptoe to try to see.

"Not until it's ready," Jackson scolded him with a grin and shouldered him out of the way.

Noah laughed. "Fine," he lamented. "I'll go wait in the lobby." He strode away from the truck down the back hallway of the arena and the front lobby. It took him a minute to find door wedges to keep the doors open.

He'd seen this place a hundred times in his sketches and at least a dozen in person while planning the exhibit. The lighting would all have to be changed out, and extra lighting added in several places. There was only one place for the sculpture: the middle of the lobby. Noah firmly believed a sculpture should never be against a wall, and this was the show centerpiece. Good – the pedestal he'd had delivered last week was already set up.

The loader rumbled its way into the room, bearing the massive crate on its metal prongs.

"Where to?" Jackson asked, and Noah indicated the middle of the room. "Really?"

Noah nodded. "You cool with that?"

"More than cool," Jackson laughed. He pivoted the loader as he entered the room, his eyes narrowed in focus. Once he maneuvered the prongs into position, he set down the crate. "I'll use the hand truck to get it off the pallet. Perfect, the pedestal's the right height."

"It's almost like we coordinated it."

They worked together, Noah directing Jackson to maneuver and twist the sculpture until it faced the right way. Then, slowly, the sculpture was eased into place on the pedestal and set down. Jackson unwrapped the plastic around it once that was done and stood back, folding his arms.

"Now can I look?"

"Turn on the lights first."

Noah laughed and flipped on the overhead light switches. When he turned around, light glimmered off steel and bronze, bringing it to life in a way even he hadn't anticipated.

"See?" Jackson smugly stated. He hauled the pallet back onto the loader before leaning against it and folding his arms. Despite his self-confidence, Noah could tell he was waiting for the final assessment.

Noah paced around it, admiring the smooth, burnished curves. It showed a hockey player caught in mid-stride. One skate was slightly off the ice, the puck delicately balanced on the edge of the stick's blade...

The face was familiar, too.

"Oh my God, you used Cam."

The model's open face mask framed Cam's distinctive chiseled jaw and narrow cheekbones, strong and slightly crooked nose, thin but full lips...

Cameron was breathtaking in bronze and steel. Noah swallowed back his emotion as his chest tightened. Was that what he looked like when he'd played on the ice? This was far more focus than he'd seen even on the hockey court last week. The sculpture's lifelike eyes even subtly narrowed in focus on a distant point.

Noah was spellbound by Jackson's skill. This showed his boyfriend's passion, elegance, and strength all at once.

He just wished he'd been able to see that in person.

So why the hell hadn't Cam wanted Noah to know about that part of him?

Thirty-Four

CAMERON

THE NEXT TIME CAMERON SAW A DARK BLUE STATION WAGON, HE had its number.

He and Bill were working at the corner lot again that sunny Saturday afternoon. They tidied up hives and finished sorting out the mess the bear had left in the bee yard. There was no reason that station wagon ought to be there, except...

"Excuse me. I'll be back in a minute, sorry."

Bill nodded and Cam set down his smoker. He strode down the length of the bee yard, through the trees, and out to the road.

The man behind the wheel was startled to be directly approached, but rolled down the window. "Hello?" He looked a few years older than Cam. He had dark stubble across his jaw, pale pink lips, and eyes that were a soft, enchanting brown. His brows were thin, dark, and low, but he looked like a goddamn model. He could get information anywhere.

Cam had no patience for the act. "Unless you want a lot of bees in your car, tell me why you've been watching me."

The man scanned his expression for a few moments. He

rubbed his face and set aside the notebook Cameron wanted to pry out of his hand. "There's no point in bullshitting you, is there?"

"Nope."

"I'm Alex. I've been asked to set up a meeting between you and a few people who want to meet you."

Cameron took a certain pleasure in seeing a few little bees crawling in through the window. He had the sneaking suspicion he knew what this was about, but he leaned back to give Alex a skeptical look. "When and where?"

"This afternoon, if possible. At the Park hotel downtown. Room 341. Say, two o'clock?"

That was a fancy-ass place for a meeting, and right next to the art gallery. Cam glanced back at the bee yard. They were just about done there, and if he explained the situation to Bill, he was sure he'd be sent home anyway. "Fine. I'll be there. Stop watching me." He strode through the trees again for the yard.

The car pulled away after he walked off,

By the time he made it back to the field, Bill was watching him. "What was that about? Someone want to talk to you?"

"Yeah. I have... my old bosses, sort of, breathing down my neck."

Bill eyed him for a moment before nodding. "If you need to leave at lunchtime..."

"If I can, that'd be great, yeah."

"Should be fine. I just have some painting to do this afternoon. I've seen that car around before, too. Nearly called the cops on it once."

Cameron's eyes narrowed. "I know. He's been watching me for a bit. Says his name is Alex – ring any bells?"

"Sorry, Cam. Lots of "Alex"s around here your age."

Cameron nodded and drew a breath. When he let it go, he cleared his mind of thoughts. "Let's get back to checking hives."

By lunchtime, he had some guesses about who it was and what they wanted. He didn't have any kind words for any of the possibilities.

He changed at Jackson's home and showered, grabbing a bite to eat. Jackson had been out almost day and night for the last few weeks, they saw each other only a few evenings a week now. That was another stressor, but he didn't have time to worry about that.

Cameron arrived at the hotel a couple minutes before the hour and headed up in the elevator.

He knocked firmly on the door of room 341. When it opened, the man who answered seemed unsurprised to see him. The gray-haired older guy was wearing a suit jacket in the kind of style that screamed "team owner".

"Afternoon," Cameron greeted. "I'm Cameron Riley."

"Darren Kolusky. Owner of the--"

"Florida. I know."

Darren raised his eyebrows and nodded. "Well done. Yes. And that's Henry Thibeault, the New Brunswick team manager. Come on inside."

Cameron firmed his jaw as he strode into the small hotel room. Three chairs were pulled cozily together. "Alex isn't here? Who's he to you?"

"Oh, he was just a private eye. We needed someone to see if you were around here."

A muscle in Cameron's jaw twitched. He remained calm and sank into one of the three seats while Darren and Henry followed suit.

"We're here to make you an offer. From what Walker told

us, you've been expecting this for a while. And you're right to expect it – you were inches away from being drafted."

"I know." Cameron watched both men.

Henry cleared his throat. "We're getting a great team together. There's a lot of talent here in the Atlantic provinces. Guys are getting tired of flying out to Toronto, Montreal, even St. John's, and that's just for home games. When you're not on the road, you want to be truly home."

"The spiel's good, but you can save it for the other guys," Cameron told them. "You've been following me around with a frigging private detective."

Darren held up a hand to Henry and nodded. "Here's the thing. All the papers say you suddenly quit, but then you wind up back here. You're keeping your skills sharp in the only quiet local venue you can. Our thought was this: you're hoping to get back into the game soon."

"I'm not playing damn games trying to pretend I wasn't drafted. That's all public knowledge," Cameron snorted. "If I had been, it'd be all over the internet by now."

"Right. But a gentleman's agreement under the table, in effect as soon as your heart's fixed..."

Cameron narrowed his eyes. "It'll take a specialist and probably surgery to fix. Ablation, they said. A wait list."

"Or you can go private, if you have a team willing to pay. We would. I bet Toronto offered."

"They looked. They couldn't find anyone."

"We know someone in Florida who will."

Cameron tightened his jaw. "And after that, there's no guarantee I'll be in fit condition to play."

"Kid," Henry told him, "look at the offer. No strings attached surgery, and if it works, you join us."

"You'll draft me after a season," Cameron told them, boldly

jutting his jaw. "I'm that good, and that's why you're so interested. How can pulling me to Florida get me closer to home?"

Henry shifted and glanced at Darren.

Darren chuckled. "Walker was right: you take no shit. Listen, you're smart. You know we get on well with Toronto. There's a trade or two we're looking at, and if we can give them something they want..."

"You get something – or someone – you want," Cameron nodded. "Like Matty?"

"Among others."

Cameron breathed out. *This isn't how I wanted my new life to go. Being traded, traveling all over the damn continent again...*

"If money and fame isn't enough, we can do a lot. We can set you up with a good-looking new boyfriend. If that's your concern, it's not a problem with us. The team's willing to accept it. Don't quit your passion over it."

How nice of them. Cameron's jaw tightened. Fuck them for trying to replace Noah with some underwear model.

"A guy your age will have a lot of fun off the ice if he's willing to put everything into his game on the ice."

Cameron shook his head. "And I'm not. My family needs me – my new boyfriend, who you *can't* just replace with some Armani model, needs me."

"If you had surgery tomorrow and you woke up fit to play again, can you say you'd walk away?"

That was Henry, his gaze knowing as he watched Cameron.

The bastard already knew the answer. Cameron hated it. He wanted the answer to be *yes*, but... This tactic wouldn't work.

"I'm not signing up."

"We called Gavin." His old agent. Cameron hadn't minded

the guy, but he'd been canny. "He told us you might take a good offer."

"Then he didn't know me. What did Walker say?"

Neither of them said anything.

"That's what I thought." Cameron rose to his feet. "Thanks for meeting me, but that was a colossal waste of time and money. If you want a star heading your team, get your ass to Toronto. There's half a dozen great guys that only need another season under someone like Coach Walker. Make your own stars."

Henry and Darren rose, too. "Is that your decision?"

"Yeah."

"If you change your mind..."

Cameron's vision went wavy around the edges. He interrupted, "I'll talk to the team that didn't hire a fuckin' *detective* to stalk me."

He hated burning bridges, especially with how fucking badly he wanted to be on the ice. Yet he couldn't let them use that as leverage.

He bit back the worst of his vitriol to be calm and polite on his way out. "Thank you for the meeting. Good luck with the team."

"Good luck with your new life," Henry answered, walking him to the door.

Cameron strode down the hall without a backward glance. His hands were curled into tight fists to keep his self-control.

That went about as well as he'd expected, and he *had* to calm down *now*.

It was the last thought he remembered. He stepped out of the elevator into the lobby and smooth marble flew into his face.

When Cameron opened his eyes, the sterile whiteness around him was the second thing to register.

The first was a warm hand in his own, fingers laced with his, and a murmuring voice. "--many months now?"

"About six weeks. It's an urgent referral."

"Good." That was Noah's voice. "Three months or more is unacceptable when he's fainting in public."

Cameron stirred slightly and rolled his head to the side as strength returned again. His heart rate was back to normal. He was dressed in a weird paper gown and he had those fucking sticky patches on his chest. Damn it, he was going to rip off circles of his own chest hair again.

"Hello," Noah greeted him with a little smile. "Fancy meeting you here."

He wasn't panicking or freaking out. Noah looked calmer than Cameron felt. He sat up with confidence as he faced the doctor.

Cameron blinked and nodded. "Hi."

"Hello. I'm Dr. Smith. I was discussing your referral with your, er--"

"My boyfriend, Noah, yeah," Cameron said. He cleared his throat and blinked as he sat up slowly, licking his lips. "And?"

"Yes. And you're being bumped up the waitlist. I expect it'll be about a month, six weeks at the outside. As soon as possible given your condition."

Cameron glanced at Noah, wondering how much of a role he had in that decision. "Oh. Oh, that's great."

"Noah explained some of the difficulties you've been facing, and we looked over your file and your activity level. You're unlikely to reduce your physical activity much. And it's obviously impractical to just *not* stress about anything at all for months on end."

"Yeah."

"Right. A nurse will be by in a few minutes to do some tests. I want to make sure you're clear to go and assess whether we need to keep you any longer."

Cameron nodded and lay back again. "Thanks, Dr. Smith."

The doctor strode out and they were alone. Beeps and babbling of voices in the background filled the air beyond the soft curtains of the emergency room space.

Cam took in Noah sitting in a chair next to his bed, still holding his hand. "How are you?"

"A lot better than you," Noah teased with a gentle smile. "You?"

"I... I didn't tell you everything," Cameron said before he stopped himself.

"So I gather. Want to tell me now?"

"Please," Cameron murmured with a nod. "I'm here because my heart condition benched me, then got me to quit the team completely. I played pro hockey in the minor leagues in Toronto. I was about to be drafted. Then this thing developed, and they couldn't diagnose it. I just... quit." He pressed his tongue against the inside of his cheek, then ran it along his teeth as he looked away. His stomach twisted into a knot of fear when Noah let go of his hand. *I shouldn't have hidden it all.*

Noah's hand pressed against his cheek to turn his face toward him.

Cameron blinked, then shifted onto his side to face Noah.

"I don't blame you," Noah said, his voice quiet but clear. There was no hint of a lisp now. Was this his curator voice? "It's life-changing. The doctor said they don't know if you even *can* play after they fix... whatever's going on. The team can't keep you on under those conditions."

"But they were willing to try. I walked away."

Now Noah's lisp came out as he clicked his tongue against his teeth and rolled his eyes to the ceiling for patience. "You were forced off the ice. I'm glad you didn't kill yourself out of some hyper-macho bullshit weakness complex."

Cameron's jaw dropped. After a second of staring at Noah, all he could do was laugh. "Don't hold back."

"I'm serious," Noah insisted. "If you'd died on the ice, I would never have met you. So you better not get yourself fuckin' killed over it. And next time, tell me about things that are important to you. Don't assume I'll apply the same bullshit macho standards to you that you apply to yourself."

Ouch. Cameron laughed again and closed his eyes as he rolled his head back to stare up at the ceiling. "Okay."

"Good," Noah chirped in that adorable upbeat voice that always made Cameron smile.

Cameron's fingers tingled: Noah's hand slid into his own again. This time, Cameron squeezed hard, and Noah squeezed back.

CHAPTER
Thirty-Five
NOAH

"I don't think I can play against Moncton."

Noah wasn't even a little surprised to hear Cam say that. It had taken him three days to work up the courage. Since being sent home from the hospital that same afternoon on Saturday, Cameron had had a lot on his mind. Even going to get tested and getting clean results together hadn't broken his funk.

Last night, Cameron had skipped their usual Tuesday evening hockey practice, and he was no doubt guilty about that.

All Noah could do was give him time to get through it.

"No problem," Noah said. They leaned into one another on Noah's living room couch. "Neither can I."

"What?"

Noah bit back a smile at Cameron's shock. "Not every guy can or wants to to play in them, you know." The thought clearly hadn't even occurred to Cam. "That charity show I'm doing in August is on the same day – same time, even."

"Oh. I never realized…"

Noah chuckled and ruffled Cameron's short hair. "I know. You've been wrapped up in your own issue, and that's understandable. It's good, even. Better than trying to ignore it."

Cameron groaned. "I wasn't ignoring it..."

"You were just putting yourself into stressful situations to prove you could beat it, right?" Noah teased, and Cameron's blush made him laugh.

"Stop being my fuckin' psychologist. I've had a sport one before. I hated it."

Noah laughed. "Okay. But you can just agree to help me out with the charity event – or be my plus-one. I'll tell the team I can't do it and... you know, maybe step back from organizing a little. All I wanted to do was play."

"Mm," Cameron nodded. "But you have to organize everything around you, don't you? You'll get physical pains if you don't."

It was Noah's turn to be taken aback, then laugh. "True. I'll talk about it with Kevin."

They sat in silence for a few more moments, watching a yogurt commercial. By unspoken agreement, they both leaned in at the same moment to press a kiss to each other's lips.

After a minute of gentle kisses, Noah's body pressed into Cameron's muscular side, Noah pulled back. "Still coming to the hockey exhibition Saturday?"

"Wouldn't miss it for the world."

Noah patted Cameron's chest lightly. "Good. Hey, I know the doctor said to keep vigorous sexual exertion to a couple times a week--"

"Now that was just bullshit," Cameron grumbled.

"--but what if I did the exertion for you?" Noah teased, sidling over Cameron's lap to straddle it. He leaned in to press a kiss to Cameron's lips, then his collarbone and neck and chest...

His knees hit the floor and his lips landed on the bulge in Cameron's jeans. Cameron already pushed up into Noah with soft, needy moans.

Noah knew the feeling: it had been a long week since their last hot and heavy moments together. They'd made out plenty, but they'd been too focused on everything else for sex. Cameron had been running around taking care of shit whenever Noah couldn't get him to sit still. The house was due to close tomorrow.

God, he loved sucking Cameron off.

Noah pulled Cameron's jeans down enough to slide Cam's thick cock out into the open air. He licked his lips pointedly and Cameron choked off a quiet sound in his throat.

No holding back. He leaned down to lick the thick length from base to tip and back down again. He enjoying the throbs of pleasure as it stiffened the rest of the way in his hand. Then, he closed his lips around the tip and sucked in the musk of Cameron's manhood as he bobbed his head down.

The thick, warm length in his mouth throbbed with need as Cameron moaned again and pushed his hips up.

Cameron's cock slid down to the back of his throat. Noah sucked and darted his tongue along the underside of Cam's cock. He pulled his head back up to the tip and back down again, setting into a quick rhythm.

Noah loved it all: Cameron clenched and shivered. His thighs twitched and feet curled and hands dug into Noah's shoulders and hair...

Most of all, he loved the sounds. Cameron grunted and moaned with overwhelmed pleasure. His harsh breaths and the wet lapping of Noah's tongue against the shaft were a background track.

Cameron's balls drew tight in Noah's hand. His shaft swelled and Noah kept his head down to swallow the quick, strong jets that hit the back of his throat. He rubbed Cameron's thigh, gazing up at those intense eyes half-closed in ecstasy.

"Jesus, Noah," Cameron whispered, his voice hoarse. His hips settled back down and Noah pulled his lips up and off his cock. "Christ, you're good. And fast. And... good."

Watching all that had made Noah's dick so hard it hurt, but he was ready to take care of that himself.

Turned out he didn't have to.

Cameron pulled him up onto the couch until he lay flat on his back and crawled over him to kiss at his groin.

"Oh, fuck, Cam," Noah breathed out. He grabbed Cam's shoulders and squeezed hard. "You're hot when you're coming."

"Yeah?" Cameron murmured. He unzipped Noah's tight jeans, wiggling the fabric down. Noah's hard cock popped free and bobbed stiffly up in the air.

Then, Cameron attacked it, grabbing and stroking the length sensually. He leaned down to kiss the side of it and rub it against his bristly cheek, a sting that Noah *adored*.

"Christ!" Noah whimpered. His stomach tensed with hot, tight need. Then Cam's hot, wet mouth wrapped around the sensitive head of his cock. That tongue tapped against that certain sensitive spot... once, twice, three times, flickering back and forth across it.

Noah's hips bucked as his head pressed hard into the arm of the couch. "Fuck – oh, fuck, yes..."

Cameron moaned, the sound sending a little vibration of pleasure through Noah's whole body. Noah's fingertips buzzed with pleasure. His cheeks burned and he pushed up into Cameron's mouth.

His cock head rubbed against Cameron's palate and Cameron didn't protest for a moment. Cam sucked his cheeks and lips in tightly and bobbed his head down until he took all of Noah in.

Having his cock enveloped by Cameron's skilled mouth was one thing. Watching the pink length slide between Cameron's even pinker lips... And the way Cameron's looked up and down his shaft hungrily...

Noah throbbed and pushed up again, encouraging Cameron to get to work.

Cameron's lips sucked up and down the shaft. He rubbed the base now and then whenever he pulled his head up to focus on the sensitive head.

"Christ, I'm only gonna – Cam, fuck, watch out..."

Noah could hardly put words together. Cam's mouth on his cock was his whole world. He slammed his hips forward as his cock pulsed and throbbed and jetted out his sticky passion straight to the back of Cam's mouth.

He still tasted Cam, and Cam was eagerly swallowing him. The tip of Cam's tongue teased his slit until he *ached* with how hard his body throbbed.

"Cam, I – fuck, Cameron... you're..." Noah trailed off. Cameron pulled his head off his manhood with a quiet, slick *pop*. "You're perfect."

A half-loopy smile spread over Cameron's face. He scooted up the couch until he braced himself over Noah, then leaned down to kiss Noah.

Noah didn't care that they tasted themselves on each other's lips; he just wanted to share the moment with him. He wrapped his arms around Cameron and kissed him hard.

I can't live without this man. The thought made him catch his breath and kiss harder, until Cameron reached up to run his callused thumb along Noah's jaw like he was touching something precious.

Noah's tension melted, his eyes sliding closed as Cameron silently told him everything would be okay.

CHAPTER
Thirty-Six
CAMERON

WITH JUST THREE KEYS ON IT, THE KEYRING WAS LIGHT, BUT ITS significance lent it weight in his palm. A quick look at Thomas and Jackson told him his brothers felt the same as they approached their houses.

"This is it. Those papers were it."

Cameron elbowed Jackson. "Thanks, Captain Obvious."

Even Thomas chuckled. "No, but... it's so weird. I've never *not* rented."

Cameron and Jackson both looked at their younger brother, then each other. They nodded with an unspoken agreement: *He should be the first one.*

"Come on, you open up your house first."

The moving truck behind them was on a clock, and they didn't have much time to be sentimental. Cameron was forced to stick to lighter boxes or sharing loads. Jackson and Thomas handled the heavier shit. It made him itch with frustration. Every time he wanted to push himself too far, though, Noah's words rang in his head: *hyper-macho bullshit weakness complex.*

Pretty accurate, even if it stung.

So Cameron took it slow as they moved Thomas in first, unloading his truck with the help of moving dollies. A few of Jackson's buddies showed up, followed by Noah and some guys from the hockey team, and Thomas's friends. People were free to come and go, but they'd promised food to anyone who stuck around to the end.

With eight of them, there were almost too many for one moving truck. They had the truck unloaded before noon. Then, they split into two groups to finish moving stuff from the sidewalk inside while the others loaded the truck with Cam's and Jackson's stuff. By the time they sent Cam for pizza, they were almost finished.

When Cam came back with a stack of four pizzas and a flat of pop, he heard them holler his name from the backyard, though he couldn't tell which.

He let himself through the side gate, then burst out laughing. A few boards had been kicked out from the fence between the three houses. "Did someone fall through or was that deliberate?" He ducked into Jackson's yard.

"Nah, that was on purpose."

"If you're sure you wanna be around my bees, then you're welcome to my yard," he winked as he set pizzas out on Jackson's lawn furniture.

"Bees?" Jackson exclaimed. "You want them at home?"

Cameron glanced over at Noah, who was glowing at him. "They've kinda won me over. Besides, they won't sting unless you're a dick to them. You can ask Bill – he's gonna be at the show on Saturday. Are you all going?"

"Duh, I'm going," Jackson snorted.

Cameron slapped the back of Jackson's head as he reached

for a pop. "Well, duh. I didn't mean you, attention hog. Notice Noah didn't answer?" Jackson's buddies cracked up and he grinned at them. "The rest of you?"

"I am," Thomas promised. "I know Mom and Dad are, too."

"We might," Kevin added, raising a slice of pizza. "I heard it's quite a show." He exchanged looks with Noah.

As they settled into eating pizza and drinking pop, Cameron couldn't wipe the stupid grin off his face. These guys were a ragtag bunch, each of them friends with just one of the brothers, but it was a sign of things to come.

It was a new life for Cam to share with his brothers... and maybe someday soon, Noah.

As he glanced at his own house, then Noah, he caught his boyfriend gazing over there, too. He leaned in to murmur, "You should stay the night Saturday. Not 'til I have the place set up."

Noah pouted. "I gotta wait?"

"Yeah. I want things to be set up first," Cameron told him.

"I already saw inside."

"Not set up yet." Cameron reached out with a napkin to dab tomato sauce off Noah's cheek and licked off his own fingers. "Trust me."

"Fine," Noah groaned, but there were others groaning, too.

Cameron looked over at their buddies, then laughed at the faces they were all making. "Hey, if you're jealous, you can go get a love life of your own," he teased them.

Thomas made a face. "I'll get right on that."

Jackson just laughed, then elbowed him. "So where's the beer?"

"Hold on. I put it in your fridge."

Cameron rose to his feet to grab the case of beer and bring

it outside, his heart soaring. *What a weird goddamn month.* But summer was almost here, and it was gonna be a thousand times better.

Thirty~Seven

CAMERON

"Yᴏᴜ ʟᴏᴏᴋ ɢᴏʀɢᴇᴏᴜs."

"You look like you belong on my gorgeous arm." Cameron grinned at Noah as he leaned against his freshly-washed car in the shadow of the arena. "Like a curator who's done incredibly against all odds and people who hate change."

Noah swatted Cameron's thigh and laughed. "Okay. The evening's already started. Come on in." He held out a hand for Cameron to take, then led him around to the front of the building.

Cam had been busy learning how to diagnose varroa mites until forty minutes ago, when he and Bill had realized the time. Bill hadn't arrived yet, but Cam had barely had time to shower, change, and wolf down a peanut butter sandwich. He'd broken a few speed limits on the way to the show.

"Don't look around until I tell you to."

So bossy. Cameron laughed and nodded. "I'll avert my gaze from anything you don't want me looking at. Except your ass. Those trousers--"

"*Cam,*" Noah hissed, but he was laughing. He paused

outside the door before he opened it to take Cameron in one more time as if memorizing his expression.

Cameron smiled and leaned in to peck Noah's lips, then past Noah to open the door. "Lead on, Mr. Clark."

"Keep your eyes to the left." Cameron obeyed and made his way to the wall where new and beautiful artwork hung.

One painting and sketch and mixed media piece at a time, Noah took him around the exhibition, explaining the significance of each piece. Cameron half-listened to his boyfriend – enough to answer a quiz about what he'd just said. Mostly, his attention was caught by the detail in each piece. It didn't make his heart ache as much as he'd thought to see these passionate representations of his sport.

Some pieces made him smile more than others. In particular, he loved the series of watercolors from that local artist Noah had mentioned several times. It showed different hockey teams playing – university teams in the oh-so-familiar university stadium, local kids on the river, even their little club on the field.

He paused for a long time by a series of painted pucks, taking in each miniature scene carefully. They were intimate portraits behind the scenes – a locker room, a janitor picking up a popcorn box in the bleachers, a Zamboni driver climbing aboard... The pucks were joined together by thin, flexible needles, producing a story out of interconnected vignettes.

"You like that one?" Noah asked, finally catching Cameron's attention.

"Yeah. A lot," Cameron admitted. There was another guy standing next to Noah in a short-sleeved black collared shirt and trousers, his arms covered with full-length tattoo sleeves. "Wow, nice tats."

"This is Chase, the artist who did them."

"Wow. Nice," Cam whistled, glancing between Chase and the pucks. "I really like this, man."

Chase glowed with pride at the compliment and reached out to shake hands. "Cam, right? I've heard a lot about you."

"Jesus, I'm not that late, am I? Should I sneak out the side door?" Cam grinned.

Chase laughed. "Nah. Your big brother had a lot to say about you. And Noah..."

"I bet they did," Cameron laughed. "It's all lies." His eye was caught by the short *about the artist* bio. "Wait, you're a tattoo artist?"

"Yep."

"And you paint?" Chase gave him a look and Cameron winced after a moment. "Sorry – I didn't mean to imply you can only do one or the other." Jackson clapped his arm. "Hey," he added.

Chase relaxed again and chuckled. "No, it's fine. A lot of people don't figure I would. But I have to know art to free-hand." He smiled and nodded at Jackson as Jackson approached.

"No, I understand. I've never gotten a tattoo, but now I know who to go to," Cameron nodded. Noah's hand slipped into his own, and he glanced at his boyfriend. "Is this one for sale?"

"To the right person, it might be," Noah winked, exchanging glances with Chase.

"Oh, yeah," Chase agreed. "This isn't one of the pieces they're keeping."

Jackson shook his head. "They ought to. I mean, I want it, but it's good enough to stay here, too..."

Noah cleared his throat. "No, I think they're happy with

their choice. The only thing here left for you to see... is Jackson's piece."

"Wait, they're buying yours? Great work," Cameron grinned at his big brother, reaching out for a manly half-hug and back slap. "Do I get to see it?"

"Turn around," Noah invited and let go of his hand.

When he spun around, Cameron wasn't even sure what he was seeing at first. The bronze and steel sculpture was so fluid and smooth that he knew it was his brother's work. It seemed to have been poured molten into a mold instead of hand-shaped by long hours at the forge.

It was a hockey player skating hard, his back foot up as if he were about to push his foot in and halt in a spray of ice. Cam could tell the puck danced on the edge of his blade, ready to fly into the upper corner of the net...

And it was him.

Cameron's jaw dropped.

"That's the same face you made," Jackson teased Noah in the background. Cameron ignored him and walked closer to the piece.

It was large as life, the stick a glimmering silvery steel while his face was bronze. The jersey was a loose practice jersey, each tiny hole imprinted in the metal. It made him want to tug the hem just to make sure it was solid.

"I was planning on modeling it after you from the start, but then after everything... I especially thought it should be," Jackson murmured, coming up beside Cameron to look up at it. "You like it?"

Cameron barely had words. He nodded and squeezed Jackson in a hard hug instead, the air rushing out of his big brother's lungs.

Jackson squeezed him back with those blacksmiths' arms, a

game he always won. He slapped Cam's back. "Love you, bro'," he muttered into Cam's ear and pulled back before the moment was *too* sappy.

"You, too." Chase was still lingering and watching with a broad smile.

Jackson nodded to Cam and strode off to join Chase and talk about tattoos. He was clearly on a high from Cameron's approval and hiding it as much as a cuddly, over-excitable hothead could. He clapped Chase's back now and pointed out spots on his arm, then Chase's. Was he thinking of getting a tattoo?

Noah grabbed Cameron's attention when he took Cam's hand again. "So, that's the main attraction."

"That's... that's stunning," Cameron told him. "I can't believe you made me wait until the end of your tour to see it! Is Jackson gonna be all right?"

Noah laughed. "I think so. He's been waiting for your reaction for freakin' months now is all. Chase will help cool him off."

Cameron laughed. "That's... That's so cool."

They'd already met most of their friends and family, but there was someone new approaching: an older guy in a suit. He nudged Noah.

"Oh, hi, Frank."

Frank... Oh, right. The asshole on the board of directors who Noah thinks was the one dragging his heels. Cameron smiled lightly, glancing between them. Frank had played for Montreal two decades ago, and he thought it gave him a name in Fredericton. Maybe it did – Frank had come to talk to his junior and senior teams about the life of a pro hockey player.

"Congratulations, Noah. This is a great exhibit."

"Thanks. You like how it turned out?"

"I had my doubts," Frank admitted. Cameron could tell Noah was resisting the urge to punch Cam in the arm and hiss, *Told you so.* It absolutely *had* been him dragging his heels. "But the way it came together... it works. It'll be a great show for the next month, and keeping this around just seemed fitting. It was a unanimous vote on buying it."

"Oh, Jackson's gonna flip," Cam grinned.

"You're his brother, aren't you? Cam Riley? You were spectacular this season. I was sorry to hear the news. It's hardest when we lose young guys, you know."

Cam nodded. "Thanks. I'm alive and well, and I got to play for Toronto, even if only the minor leagues. A lot of people never get that far."

"Good perspective," Frank approved. "Anyway, I've gotta go, but I wanted to congratulate you, Noah." Noah and Cam shook hands with Frank as they saw him off.

Then, Sarah approached. She wore a distinctive dark outfit like Noah's that just screamed 'curator' plus a name badge. "Hey, Noah. That's it for all the local celebrities, then. You should head home."

"What? There's still another half hour, and then cleanup, and the – the empty cups and cheese trays..."

Cameron grinned. Noah couldn't stand leaving others to clean up, either, apparently.

"No, we've got it," Sarah assured Noah with a laugh. "You've put a lot of hours into organizing this. Go and relax now. You've more than earned it. First solo show – great job."

She leaned in to hug him and Noah let go of Cameron's hand to hug her back. "Thanks, Sarah. Fine. We'll go."

Sarah smiled at Cam, too, and nodded. "Thanks for coming out. I'm sure I'll see you at the next event, if not sooner."

"Of course," Cam agreed with an easygoing smile back at

her. "I'll make sure he rests."

"It'll be easier now that I'm not fretting about keys and paperwork and – oh, but I still have to do Jackson's paperwork--"

"I've got it," Sarah assured him with a laugh. "There's nothing that can't wait anyway."

Cameron gripped Noah's hand. "Besides, I have a new house to show you."

"So I heard!" Sarah agreed. "Go show off your new house. Congratulations on that, too, by the way."

"Thanks. See you," Cameron waved. His parents were chatting with Thomas, Jackson still talked to Chase over in the corner, Jackson's buddies mingled with Kevin from the hockey team...

He'd see everyone else some other time. It was time for him to be alone with Noah.

Even Noah sensed it; he led Cameron out of the arena without any further protest, his expression calmer than it had been in weeks.

"That was great," Cameron murmured with a fond smile once they reached the car and he started it up.

"Next project: your house." Noah clapped his hands together. "Let me see what I'm working with."

Cameron laughed and turned on his headlights. If Noah needed a project, he'd give him one... but that would come later.

He had other plans for tonight.

Just as he'd hoped, Noah's first reaction upon seeing the living room was a quiet, "Wow."

He'd swapped out the chandelier for a better one – a cascade of glass shards on a dimmer circuit. Now Cameron could turn the living room lights to just a gentle, romantic glow that bathed the main floor and the upper hallway. He'd set up his newly delivered furniture cozily around the living room fireplace. Even the kitchen was neat and tidy, though he'd only finished unpacking that this morning before work.

"I got something to celebrate your show, too... and the house." Cameron left his shoes and jacket by the door. He brought Noah to the kitchen island where he'd set up a thin vase with a single rose and two wine glasses.

"Oh, you didn't have to!" Noah relaxed into the bar stool at the kitchen island.

"Want anything?" Cameron added. "I think I filled up on cheese and crackers and fruit at the show, but I've got nibbles..."

"I did, too," Noah laughed. "I'm fine. Just... a glass of wine, and you."

Cameron smiled and leaned in to press his lips against Noah's. He popped the cork on the wine bottle and poured them each a glass.

"You learned fast. This is my favorite," Noah murmured as he swirled his glass around and raised it to his nose.

"I made a note of it in my phone," Cameron confessed, and Noah laughed. "I'm a meticulous romantic."

Noah smiled, raising the glass to his lips to sip. He closed his eyes in the kind of pure enjoyment Cameron loved seeing on his face. "I like all your romantic habits."

Cameron sank into his seat and sipped his wine. Their knees bumped as the two of them swiveled in the chairs to look around.

"This is already a beautiful space," Noah admitted. "But

with that vaulted, open ceiling... there's so much I can do with the living room. And I already see the perfect spot for that hockey puck piece."

"Yeah?" Cameron smiled.

"Mmhmm."

They finished their glasses of wine in contented silence, sometimes reaching out to touch each other's arm. Each time they did, Cameron's nerves buzzed with a pleasant tingle.

By the time their glasses of wine were done, he had a good idea he knew what Noah wanted, too. "Shall I take you on a tour?"

"You can skip the rest of the house and bring me to the bedroom," Noah teased. "The rest of the tour can come tomorrow after I've slept."

"Aye aye, sir," Cameron winked. He took Noah by the hand to lead him up the open staircase to the bedroom, pausing at the top of the stairs for a quick kiss.

When they reached the bedroom, Noah nudged the door closed and glanced around the room. The walls were a soothing, yet sexy burgundy. The elegant, low bed frame Cameron had chosen emphasized the spacious room and glossy hardwood floors. "This is nice."

"Much better than it would have been on moving day," Cameron added with a wink.

Noah slid his arms around Cameron's waist and leaned into his body to silence his teasing with a long, slow kiss. His lips sucked Cameron's lightly and his tongue danced at the tip of Cam's. Then, he whispered, "Fine. You were right."

Cameron's lips tingled so much he could hardly speak. "Can I get that on tape? In case I need it again?"

Noah snorted. "Take me to bed, Cam."

Cameron shivered. Despite the short distance between the

door and bed, Cameron swept Noah off his feet. He carried him the whole half-dozen steps to bed, then gently laid him down and crawled over him.

Noah pulled him down with his hands wrapped around his waist. Cameron nestled between his thighs. Their bodies were warm together, thin trousers not hiding much as their groins bumped together. Their cocks were already throbbing to life.

Indeed, it only took one more slow, sensual kiss from Noah. Cameron ground against Noah's thigh and moaned, pulling back from the kiss for breath. "Jesus."

"I love how much you swear," Noah informed him with a grin. "You try to be a gentleman and not curse in public, so I know I'm doing things right in bed..."

Cameron kissed the smirk off his lips, sucking Noah's lips between his one at a time. He loved to flick his tongue along them, nip them, then kiss them so thoroughly Noah barely breathed.

When Noah was hard and twitching against his hip, they pulled each other's clothing off. Cameron's suit jacket, Noah's waistcoat, both of their collared shirts came off one piece at a time. By the time their bare chests rubbed, Cameron's heart pulsed with excitement. He leaned in to kiss at Noah's neck, then licked his way to his throat to kiss up it to his chin, then down to his collarbone.

If they couldn't fuck like animals every day, he'd take it slower with Noah. At least, until he got the letter with the date of his specialist appointment. They had all the time in the world together now.

Noah unfastened Cam's trousers and slid them down along with his underwear, then Cameron did the same for Noah. They kicked their way out, pants and socks and all, until they were naked together on the freshly-made bed.

Noah arched into Cameron and wrapped his legs around his waist, then pressed his lips by Noah's ear. "Make love to me."

Cameron didn't waste a second grabbing lubricant. As he pushed his fingers into Noah's tightness and the man firmly sucked on his neck, he took it slow. He wanted Noah to remember this moment for years to come.

They'd always shared a deep intimacy in bed, even during their fast and hard sex, but this time was different. There was something deep, yet unspoken here.

Cameron rubbed the bump inside gently as he pushed his fingers in and pulled out, simulating the motion of sex. He kept Noah's body pinned flat to the bed with his weight. Noah's chest rapidly rose and fell. Quiet sounds of approval spilled from his lips with each little thrust of Cam's fingers.

Noah slapped his wrist after a couple minutes. "That's good."

I'll find a time to make him come with only my fingers... but now isn't the right time. Cameron grinned and wiped his fingers off, then stroked himself. "You sure you don't want a condom?"

"No condom," Noah murmured simply and firmly, smiling up at him.

Cameron's heart soared. He leaned in for another spontaneous kiss as he stroked his lubed hand up and down his shaft until he was sure he was ready.

When he brought his fist between Noah's leg and let his tip press into him, Noah opened up perfectly for him. His body was tight and warm around him. Cameron thrust in slowly, enjoying the naked sensation of skin on skin, his body locked together with Noah's.

One thrust at a time, he plunged deep inside Noah and pulled out again with skilled thrusts of his muscled hips. Noah clearly loved the power behind them. His hands curled around Cam's hips and nails bit into his thighs.

Within a minute, Cameron found the perfect rhythm to make Cam's cock throb and Noah's body shudder with each thrust.

"Cam... I love you," Noah whispered.

Cameron's eyes widened, but he didn't hesitate to whisper back, "I love you, too, Noah." He'd never been more certain of anything.

A grin cracked Noah's lips, and then he clicked his tongue. "You can make love a little harder, then."

Cameron laughed and braced himself on his arm to thrust deeper and faster. His own itch had to be satisfied, but more importantly, he wanted to make Noah moan until he lost his senses.

It didn't take long: Noah's body arched with each good thrust. His leg wrapped around Cameron's thighs while his other foot pressed into the bed. One arm tightly wrapped around Cameron's back, their chests pressed together as Noah was blanketed with Cam's weight.

"Yes...!" Noah moaned, panting harshly for breath. Before he could even ask, Cameron reached between them to close a hand around Noah's cock and jerk his hand up and down.

Noah's body quivered and clenched around Cam. Cam's own thighs clenched, his balls drawing tight.

Not yet... Not yet, hold out...

"I fuckin' love you," Cam growled, leaning in for a possessive, hot, hard kiss to take Noah's breath away. Then, he twisted his hand around Noah's shaft just right.

"I lo-- uh! Cam!" Noah came hard, moaning and whimpering as he pushed his head back into the pillow. His whole body arched up against Cam – not hard enough to lift him, but hard enough to rub their bodies and stimulate Cam's whole body with just the extra tingling tension he wanted.

"Yes...!" Cam grunted as warmth splattered between them. The tight clenches pushed him over the edge, too. He thrust hard into Noah with each burst of heat and warmth through his body until the bed creaked, his claim laid inside Noah's body.

When his cock finally softened and slipped out, Cameron's chest still heaved as he lay still on top of Noah to catch his breath.

Noah wouldn't let him go anyway, his arm still around his back.

"I love you," Noah whispered, finally finishing the sentence again. "I really do."

Cam's heart soared. "I'm so glad I met you."

"Me, too," Noah murmured, kissing Cameron's cheek and neck until Cam rolled onto his side. Noah just followed, rolling to straddle Cameron and press kisses against his lips.

Cameron grinned against Noah's lips and wrapped his arms around his back as Noah's weight pressed against his chest.

It was almost time to make Noah relax for the night... perhaps after one more round. This time, Noah was taking the lead. He ground in small circles against Cameron, giving him a playful grin that made Cameron laugh.

"Again?"

"Again."

They had already been through so much, but there was so much more to look forward to; Cameron was certain of it.

Clang (The Riley Brothers #2)

"I CAN'T LET YOU FACE THIS ALONE."

When blacksmith Jackson Riley asks his friend Chase for help with his dating profile, their friendship stirs into more. Jackson wants a family tattoo and Chase's skilled hands can deliver. But when Chase asks him to forge a sword, Jackson worries: what could he need protection from?

Tattoo artist Chase MacLeod thought he'd escaped his abusive family, but one letter throws his world into disarray. He's taking fencing lessons to grow more confident, but that's not enough. New flame Jackson defends Chase, and even opens his home and heart to him. Chase just has to find the courage to face his past.

Chase wants to find a place to call home, and a family to call his own, but the enemy fights dirty… and his worst enemy might just be himself. With Jackson by his side, can he take on the world? Or will his scars forever close his heart?

Clang is the second book in The Riley Brothers, a low-angst series filled with brotherly banter and small-town smiles. This steamy, standalone gay romance novel can be enjoyed on its own, and promises a happily-ever-after ending.

About the Author

E. Davies writes feel-good, low-angst romance that never fades to black when the going gets good! Born in Canada, after 16 moves and counting, Ed has finally put down roots in north London.

He emerges from his writing nest to coo over fuzzy animals, flee from cute guys, dance through the streets with his chosen family, put together fierce looks, and—most of all—befriend local flowers.

You can find all available titles at: www.edaviesbooks.com

FOLLOW E. DAVIES ONLINE:

amazon.com/author/edavies

bookbub.com/authors/e-davies

facebook.com/edaviesauthor

goodreads.com/edavies

instagram.com/edaviesauthor

x.com/edaviesauthor

Grind

Brooklyn Boys:

Electric Sunshine

Live Wire

Boiling Point

F-Word:

Flaunt

Freak

Faux

Forever

Freedom

After:

Afterburn

Afterglow

Aftermath

Shared Universes:

Shelter

Adore

Miracle

Redemption

Limelight

Barely Regal